A Marcus Cor

BODIES POLITIC

David Wishart

PlashMill Press

Published in the United Kingdom in 2010
by PlashMill Press

First Edition

A CIP catalogue record for this book is available from the British Library.

ISBN-13: 978-0-9554535-5-5

Printed by Robertson Printers, Forfar

PlashMill Press
The Plash Mill
Friockheim
Angus DD11 4SH
Scotland.

www.plashmillpress.com

Author's Note

The story is set between June and September AD38: I feel slightly guilty about the length of time separating my fictional date for the uncovering of the Gaetulicus conspiracy - or at least the point where Gaius becomes aware of it - and the probable historical one of almost a year later, but I needed to have Corvinus in Alexandria at a time before the rioting and the arrest of Flaccus, so this was unavoidable. Otherwise the chronology (as far as I'm aware) is accurate.

Which leads to the usual (important!) question of what is historical fact in the story and what is pure fiction. I've tried, as I like to do in all the political books because the 'Times' crossword solver in me finds it fascinating, to combine ostensibly disparate real events into a single plot-line; which means that although the events themselves, taken individually, are historical the links I make - together with their circumstantial details - are my own invention. The result may be plausible in real, historical terms (at least I hope it is) but it remains an artificial construction.

In this instance, the deaths of Macro, Gemellus and Silanus are real, but although an actual conspiracy - false or otherwise - involving them together is certainly possible it is not a matter of hard fact. Similarly, Gaetulicus and Lepidus were actually executed in the course of Gaius's journey to the Rhine in September AD39, while at the same time Agrippina and Livilla were banished (for fuller details, plus the fates of Seneca, Anteius and Vinius, see below). Thus far - but no further - historical fact; even if they were all implicated in a single conspiracy (which seems a reasonable assumption) its circumstantial details must lie within the realm of theory. As those of my Lepidus/Agrippina strand most certainly do.

The Alexandrian plot is a complete fabrication, albeit one I feel proud of because it fits in really nicely with the facts that underpin it. Historically, Tiberius Claudius Helicon was the leader of an Alexandrian Greek faction in the fledgeling civil service; he did try to put the Alexandrian Jews down with his close friend Gaius at every opportunity; Isidorus did reappear in Alexandria, became an intimate of the previously-hostile governor Flaccus, and suddenly, unaccountably, persuaded him to reverse Roman policy vis-à-vis the Jews, with catastrophic results (again, see below for details); and Flaccus was a friend of Macro's and one of Gemellus's few named supporters. All in all, one of those instances where if the explanation isn't actually true then it should be.

The one-year gap I mentioned above between the timings of fiction and fact meant that, unusually, I couldn't integrate the larger part of the results of Corvinus's investigations into the story itself. For the sake of completeness, then, they need to come here.

Alexandria

Between early August and September AD38 - ie starting immediately Corvinus left the city - the rioting became much more serious. Greek mobs roamed the streets, destroying Jewish synagogues and property, with Flaccus at best turning a blind eye and going himself to the extreme of issuing a proclamation confining Jewish residence to the original eastern quarter; in effect, creating a ghetto. Since this entailed a huge influx of Jews from the other parts of the city who had lost everything in the process, the result was severe overcrowding in insanitary conditions; the problem being aggravated by mob savagery on the part of the Greeks, who beat or burned to death any Jews found outside their quarter. Any attempt at retaliation was ruthlessly suppressed, and the ringleaders were publicly executed. In October, troops arrived to arrest Flaccus. He was taken to Rome and - despite an attempt by Lepidus to have him exiled to the relatively-comfortable island of Andros - was sent to its fly-speck neighbour Gyaros. At about the same time as Lepidus fell (the following September), Gaius sent men to have him killed.

Germany

Gaius left Rome for the Rhine - and his intended British campaign, which came to nothing in the end; that had to wait for Claudius - in mid-September AD39, taking with him Lepidus, his two sisters, and the freedman Tiberius Claudius Etruscus. However, he went only as far as Mevania in central Italy, less than a hundred miles from the capital. Troops were sent forward to arrest and execute Gaetulicus at Mainz, while Lepidus was executed at Mevania itself. Agrippina and Livilla were exiled, but first - as her mother had her father's - Agrippina was forced to carry Lepidus's ashes back to Rome.

On his own return to Rome, Gaius dedicated three daggers in the temple of Mars Ultor ('Mars the Avenger').

Other fates

Calvisius Sabinus, the Pannonian legate, and his wife **Cornelia** - genuinely Gaetulicus's daughter - were recalled to Rome. Cornelia was charged with trying to suborn the troops (in the euphemistic phrasing of the charge, 'going round the sentries') and with an act of adultery on the *tribunal* (the sacred platform where the standards were set, which would add the frisson of impiety needed to raise the crime to another level), her partner being the tribune **Titus Vinius**. Whether Vinius himself was punished is not known, but he was certainly still alive in AD69 so he may have escaped, possibly (as I have it) by turning informer. Cornelia and her husband both committed suicide.

Annaeus Seneca, the later philosopher, tragedian and principal tutor/advisor to Agrippina's son the emperor Nero, was originally sentenced to death but had the sentence commuted to exile; the historical reason given being that he had been too successful in defending a man whom Gaius wanted to see condemned. Whatever Gaius's true reason for getting rid of him in 39 was (and surely it could not have been anything as trivial as pique, especially since at the time so much was happening within the imperial circle of which he was a member in the way of intrigue), two years later he was exiled again at the instigation of Claudius's wife Messalina; this time on a charge of adultery with Livilla. I have simply blended the two historical facts to provide him with a plausible role in the story.

Anteius was a senator recorded as being implicated in the plot against Gaius; precise details are unknown, and I've used nothing that is factual about him except for his name and rank. He was first exiled then - like Flaccus - killed by soldiers sent for the purpose.

Helicon was executed under Claudius. **Etruscus** survived, amazingly, into the reign of Domitian (AD81 - 96), and died at the age of ninety.

Finally, two recommendations. If you're interested in the history of the period *per se*, then I cannot recommend highly enough Professor Anthony Barrett's book 'Caligula: the Corruption of Power' (Batsford 1989, reprinted Routlege 2000). Comprehensive, thorough, beautifully written, and a tremendously good read. The same goes for 'Philo's Alexandria', by Dorothy Sly (Routlege 1996), to which I am seriously indebted for the topographical details of the city. My grateful thanks to Professor Harry Hine, of the School of Classics, University of St Andrews, for pointing me in its direction.

Dramatis personae

(Only the names of the main characters are given. Historical characters are in upper case)

Corvinus's family, household and friends

Agron: Corvinus's Illyrian friend, resident in Ostia. His wife is **Cass (Cassiopeia)**.
Alexis: the gardener.
Bathyllus: the major-domo.
Clarus, Publius Cornelius: Marilla's fiancé.
Marilla, Valeria: Corvinus's adopted daughter.
Perilla, Rufia: Corvinus's wife.
Secundus, Gaius Vibullius: an old friend of Corvinus's, currently a senior military administrator.

The imperial circle

AGRIPPINA, DRUSILLA, LIVILLA: the emperor's sisters (Drusilla is now dead).
ANTEIUS, Gaius: a young finance officer, a friend of Seneca's.
GAIUS CAESAR: the emperor (Caligula).
GEMELLUS: Tiberius's nephew and Gaius's adopted son. Now dead.
HELICON, Tiberius Claudius: a freedman, prominent civil servant and close friend of Gaius.
LEPIDUS, Marcus Aemilius: a close friend of Gaius and the husband of his dead sister Drusilla.
MACRO, Naevius Sertorius: commander of the Praetorian Guard and one of Gaius's chief advisors, now dead. His wife was **ENNIA**.
SENECA, Lucius Annaeus: the later philosopher, tragedian and advisor to the Emperor Nero.
SILANUS, Marcus Junius: Gaius's former father-in-law and advisor. Now dead.
VINICIUS, Marcus: Livilla's husband.
TIBERIUS ('The Wart'): the former emperor.

Rome, Italy and the Rhine

Crispus, Caelius: a professional scandal-merchant.
ETRUSCUS, Tiberius Claudius: an important civil servant, aka **Dion.**
GAETULICUS, Gnaeus Cornelius Lentulus: legate (governor) of Upper Germany.
SABINUS, Calvisius: legate (governor) of Pannonia. His wife is **CORNELIA:** Gaetulicus's daughter.
VINIUS, Titus: an ex-tribune of the Pannonian legions.

Alexandria

AGRIPPA, Herod: newly-appointed king of Judea, and a close friend of Gaius.
Cineas: a merchant.
FLACCUS, Aulus Avillius: the Roman governor.
Gallius, Marcus: a tribune with the XXII legion.
Glabrio, Sextus Acilius: Flaccus's aide.
ISIDORUS: a Greek demagogue.
Mika: Agron's sister-in-law.
Stratocles, Fabius: Corvinus's host.

One

Trust me. Organising a wedding is a pain in the rectum.

Not that there was any great hurry now. Perilla's Aunt Marcia had passed away just after the Winter Festival, bolt upright in her chair where she'd nodded off after dinner. Hyperion the doctor had been there at the time, as well as Clarus and Marilla, and he'd said in his letter that it had been the best way for her to go. Still, it was the end of an era: Marcia and the villa in the Alban Hills had been a fixture for more years than I liked to count. The villa itself wouldn't be gone, mind, Aunt Marcia had made sure of that. Once Clarus and Marilla were hitched in four months' time the couple would take it over lock stock and menagerie as the old girl's posthumous wedding present.

So there I was, holed up in my study with an abacus while Perilla was scouring Rome for dress material to kit out the bridesmaids. I'd just added up the column of figures for the sixth time and got my sixth different answer when Bathyllus scratched at the door and sidled in. He had his propitiatory face on, which was fair enough because in the Corvinus household interrupting heavy arithmetic is the domestic equivalent of invading Parthia.

'Yeah, Bathyllus,' I said. 'What is it? Plague of rats in the kitchen? Housemaid gone berserk with a cleaver?'

'No, sir.' Not a flicker. 'A visitor.'

I laid the tablet down and brushed the torn-out hair off the desk. 'What kind of visitor?'

'A freedman by the name of Dion.'

'Who the hell's Dion?'

'I don't know, sir, and he wouldn't elaborate. I did ask him to call back tomorrow but he says it's important.'

'Is that so, now?' Odd, but then I could do with a break. Whoever

1

the guy was, and whatever he wanted, it couldn't be any worse than another bout of wrestling with prenuptial arithmetic. Mind you, I'd take that to cruising the shops with Perilla any day. 'Okay, then. Wheel him in.'

I poured myself another cup of well-watered Setinian - abacus-wrestling needs a clear head, but you can take abstinence too far - and sat back in my chair just as the door opened again and the distraction came in. He was a middle-aged guy, Asian-Greek by the look of him, very prim and proper, on the plump side and with a definite lack of hair under the freedman's cap.

'Marcus Valerius Corvinus?' he said. Educated voice, with a slight Greek accent. 'It's kind of you to see me. I'm Naevius Sertorius Dion.'

If the last name meant nothing to me, the first two certainly did. I set the cup down. 'Naevius Sertorius? As in Naevius Sertorius Macro?'

'Yes, sir. I was the commander's secretary. He freed me in his will.'

I knew Macro, sure: ex-commander of Praetorians, Gaius's right-hand man until our fledgeling emperor told him and his wife to kill themselves, and one of the most dangerous bastards I'd ever met. 'So?' I said.

'He left a letter for you, sir.' He drew it out from his belt and laid it carefully on the desk.

I looked but didn't touch. Odd was right. 'Why should Macro write to me? And the guy's been dead for almost three months.'

'He thought it better that there should be a delay, sir. I'm sure the letter will explain, if you'd be good enough to open it.'

Polite but firm; very firm. And from his tone of voice and the expression on his face I knew that freedman or not the guy wouldn't be fobbed off by a promise to read the thing later. If I wanted him out of my study, letter unread, it'd mean calling in the bought help to drag him through the door by the heels. I was beginning to get a bad feeling about this.

Bugger.

I reached for the roll of paper and broke the seal:

2

'Naevius Sertorius Macro to Marcus Valerius Messalla Corvinus. Greetings.

When you read this, Corvinus, both I and Ennia will be dead, on the emperor's orders. What excuse he'll offer publicly or in private I don't know, but whatever it is it will be the product of misinformation and calumny.

I fully realise the extent of the favour I am asking you to perform for me. We were never friends, you and I, but even when circumstances inevitably placed us on opposite sides I have always had the greatest admiration for your integrity, your persistence, and your skill in sifting truth from fiction. As indeed has the emperor. That last is important, and the prime reason for this letter, since if anyone can clear my name with Gaius then it is you.

Accordingly, I beg you (and you know that I am not a man who begs easily) to try to do so if you can, to the best of your abilities. I can give you no prior help; or rather - since of course I have my own suspicions on the matter - I will offer you none, because these suspicions are subjective and may be unfounded. Better that you are left to yourself; that approach has served admirably hitherto, and I therefore see no reason to depart from it.

I have asked Dion to keep this letter back - he is aware of its general tenor - until such time as my death is no longer recent, and so as an issue of general concern and interest: I think that, given Gaius's present state of mind, this would be the wisest - and the safest - course of action. Our new emperor is very young and has his foibles but at root he is a decent and fair-minded man, and once time has distanced him a little from events I am sure that, if supplied with the appropriate evidence, he will be amenable to their reassessment. If nothing else, my rehabilitation will remove the stain from our children, and knowing that you will be working towards it when we are gone will ease both my and Ennia's minds greatly.

Believe me, Corvinus, that whatever the outcome you have my grateful thanks and my very best wishes.
Macro.'

I let the page fall. Shit.

Dion was watching me closely. 'Well, sir?' he said.

'Well what?'

'Will you do it? Look into the circumstances of the master's death?'

I sighed. 'Listen, pal. Contrary to what your ex-master seemed

3

to assume I'm not a complete idiot.' *Decent and fair-minded*, right? From what I'd seen of the bugger - and I'd seen a fair amount of him over the years - the adjectives fitted Our Gaius like bedsocks did a snake. 'Macro was chopped by the emperor's order. End, finish, close the book. Even if there is any dirt to be dug I put one spade in the ground and I'll find myself told to slit my own wrists. Quite rightly so.'

'But he's innocent! He didn't do anything!'

'Calling someone like Macro innocent is like saying Brutus and Cassius were old Julius's bosom chums. Now come off it, Dion, you know I can't help, even if I wanted to. Which I don't. I'm sorry, but if the guy didn't deserve chopping this time he'd already deserved it a dozen times over.'

'If he had,' - Dion was angry, but he was holding it in - '*If* he had, then he was acting for the good of Rome. Sir.'

Yeah, well, I'd heard that one before, too. It was funny how often the good of Rome coincided with the good of whoever claimed it as an excuse, and Macro had been as altruistic as a fox in a hen-run. 'Fine' I said. 'I won't argue. But the answer's still no. And that comes with bells on. Now just go, okay? Thanks for coming, but I'm busy.'

Dion drew himself up. 'Valerius Corvinus,' he said, 'I am gravely disappointed in you. And so would the master be.'

'Yeah. Yeah, right.' I reached for the abacus. 'The door-handle's behind you. Just turn it and push.'

'Whoever poisoned the emperor's mind against the commander had reasons of his own for doing it. Thanks to you it would appear that he will get clean away, and *that*, sir, might not in the end be to the good of Rome at all. Forgive me, but from what Macro said about you I'd expected far, far more. Evidently I was wrong and so was he. You couldn't care a fig for the truth.'

He turned and left, slamming the door behind him, and the slap of his sandals echoed along the corridor.

The echoes faded.

I stared at the door's panelwork for a good half minute. Then I picked the letter up and read it through again, twice.

Hell.

Watery Setinian's no food for the brain. I got up, opened the door and yelled for Bathyllus to bring me half a jug of the proper sort.

4

Then I lay down on the reading couch to think.

I was a good half way down the jug when Perilla got back hot, tired and material-less an hour later.

'That was a complete waste of time,' she said as she collapsed onto the other couch. 'I have been in every material shop in the city including that big new one by the Livian Porch that everyone's talking about and there's simply nothing suitable. You'd think you could find *something* the right weight and colour for bridesmaids' dresses in Rome.'

I grunted. Me, when I want a new cloak or a pair of boots I just go out and buy them, and so long as they fit and do the job they're supposed to do I couldn't care less about finicky details like colour and style. Hell is a woman shopping. And a woman shopping for wedding supplies is hell with frills on. Still, a sympathetic grunt is all they want, usually.

'So,' she went on, 'It's a nuisance but I'm afraid we'll just have to try elsewhere.'

Well, so long as the 'we' wasn't used inclusively she could try where she liked. 'Fine by me,' I said. 'You have anywhere particular in mind?'

'I thought Alexandria.'

I almost swallowed my winecup. '*What?*'

'Alexandria, dear. The big city on the coast of Egypt?'

Oh, gods! She wasn't joking, either. Bring weddings and women together and you kiss sanity goodbye. The Macro problem could wait. 'Perilla...'

'We can take Marilla and Clarus. They'd love it. They've never been abroad.'

This was getting surreal. 'Lady, just listen to yourself! Capua or Naples, fine, although why the shops there should be any better than the Roman ones beats me. Alexandria's the other side of the fucking Mediterranean!'

'I'm quite well aware of that, thank you, Marcus. But the sea connections are excellent. And we could stay with Stratocles. He wouldn't mind if we turned up on spec, I'm sure.'

'Who the hell's Stratocles?' I was seriously worried now. Once the lady gets an idea into her head she's like a terrier with a rat. And, like I say, where wedding shopping's concerned women aren't rational.

'You remember. Uncle Fabius's old freedman.' Fabius had been Aunt Marcia's husband, dead over twenty years before. 'He owns a paper factory that supplies half the copyists in Rome. And he's got a huge house near the city centre. There would be plenty of room.'

Forget the rat and terrier; we were operating on a whole new level here. If she'd got down to the fine details of accommodation then we were in real trouble. This thing had to be knocked on the head right now before she started asking what socks I wanted packed. 'Perilla, watch my lips. We are *not* chasing off to Alexandria just so you and Marilla can go on a shopping binge. It's ridiculous!'

'No it isn't. I told you. There are plenty of boats, and it wouldn't take long at this time of year. Twelve or fifteen days at most.'

'Plus the ten it'd take to get down to Brindisi. Plus the shopping binge. Plus the journey home. We'd be lucky if we got back in enough time to chill the wine for the sodding reception. Jupiter, lady, have some sense!'

'Well.' She sniffed. 'We can think about it, at least.' Right. Keeping an eye out for flying pigs all the way. 'So how was your day?'

Ah. I told her, as gently as possible. Not that that helped much.

'Marcus, you can't!' She was staring at me in horror. 'Whatever the reasons, Macro died by direct order of the emperor. If you start poking around Gaius will be livid, and if there is anything to find it'll be even worse. You did say no, didn't you?'

'Yeah, but -'

'Listen. Macro's death is nothing to do with you. You didn't even like the man. And Ennia was Gaius's mistress, everyone knows that. Their suicides were the emperor's business, no one else's, and they're finished and done with. Now don't be stupid.'

'I've been thinking it through. Macro's wasn't the only enforced suicide round about that time. There were Gemellus and Silanus just before the new year. If all the deaths were connected then -'

'Juno! Will you *listen!* Macro was Praetorian Prefect and the emperor's chief advisor. Gemellus was Gaius's co-heir, at least Tiberius named him as such in his will. And Junius Silanus was Gaius's father-

6

in-law and the most powerful man in the senate.'

'Right. Full marks. So what if -'

'Stop it! Just...bloody...stop it!' I blinked: the lady never, ever swears, not even mildly. 'I'm not dense, and it doesn't need half a brain to see the *what if* here. You're going to say that they were involved together in some sort of plot against Gaius, yes? That they were, in effect, executed for treason but it wasn't made public.'

'Ah...yeah. Yeah, that would just about cover it. Or at least -'

'Fine. So what?'

'How do you mean, so what?'

'Marcus, what on earth business is it of yours? This is *political!* Gaius may be a lot of things but he isn't a fool. If he does something he does it for a reason, and even if it's the wrong reason he's still the emperor. Start grubbing around in the whys and wherefores of politics just for the fun of it and you'll find yourself ordered into suicide as well. What's more, you'll deserve to be.'

Yeah. True. All of it. Even so -

Silently, I passed her the letter. She read it through. Twice. Then she said, very quietly:

'Oh.'

'Doesn't sound like an admission of guilt, does it?'

'No, but all the same.' She handed the roll back. *'All the same,* Marcus. Don't do it. Don't get involved. I mean it; please, not this time. It's far too dangerous, and it isn't worth it.'

'No arguments,' I said. 'None at all.'

She smiled. 'Good. That's a huge relief. The best thing you can do with that letter is burn it.'

I reached over for the wine jug and topped up my cup. Bugger; this was going to be tricky. 'None the less,' I said. 'I, ah, was thinking I might go round for a word with old Cornelius Lentulus tomorrow. Just to set my mind at rest, clear the air a bit. That wouldn't hurt, would it?'

Perilla's smile faded and she turned away.

'Yes,' she said. 'Yes, I think it would. Very much so. And, Marcus Valerius Corvinus, I think you are a complete fool.'

Ah, well, I couldn't disagree there, either; but then I always had been, and it was too late to change.

7

Two

I'd first met Lentulus years before, the time of the Ovid business: he'd been one of my father's cronies, and a lot more human than the average specimen of that pokered-rectum bunch. That first time he'd told me he never wanted to see me again, but we'd bumped into each other since at various social get-togethers - Lentulus was the party animal's party animal - and the guy had mellowed like a ripe cheese. Although he was getting on now, pushing eighty, he was still a heavyweight on the senate benches: literally rather than politically, because the guy must've weighed as much as a rhino. How they got him into his seat I don't know. Probably with a crane.

There was nothing wrong with his mind, though. What Cornelius Lentulus didn't know about the ins and outs of politics over the last sixty years you could write on a bootstrap. But - and this was what was important - he had a mouth as loose as a cat-flap. Especially when he was half-pissed, which was most of the time.

Lentulus lived just up the Caelian Hill from us, in an old rambling property that must've been one of the first ones built. Which was where I found him the next day, sitting in the shade of the peristyle garden with a jug of wine and the best part of a bushel of fruit beside him.

'Corvinus, my boy! This is a surprise! Sit yourself down!' He snapped his fingers - or tried to; half-pissed was right - at a hovering slave. 'A cup for the lad, you! Quick, now! Chop-chop!'

There was a wickerwork chair by the nearest pillar. I pulled it over and sat. Lentulus's chair was solid oak and practically the width of a bench. It looked like it'd been reinforced.

'How are you, Lentulus?'

'Very bonny. Very bonny indeed. Soaking up the sunshine and the booze in unequal measures. How's your Rufia Perilla?'

'She's fine.' I was always impressed with Lentulus's memory

8

for names. He might've met Perilla once or twice at most, but half-cut as he was the guy hadn't even skipped a beat.

'Don't go out much, the pair of you.' He pushed over the tray of fruit, but I shook my head. 'Least, I don't see you around. You missed a party last night at Quintus Largus's place, young Corvinus, by the gods you did! Palmyran belly-dancers, naked mud-wrestling and the sweetest little boy-band from Ascalon. Of course, I can only watch now. Comes to us all.' He chuckled. 'Or rather it doesn't, more's the pity. Ah. Here's your cup. Try this one, see what you think. Pour, Desmus, you idle bugger! Mine too.'

The slave who'd brought the cup filled it from the jug. I sipped...

Beautiful.

Lentulus was watching me. 'Good, yes?' he said.

'Yeah.' I took a proper swallow. Not Italian. Easily top-range-Alban standard. If I were pushed I'd say east of Sicily, but it wasn't Greek, or at least not one of the Greek wines I recognised. On the other hand, as an offside chance, it could be small-vineyard Gallic; they were producing some nice individual stuff these days in Gaul, if you were careful about your shipper. The fact was, though, I hadn't a clue, and that doesn't often happen.'What is it?'

'Mareotic. Egyptian. Alexandrian, rather. They use a different process from us, but by hell it works. I had two dozen gallons delivered yesterday of different vintages and I'm working my way through them. Take a flask home with you if you like. I'll tell one of my lads to carry it down the hill for you.'

'Thanks, that'd be -' I stopped. 'Ah...maybe not. Thanks all the same.'

'*No?*' Lentulus's piggy eyes widened. Then he shrugged. 'Suit yourself, boy. Never known you turn down good wine, though. Not sickening, are you? There's a lot of it about just now.'

'No, I'm fine.' With Perilla on her Alexandrian jag maybe a reminder like a freebie flask of the local wine was a bad idea. Pity. It was lovely stuff.

'Good. I'm glad to hear it.' He took a swig from his own cup and shifted his huge bulk. The reinforced chair creaked. 'Now, young Marcus Valerius Corvinus, you can just cut to the chase, please.'

Yeah, well. No flies on Lentulus; there never had been. 'Tell you the truth,' I said, 'I was wondering about Sertorius Macro's suicide.'

'Were you, indeed? Wondering what?'

'Why he did it.'

'Because the emperor told him to.'

I grinned; I'd always had a soft spot for Lentulus. 'You know what I mean, you old bugger,' I said. 'What had he done?'

'Why do you want to know?'

'Call it curiosity.'

'I'll call it no such thing.' Lentulus emptied his cup and without looking at the man held it out for the slave to refill. 'I don't play *ingénus*, Corvinus, and I'm not senile. You're digging the dirt, same as before. Only this time - trust me - there's nothing to dig for.'

He had suddenly gone serious. I remembered the first time, and I warned myself to be careful. He was an okay guy, Lentulus, but like I say he was no fool.

'Fine,' I said. 'Fair enough.' I took out Macro's letter and handed it over.

He read it carefully, then handed it back. 'Load of rubbish,' he said. 'Macro was guilty of conspiracy and treason.'

'But he wasn't charged with treason.' Even I knew that. With the wedding arrangements taking up all my time I hadn't been following events all that closely, but I couldn't've missed the Commander of Praetorians and the emperor's closest friend being arrested on a conspiracy charge.

'Of course he wasn't. Nor were the other two, Silanus and that poor specimen Gemellus. How could they be? The treason charge doesn't exist any more.'

I sat back. Oh, Jupiter, neither it did: when Gaius had come to power he'd abolished it, and burned all the incriminating documents gathered under the Wart's regime publicly in the Market Square. Uness they were copies, of course: as a PR exercise for the new management it was effective enough, but clean government has its limits. 'So what reason did Gaius give?' I said.

'A word of warning; don't call him Gaius, boy, not to his face, not now he's emperor. He doesn't like it. Stick to Caesar.'

'Fine. But you haven't answered the question.'

10

'Neither I have. Not intentionally, I'll do it now. Macro was accused of pandering his wife to gain influence. Silanus - well, the emperor just claimed that he was becoming too pushy. Gemellus had, and I'm quoting the bloody bulletin verbatim, "anticipated the emperor's death and waited for the chance to profit from his illness". There you are. That do you?'

Gaius's illness. That'd been almost a year ago, when he'd come down with a month-long fever that had nearly killed him. Gemellus had represented him at the Games, major religious ceremonies and so on; on any occasion, in other words, where politics or political decisions weren't involved...

Bugger that for a valid reason to chop the kid. Bugger it twice, and five times on the Kalends.

'No, it won't do me,' I said. 'As an excuse it's thin as hell.'

Lentulus chuckled, his jowls heaving. 'Right. Agreed. But I told you: a straight charge of treason wasn't an option. Gaius had to do the best he could with a bad job, leaving the juicy bits out. And, like I say, the whole shower were guilty as sin, barring Gemellus who wouldn't recognise a conspiracy if it bit him in the bum.'

'He wouldn't? And why would that be, now?'

'Because the boy was an idiot. Literally an idiot, even more lame in the head than Claudius, which believe you me is saying something. Half the time he didn't know what day it was.'

'So why did he have to die?'

'Don't be simple yourself, Corvinus! Tiberius had named him in his will as co-heir. Even though Macro had the senate set the will aside that still meant something. Oh, not for Gemellus personally; he wouldn't've made a decent shopkeeper, let alone an emperor, and the senate wouldn't've touched him with a ten-foot pole. But if Gaius were dead he'd make someone a damn good puppet. Besides' - he held out his cup for another refill - 'you can't have two king bees in a hive. Gaius was quite right to be rid of him. Not before time. I didn't blame him myself, and I don't know of anyone who did.'

'For the gods' sakes, Lentulus!'

'Practical politics, lad. Welcome to the world.'

'Okay,' I said. 'So what was the real story?'

Lentulus shrugged. 'No secrets there. At least for all but

11

public consumption, and you remember that qualification when you leave here, boy, or you'll be in real trouble. You and me both, and I'm too old to take the hassle. All this is just between ourselves, right?' I nodded. 'When Gaius fell ill and looked like dying Macro and Silanus got together with the plan of using Gemellus as a figurehead emperor. Maybe going so far, if they could arrange it, of giving the emperor a push into the urn. Only Gaius recovered, found out, and that was that.' He drew his finger across his throat. '*Tsikkk!* Served the pushy bastards right. Gaius has his faults, but he's a smart young bugger with his head screwed on, and he doesn't stand for any nonsense. That's what we need in an emperor. Silanus was a pompous fool with more breeding than sense. Macro was the other way about, and the last thing we - I mean the senate - wanted was another Sejanus. Which is what we would damn well have got if the conspiracy had succeeded.'

'And Ennia?'

'The bitch was getting to be a bore, and she was in the plot up to her neck. Gaius was well rid of her, too.' Lentulus drained his cup. 'You're not drinking, boy.'

Obediently, I took a swig and held the cup out for Desmus to refill. Well, food for thought right enough, although it was all pretty predictable. Still -

'To change the subject, I hear your adopted daughter's getting married.' Lentulus tapped the rim of his cup and Desmus refilled it. Jupiter! The old guy could sink them! And he'd probably been doing it since breakfast. If Lentulus bothered with breakfast. 'Valeria Marilla, isn't it? Lives with old Paullus Maximus's widow up in the Alban Hills?'

'Yeah,' I said. 'Yeah, that's right. Only she died last December.'

'I'm sorry to hear it. She was a fine-looking woman in her day, Marcia. Completely wasted on a dry stick like Paullus. Getting an invitation, am I?'

I grinned. 'If you like. But they want a quiet wedding, in Aunt Marcia's villa.'

'Bugger that, then. I haven't been out of Rome in years, and I'm not built to climb hills. Or be carried up them. Who's the groom?'

'His name's Clarus. Publius Cornelius Clarus.'

'One of our lot?' Lentulus's eyebrows rose. 'Well, well. Don't know of any relations by that name.'

'Maybe because he isn't one. One of the Cornelii, I mean. His family's from Boeotia, originally. They had the citizenship from Africanus.'

Lentulus blinked. 'Good gods! You're telling me that he's a bloody *Greek?*'

'Not for ten generations, no. His father's the local doctor.'

'A doctor?' Lentulus laughed. 'Corvinus, boy, your father'll be spinning in his urn!'

'Yeah, well.' Actually, though, I doubted it: when it came to the crunch, Dad was okay. Still - remember that Lentulus, for all his upper-class background, was pretty tolerant as far as the Roman social milieu went - it was a foretaste of what Clarus would have to face in the way of prejudice, if he ever decided to move to Rome. Not that he ever would, I was pretty sure of that. He and Marilla were happy in Castrimoenium.

'I'm sorry.' Lentulus must've read the expression on my face, because he was suddenly serious again. 'That was in bad taste. I didn't mean it.'

I shrugged. 'No problem.' I held out my cup for more of the Mareotic. 'So tell me about these Palmyran belly-dancers.'

He did, and we got quietly smashed. I managed to ask one more question, though, before I left a couple of hours later.

'Dion?' Lentulus frowned. 'Can't remember Macro having a secretary by that name, let alone tell you where to find him. But then I didn't really know the man socially. I kept my distance. His major-domo was a man called Antiphon. He might be able to help. Old Caecilius Cornutus took him on when Macro went. You'll find him on Broad Street, near the junction with Pallacinae.'

Fine. Well, I reckoned it had been a fair morning's work, albeit pretty disquieting.

I didn't believe that stuff about Macro and Silanus, for a start.

13

Three

'Macro wouldn't've done it, lady. No way. And I've got my doubts about Silanus as well.'

Perilla dunked her chickpea rissole viciously in the fish-pickle-and-mustard dip. Half of it broke off, and she scooped it out with her spoon. 'Marcus, I am *not* getting involved,' she said tightly. 'You know what I think. When - not if, when - the emperor gets to hear that you're shoving your nose into matters of high politics you'll be out of Rome before you can say "exile". And that's if you're lucky and don't have to slit your wrists.' She glared at me. 'And it's not as though you're at a loose end at present. We've got a wedding in four months' time to organise, and it's not going to be much fun for Clarus and Marilla if you're dead or stuck on some island or other. Nor for me either, for that matter. Leave it alone!'

I shifted uncomfortably on the couch. She was right; sure she was. I didn't owe Macro anything, quite the reverse, and messing around with the system, especially when the system was Gaius, was tantamount to putting your head in a crocodile's mouth in the hopes that it had gone vegetarian. Even so, I had my self-respect to consider. And that last exchange with Dion had hurt.

'Yeah, well,' I said. 'I'll be careful. I promise.'

Perilla reached for the bean casserole and said nothing.

'Look, how would conspiring against Gaius help Macro?' I de-shelled a snail. 'He was sitting pretty as it was, and he couldn't go any further. He's a no-account Italian provincial from the sticks, his family are nobodies, the great and good in Rome hate him worse than poison and think he's another Sejanus in the making. Gaius is the only future he's got. And he's not a fool, he knows it.'

No reaction. The lady wasn't even looking at me.

'Silanus, now, at least he has form, sure. He's got family connections with the imperials that go back to Augustus and the

Wart married his daughter to Gaius when he was on Capri. Plus he's a political animal. If Macro was one of the guy's chief advisors when he took over then Silanus was the other. Silanus I can believe as a conspirator, just, although he'd be a bloody fool to try anything unless he was hundred percent sure of his ground. But not Macro.'

Perilla laid her spoon down. 'Have you considered that he might not have had any choice?' she said.

'How do you mean?'

'Gaius was ill. Possibly - probably, from all indications - terminally so. Macro was about to lose him anyway. There needn't have been any conspiracy at all. If the only heir was Gemellus, who you say Lentulus told you wasn't up to the job, then it makes perfect sense for the emperor's advisors to make contingency plans. After all, someone would have to run the empire if Gaius died.'

I grinned to myself. Well, at least the lady was talking. And dangle the bait of an intellectual puzzle in front of Perilla's nose for long enough and she'll go for it every time. She's like me that way; the difference is she doesn't admit it, not even to herself. Still, I had to play this careful. I helped myself to some of the beans and took a spoonful.

'Okay,' I said. 'So why not just present it like that to Gaius when he recovered? I mean, he's a long way from stupid. And he's an imperial born and bred, he knows how important making sure of the succession is, that's built in with the brickwork. What else could he expect? Why chop the poor bastards just for doing their job while he was out of things?'

Perilla sighed. 'I don't know, Marcus,' she said. 'And unlike you I don't think it's any of my business to guess. Now eat your dinner before it gets cold.'

We ate in silence for a while.

'So,' Perilla said finally, her eyes on her plate. 'What are you going to do now? I mean, you are going to do something, I assume, whatever I say.'

I grinned to myself again. Got you! It was just a matter of waiting.

'Find Dion,' I said. 'He may not know much, but he was Macro's secretary after all. And he was pretty insistent that the guy

15

had been set up. He must have a reason for thinking that, other than simple loyalty. Besides,' I took another spoonful of beans, 'he's the best I've got at present.'

'He didn't give you a contact address?'

I shook my head. 'I didn't ask. And I'd just turned him down flat. But Lentulus said Macro's major-domo might be able to put me on to him. Guy called Antiphon, sold on to a household on Broad Street.'

She was quiet for a long time. Then she said, softly, 'Marcus, you will be careful, won't you? That's a promise?'

'Sure.'

'And if - well, if things do begin to turn nasty, you will give this up straight away?'

'Cross my heart and hope to die, lady.'

She set her spoon down. 'Don't say that!' she snapped. 'Ever!'

I went to call on Antiphon next morning.

Drusilla, the second of Gaius's three younger sisters, had died from a sudden fever at the beginning of the month and although the regulations governing the public mourning were still technically in force not even Gaius could keep the ordinary Roman punter po-faced for long, and things were slowly but surely getting back to their noisy, chaotic normal. Still, the city centre was quieter than usual, and I made good time through the thin crowds. It wasn't all that far, either: Broad Street runs north of the centre parallel with the Saepta as far as the Pincian, but the corner with Pallacinae is right at the market-place end.

The Cornutus place was one of the old upper-class houses you get in that part of town, that rub shoulders with more run-down properties like a dowager out of her place and forced to mix with the riff-raff. The slave parked on a stool in front of the door stood up when I went to knock.

'The master's in Capua, sir,' he said. 'And the rest of the family. They won't be back for another month.'

'That's all right, pal,' I said. 'I wanted to talk to Antiphon, if he's around.'

The guy blinked, which was fair enough: you don't often get

purple-stripers turning up on the doorstep and asking to speak to the bought help. However:

'Yes, sir, he's here. If you'd like to come in and wait I'll bring him to you. Who shall I say?'

'Valerius Corvinus. He doesn't know me.'

'Very well.' He took me inside and through to the atrium. 'Make yourself comfortable, sir. I won't be a moment. What was it about?'

'It's in connection with his last master, Sertorius Macro. I'm trying to trace one of his freedmen.'

The guy blinked again when I mentioned Macro, but he simply nodded and left.

I sat on one of the couches. I didn't know Cornutus, but the guy was clearly old money with a penchant for art: there were some nice paintings on the walls, seascapes, mostly, but a few architectural ones too. Good solid traditional stuff, with none of the risqué nymphs-and-satyrs jobs you find in the more adventurous houses. The statues matched, too, all decently draped, but if they were copies they were top of the range.

'Valerius Corvinus, sir?'

I turned. Antiphon was younger than I'd expected, but he fitted the decor: solid, respectable, no flash.

'You're looking for one of my ex-master's freedmen, I understand,' he said.

'Yeah. His secretary Dion. He brought me a letter a couple of days back and I need to check up on a few things. I didn't get his address and I was wondering if -' I tailed off. The guy was looking puzzled.

'What was the name again, sir?' he said.

'Dion. Like I say, he used to be Macro's secretary, and -'

'But the master didn't have a secretary, sir. Not a personal one. He used the Praetorian clerks.'

'Okay. So maybe I misheard him.' I hadn't; there was something screwy here. 'Anyway, the guy's name was definitely Dion, so -'

'He had no slave or freedman by that name at all, sir.'

Oh, Jupiter! This just didn't make sense! 'You're sure?'

'I was with the master for ten years, and I am absolutely sure.'

17

Bloody hell! But Dion's name had been in the letter! If the guy didn't exist, then -

'Hang on, pal.' I'd brought it with me, just in case I did get to talk to Dion. I took it out of my mantle-fold and handed it over. 'Take a look at this for me, will you?'

He unrolled it and read. Then he looked up.

'The master didn't write this, sir,' he said.

'*What?*'

'Oh, the handwriting is similar, but it's definitely not his. The *s*'s are wrong, and the *t*'s. And I'm afraid - well, the master was no scholar, to put it mildly. Half these words he wouldn't even know, let alone use. I'm sorry, but I don't understand.'

I took the letter back. 'No more do I, pal,' I said. 'No more do I. Thanks for your help, anyway.'

I left, my brain numb.

Gods almighty, what the hell was going on here?

Four

What I needed now was a half jug of wine and a think. In that order. Renatius's wasn't too far, on Iugarius, but there was a new place I'd thought I might try off Augustus Market. Besides, this time of day Renatius's would be packed with familiar punters and I'd just get sucked into a conversation I didn't want.

The place had tables and stools outside, under a shady trellis - late June in Rome's no time to be sitting out in the full sunshine - and if it wasn't exactly busy it wasn't empty either. A good sign. I sat down and the waiter came over.

'You have such a thing as Mareotic, pal?' I said.

'Just what's on the board, sir.'

I looked. 'Make it a half jug of Massic.'

'Half of Massic it is.' He went off.

Okay, so what was I to make of this, then? I was used to a puzzle at one end of the line, but not at both. Who the hell was Dion, what connection, if any, did he have with Macro, and why was he so anxious - as anxious he obviously was, to go to all this trouble - to have me look into the bastard's death? Above all, what the hell was the point of this faffing around? He must've known that, if I did start an investigation, his porky about being Macro's secretary and the whole whacky letter business would hold up for about as long as spit on a hot griddle. As indeed it had. So why tell the porky in the first place?

Because although the investigation was important for some reason so was keeping himself - or whoever he represented - out of it. Obviously.

'Your Massic, sir.' The waiter, back with the half-jug, cup and a complimentary plate of olives. Well, I couldn't complain about the speed of the service. And when I tasted it the Massic wasn't bad either. The first cupful didn't even touch the sides, and I poured myself a second and took a good swallow.

19

So. What had we got?

First of all, he was pretty well-informed. He knew me, where to find me, and that I'd known Macro and we hadn't got on. He knew how to get me hooked despite myself. He knew Macro's handwriting well enough to produce a passable forgery, but not well enough to do it absolutely right. He'd got an axe to grind, maybe even a personal axe, because if not - again - why the hell bother in the first place? On the other hand, he wasn't in a position to do anything himself. That much fitted, at least: he'd been a Greek, probably an Asiatic Greek, not a Roman, and if he wasn't freedman class he'd been a damned good actor. Smart freedman class, though: 'secretary' had hit it nicely. I reached for the winecup. Then again -

A hand grabbed my wrist. I refocused.

'Marcus Valerius Messalla Corvinus?'

'Yeah.' The guy who'd sat down on the stool across from me was built like a slab of the Capitol, if a slab of the Capitol had had that much hair growing in its nostrils. 'Who the hell are you?'

'Just someone who wants to keep you still living, pal. And your wife Rufia Perilla. And your adopted daughter and her fiancé up in the Alban Hills. Castrimoenium, isn't it? Nice place.'

My belly went cold.

'Course, that'd depend on whether you were sensible or not.' He leaned forwards and I could smell his early lunch on his breath. Raw onions and cheap wine had figured prominently. 'Asking questions, poking your nose into things - well, that's not sensible, is it, sir? Give it up now, that'd be my advice. Before someone gets hurt.'

I pulled back on my hand, but I might as well've tried to shake off a vice. 'Touch my family, you bastard, and you're dead meat. You and whoever sent you.'

'Oh, I don't think so, sir, I really don't. Believe me. And like I say this is just a friendly warning. Next time - well, let's hope there's not a next time, for everyone's sake, eh?' He leaned over and patted my shoulder. 'I'll see you around. Be good. Enjoy your wine.'

And he was up and off, striding into the crowds that packed the entrance to Augustus Market. I stood up myself, but he'd already disappeared and I knew I hadn't a hope in hell of following him let alone catching the bugger. And there wasn't a lot I could do to him

20

even if I did.

I sat down again and swallowed the wine in my cup at a gulp, brain and guts both churning.

When I got back home Perilla was in the garden going through what I just knew was the wedding checklist for the umpteenth time.

'Okay,' I said. 'You win. I'm giving it up.'

'*What?*' She set the tablet and stylus down on the table beside her.

'The investigation. I'm giving it up.'

She looked scared. 'Marcus, what's happened?'

I told her.

'The guy was a plain-clothes Praetorian,' I said when she'd finished biting her knuckles. 'Or if he wasn't he behaved like one. Perilla, he knew the lot! My name, your name, about Marilla and Clarus. He even knew where Marcia's fucking villa was.'

'Gently, dear,' Perilla said.

'And that bugger Dion was a fake. Macro's major-domo had never heard of the guy. The same goes for Macro's fucking letter. He didn't write the fucking thing at all.'

'Marcus. Please. Sit down.' I did. 'Take a deep breath, hold it to a count of five, and let it out.' I did. 'Good. So. Now exactly what are you going to do?'

'Give up. I told you. It isn't worth it.'

She was frowning. 'You're sure? Absolutely sure?'

'Lady, I'm not a complete idiot, or a potential suicide. If the warning came from Gaius - and six gets you ten it did - then I can't go head-to-head with the emperor, whatever the rights or wrongs might be. Besides, I promised.'

'Yes, that's true. Still, when has that ever mattered?'

I stared at her. 'Whose side are you on?'

'Yours. That's the point.' She picked up the wax tablet again. 'Fine. So if you think the emperor wants to stop you then your logical next step would be to confirm it with him.'

'*What?*'

'Go and see him.'

'Gods almighty, Perilla -!'

21

'Why not? It would save everyone a lot of grief and heartache, wouldn't it? If the wineshop man was a Praetorian, and Gaius had sent him, then why shouldn't the emperor confirm it? Then you can say, Yes, Caesar, all right, I'm sorry, I'll stop being such a nosey bastard from this moment on, and you're both happy. Or at least you'll know where you stand. Or am I wrong?'

I was laughing despite myself. I leaned over and kissed her. 'Absolutely right, lady. We have a deal.' I turned and raised my voice. *'Bathyllus!'*

The little guy had been hovering as usual. I'd hardly got the last syllable out when he shimmered over.

'Wine, sir?'

'Yeah, but then I want you to put on your cleanest socks and go on over to the palace. Make an appointment for me to see the emperor.'

Bathyllus doesn't faze easily, but he did now. 'Ah...'

'You heard me, sunshine. I'm not joking. The palace, appointment with the emperor, asap.'

'Yes, sir.' He hesitated. 'Could I suggest, though, that when you do go you wear a mourning mantle?'

Oh, bugger; I'd forgotten about that. Rome might be getting back to normal after Drusilla's death, but she'd been far and away Gaius's favourite sister. From all accounts her death had hit him hard - he hadn't even been able to attend the funeral on Mars Field - and he was still a long way from getting over it. Turning up looking crisp, summery and well-barbered, smelling of roses and with a broad grin on my puss, would go down with the guy like a six-day-old anchovy in a heatwave. If, that was, he agreed to see me at all. Still, things were urgent, and I had to try.

'Well reminded, Bathyllus,' I said. 'Off you go. Spit spot.'

He left.

'Flute-players,' Perilla said.

I frowned. 'What?'

'For the wedding, Marcus. I'd thought of getting them from the guild in Rome, but Marilla says she'd rather use ones from Bovillae. What do you think?'

'Ah...Bovillae's fine with me. If that's what Marilla wants.'

22

'Very well.' She made a tick on the list. 'Clarus can arrange that. He has an uncle in Bovillae. Now what about Patinius Cruso? I'm a bit worried about him.'

'Who the hell's Patinius Cruso?'

'You know perfectly well, dear. The priest. He was a very close friend of Aunt Marcia's and he's known Marilla all her time in Castrimoenium. He must be well over eighty.'

'So?'

She sighed. 'Marcus, he's completely senile. The last time I saw him his major-domo was trying to convince him that a loincloth and hobnailed boots were not appropriate dress for a dinner party. We'd be far safer with someone else, agreed, but he's a lovely old man and he'd be desperately upset if we passed him over.'

'It'd make for an interesting ceremony. Not many people get married by a priest in a loincloth and boots.'

'Be serious.'

'Okay. So make sure the major-domo rides close shotgun on the day and have one of the other priests primed to take over. If necessary we can bundle the old guy up in his mantle and lock him in a broom cupboard until the reception.'

'Hmm. Well, if you're sure.' She made another tick. 'What about flowers?'

'Your wine, sir.' Bathyllus must've gone off to the palace; the slave with the tray was one of the skivvies.

I took the wine and sipped. Well, there was nothing I could do now until Gaius agreed to see me. Or not, as the case might be. And at least Perilla was off the Alexandrian jag.

I was still puzzled over this Dion business, though. That made no sense at all.

Five

I got my appointment two days later.

I was nervous as hell; sure I was. We'd got on well enough in the past, Gaius and me, on the occasions that we had met, and although Macro's letter had been a fake the bit about him being well-disposed had seemed true enough. Even so, the guy was emperor now, he could break me with no more trouble than swatting a fly. And he was about as reliable as an adder with fang-ache.

Besides, we'd had four enforced top-bracket suicides inside of eight months. Those sort of statistics aren't exactly encouraging.

I'd let Bathyllus choose the wardrobe. Going unshaven for the two days, which is proper mourning etiquette, had seemed a bit OTT - the guy didn't like crawlers, I knew from past experience, and Drusilla hadn't been family - so I didn't do it; but a plain mourning mantle and no barber's powder was only sensible. I took the litter, too: walking from the Caelian to the Palatine in the afternoon heat of summer can leave you humming, and that I didn't want either.

I gave my name to the palace flunkey - like all the slaves in the imperial quarters he was in a mourning-tunic himself, and half his fringe was missing - and he took me in to the Presence.

Gaius looked terrible. Yeah, well, he usually did - not a good-looking guy, our emperor - but I'd seen privy-slaves in better nick. If I'd had any doubts about his grief over Drusilla, I didn't have them any more. Oh, sure, his mourning-tunic would be top-of-the-range quality, but even at a room's-distance in the poor light I could see he'd had the same one on for days. From the length of his stubble he hadn't shaved since Drusilla's death; hadn't eaten all that much, either, because he looked like a half-starved goat. Skulls came to mind. Mildewed ones, at that. The room's curtains were closed, there were only a few lamps lit and the place smelled of stale sweat and incense.

I bowed my head as the slave closed the door behind me.

'Caesar.'

'Hello, Marcus.' Well, at least he sounded brighter than he looked, which admittedly wasn't saying much. The usual bright, brittle drawl was missing. 'Come in. Have a seat, if you can find one. I'm afraid the place is a bit of a mess. The slaves want to tidy it, but I just can't be arsed. I've told them to stay out.'

I moved over to the couch opposite his. There was a tray on it, with bowls of untouched food that looked like it'd been there for days. I lifted it out of the way, onto a side table, and sat down.

'I'm sorry about your sister, sir,' I said.

'Yes. Yes, thank you.' He gave a brittle smile that didn't touch his eyes. These I didn't like the look of at all; they shifted, and they glittered in the lamplight. 'Mind you, she's a goddess now, you know. Or she will be shortly, as soon as I can make her one. I thought Panthea would be a good name - the Universal Divinity. Venus, sort of thing. In fact, she could share Venus's temple in the Julian Market, in the short term, anyway. What do you think?'

My stomach went cold. 'Very nice, Caesar,' I said.

'Yes. She'll like that. Still, it's hard, not having her around in the flesh any more. She was a lovely girl. We're all quite devastated.'

I said nothing.

'Life, however, must go on, I suppose.' Another brittle smile and a shrug of the shoulders. 'Now. What can I do for you?'

This was the tricky bit. I cleared my throat.

'I had a letter the other day, sir. From Sertorius Macro. Only it turns out that it wasn't.'

The smile had become a frown. 'Macro? He's dead. Been dead for months.'

'Yes, sir. I know. It was delivered by someone who claimed to be his secretary. That wasn't right either.'

'Marcus, petal, you're not making sense.'

I took the letter out and handed it over. 'Read it yourself, sir. But as I say it's a forgery.'

'How very odd.' He unrolled it. 'Bring some light over, would you? It isn't very bright in here.'

I got up and fetched the nearest candelabrum closer - half the lamps were out of oil - then waited until he'd read the thing through.

25

He chuckled.

'It's a load of balls,' he said. 'Patronising to boot. I mean, what "foibles" do I have, for goodness' sake? And I certainly was not "misinformed". The man was a scheming bastard, and that wife of his was worse. I should never have given either of them house room. Especially her.'

'You're sure of that, sir?'

'Absolutely sure. Macro pushed his overblown bedmate at me to worm his way into my confidence, then when I fell ill the two of them got together with that pompous idiot Silanus and stinky young Gemellus to get rid of me altogether. Only it didn't work. I was protected, you see. The gods of Rome protected me.'

'So there was an actual conspiracy?'

'Of course there was. They were completely guilty, all of them. Naturally, I couldn't make it public, not after making such a song and dance about scrapping that dreadfully unpopular treason charge. But I could kill them all anyway.' He grinned. 'By the gods, I could! I was a bit sorry about Gemellus, mind, he was just two tiles short of a roof, poor lamb, but I'd've had to do it sooner or later anyway, and he wasn't much of a loss.'

My belly went cold again.

'So.' He handed back the letter. 'If that's all that's worrying you -'

'Not quite, Caesar,' I said.

'You mean there's more?'

'I - well, I sort of got interested.' I swallowed.

'Really?' He raised himself on his elbow. 'You surprise me.'

'I mean, why the letter in the first place? I know it's a forgery, but -'

He laughed. 'Oh, Marcus! *Marcus!* You don't change, do you? Now *don't* tell me you want to take this further! I said: it's absolute balls!'

'So why when I start asking a few questions should some heavy go for me in a wineshop and threaten me and my family to get me to stop?'

The laughter died. 'What?'

'It happened a couple of days ago, sir. I, uh, wondered at the

26

time if you hadn't sent him yourself.'

'Why on earth would you think that?'

'He was pretty well informed. And he looked like a Praetorian.'

He laughed again. 'Marcus, petal,' he said. 'If I wanted you to stop pushing your fucking long nose into something then I'd've hauled you over here and told you myself. Or sent someone who not only looked like a Praetorian but was one to do it for me in no uncertain terms, with a nasty great sword in his hand to stress the point. That's what this is all about.' He gestured round the room. 'I'm the emperor, for the gods' sake, I don't need to be subtle. Besides, I know you and it wouldn't work. You wouldn't take a telling. So I'd've ordered the Praetorian with the sword to use it there and then or had you use it for him and saved us all a lot of trouble.' The hairs crawled on my neck. 'Not guilty, love. It wasn't me, I promise you.'

Well, that was a relief, anyway. Still, we weren't through the woods yet.

'If you do want me to stop, Caesar,' I said, 'then I will.'

He looked at me for a long time, frowning. Then he chuckled.

'Really?' he said. I didn't answer. 'Do you want to? The truth, now!'

'Not particularly.'

'There you are, then. That's settled.' He reached forward and clapped me on the shoulder. 'So don't. It's no skin off my nose. You're a fool, Marcus, because there's nothing to find and you're wasting your time, but that's your business. Besides, past experience has taught me that your long nose finds its way into very unexpected places. I may be wrong, and that would be interesting.'

I breathed out. 'Thank you, Caesar.'

'Oh, tush, petal! Enjoy yourself. You've got carte blanche. You can't do me any harm, and who knows? You might do me some actual good. I told you: the gods are protecting me. Now push off, there's a lamb. Give my regards to that wife of yours.'

'Yes, Caesar.' I got up and moved towards the door.

'Oh, and Marcus?'

I turned. 'Yes?'

'Don't worry. I'll look into this Praetorian business. You think the man was a Praetorian?'

'I'm not sure, sir, but yes.'

'Then I'll put the word out. You won't have any more trouble in that direction, I promise you. And if I find the bastard he'll be on the menu at the next Games. I'll send you a special ticket.'

That was a relief, too. It's nice to know you have an emperor on your side, even if he is Gaius. 'Thank you, sir.'

I left.

Six

'It wasn't the emperor.'

I'd changed out of my mantle and joined Perilla for a pre-dinner drink in the garden. Bathyllus had brought a half-jug of Setinian for me and a fruit juice for Perilla. Wine had never tasted so good.

'You're absolutely certain?' Perilla said.

'Yeah. He even gave me carte blanche for carrying on the investigation.' I stretched out my feet and rested them on the footstool. 'Maybe Gaius isn't so bad after all.'

'But that's absolutely marvellous!' Perilla was beaming.

'Isn't it? So we're off the hook and running, lady. All we're left with now is the problem.'

'Oh, good. And that is, precisely?'

Yeah. Right. Good question. This thing wasn't like a straightforward murder, with a definite victim and a definite perp. Oh, sure, there were bodies enough, but they were bodies politic and they'd killed themselves on Gaius's orders; no difficulty there. It wasn't a matter so much of whodunit at this point as why was it done.

And then there was the whole business of Dion. Or whatever the bastard's real name was.

'Let's start with the conspiracy,' I said.

'There was a conspiracy after all?'

'So Gaius assured me, and he was telling the truth as far as he knew it, I'm convinced of that. More or less along the obvious lines: Junius Silanus was intriguing with Macro to get rid of Gaius and use Gemellus as a puppet emperor. Although that doesn't work, does it, for the reasons I gave you, not where Macro was concerned, anyway, and he's crucial. So, me, I don't think there was a conspiracy at all, whatever Gaius says, because it doesn't make sense. I think the three of them - Macro, Silanus and Gemellus - were set up.'

'As it says in the letter. Implies, at least.' Perilla was twisting a

29

strand of her hair. 'Very well, Marcus, I'll accept that, as a hypothesis anyway. Why?'

'That's nursery-slopes stuff. Macro and Silanus were Gaius's top advisors, had been ever since he became emperor, and Macro since well before that. You could even say his only advisors, because they were responsible for most of the policy decisions. Gemellus, fine, he was a poor stick who hadn't a hope in hell of being approved as emperor by the senate if they'd any choice in the matter. Only with Gaius dead they wouldn't have: at least Gemellus was an imperial, Tiberius had named him as co-heir, and he was Gaius's legally-adopted son. Who else was left with a legitimate claim? Claudius? The day that guy gets the purple there'll be a blue moon. And Gaius's only child died with his mother at birth, so there was no direct heir at all.'

'So what you're saying,' Perilla said, 'is that the conspiracy, once it was detected, cleared the field completely. Of both potential heirs and advisers. And the conspiracy was a fake. Someone put the idea of it in Gaius's mind just for that reason.'

'Right. Macro's - or Dion's - "misinformation and calumnies". The question is, who did it clear the field for? Cui bono, in other words?'

'You said. There was no one left.'

'What about the sisters?'

'Oh, Marcus! They're women!'

'Yeah, but they've got husbands, haven't they? And Livia was a woman too. You telling me that bitch wasn't political?'

Perilla went very quiet and reached for her fruit juice.

'Go on,' she said.

'So let's take them one by one. Agrippina. Drusilla. Livilla.'

'Very well.'

'Youngest and most unlikely first. Livilla. Her husband's Marcus Vinicius. He's got about as much drive and ambition as a hamster, his idea of the perfect evening is to curl up with a good book, and he wouldn't say boo to a gosling. And she's a bubble-headed moron.'

Perilla smiled. 'Actually I know Vinicius quite well; we see each other at poetry readings and he's a very nice man indeed. I quite agree, he's not conspirator material. Neither, for the reason you gave, is his wife.'

30

'Scrap them, then. Next, Drusilla. Gaius's favourite sister. Recently and suddenly dead at, what, twenty-two? Twenty-three? If Gaius hadn't been obviously so cut up and if he hadn't been so unconcerned about me poking around then I'd be wondering about that, personally. A fifth death in the imperial circle hard on the heels of four compulsory suicides is stretching coincidence too far.'

'Your paranoia's showing, dear. It was scarcely hard on the heels; Macro and Ennia have been dead for over two months, the others for much longer. And summer in Rome's a bad time for fevers. These things happen. There's no reason to suspect that Drusilla's death wasn't natural.'

'No. Right. Or at least that the emperor was responsible. Even so, I'd take an outside bet there's something fishy there. Mark it for later. Anyway, her husband's Aemilius Lepidus. Same age as Gaius, from a good family with strong imperial connections: his father was tipped as a possible successor to Augustus and his sister was married to Gaius's brother Drusus. Plus, he's in thick with the emperor. Gossip says they're even lovers.'

'Gossip will say anything.'

'Yeah, well, he's pretty eclectic in his tastes, our Gaius. And at least he'd be keeping it in the family. Anyway, Lepidus is a better bet than Vinicius, if only just because from all reports the guy's a mental and political lightweight, and his late wife wasn't a particularly pushy type either, despite her closeness to her brother.' I paused. 'He's making her a goddess, by the way. Gaius is, I mean.'

'*What?*'

'True. He told me himself. She's to be called Panthea and she's sharing a temple with Venus the Mother, presumably until he can build her one of her own.'

'But that's ridiculous!'

'You heard it here first, lady. Watch and marvel.' I took a swig of wine. 'Okay. So we're left with the eldest sister. Agrippina.'

'Ah.'

'Ah is right. Agrippina's married to Domitius Ahenobarbus, and from past acquaintance we know all about him, don't we? They're the dream team. He's ambitious, ruthless, political to his back teeth, a total bastard, and with form to boot, and she's a pushy little bitch,

31

smart and devious as hell and hard-nosed as they come, just like her mother and Livia. Plus they've got a son now, young Nero. He's only six months old, sure, but he's a five-star imperial on his mother's side, the sainted Germanicus's only grandson, and with Gaius dead that'd weigh with the senate.'

'Wait a moment, dear. I thought the plan was to make Gemellus into a puppet emperor.'

'Yeah, and how long do you think he would've survived with Agrippina and Ahenobarbus pulling the strings? If we're looking for a cui bono, or rather a quibus bono, I reckon that pair of beauties are top of the list.'

'Hmm.' Perilla was still twisting at her hair. 'Yes. Mind you, I'm not sure where all this is getting you, Marcus. Even if Agrippina and Ahenobarbus were responsible for this pseudo-conspiracy then what can you do about it? They're imperials, Macro and the rest of them are dead and buried, and equable as Gaius seems to be he's not going to take kindly to you accusing his sister and brother-in-law of treason, not if you haven't a shred of actual proof. I'm sorry, but whether you're right or not the whole thing's impractical.'

Yeah; it was. I frowned and reached for my winecup. Bugger. So how did we get the proof? Finding Dion and talking to him might be a start, sure, but I hadn't the least idea how to go about that. And if he didn't want to be found then I was on a hiding to nothing.

Bathyllus shimmered through the portico. 'Excuse me, sir. Madam.'

'Yeah, little guy?' I said. 'What is it now? A delay with the dinner? Don't worry, we're fine out here for the present. Just tell Meton -'

'Your mother and Helvius Priscus have arrived, sir. Should I bring them through or would you rather come inside?'

I groaned. Oh, hell. 'Bring them out, Bathyllus. And tell the skivvies to fetch a couple more chairs.'

But Mother had already appeared, with Priscus in tow. Despite the heat she looked her usual carefully-groomed and mantled self, and a good ten years younger than her real age, which was sixty that year. Priscus, on the other hand, was doing his usual impersonation of a sartorially-challenged tortoise.

I got up.

'Hello, dear, how are you both?' Mother swooped over and air-kissed me on both cheeks, then did the same for Perilla. 'I'm sorry to come unannounced, but I knew you wouldn't mind.'

'I thought you were on your way to Baiae,' I said.

'We're leaving tomorrow morning. You should join us, you know. Summer in Rome is absolutely dreadful.'

'It's okay.' Given the choice between frying in Rome and being bored out of my skull in Baiae surrounded by the top five hundred's glittering best I'd take the big city every time.

Bathyllus had reappeared with the chair-toting skivvies. He hovered while Mother and Priscus settled themselves.

'I'll have a vervain mint, Bathyllus,' Mother said, arranging the folds of her mantle. I winced. 'Chilled, if you can manage it. Helvius Priscus will have the same.'

I glanced at Priscus, who was doing his sad tortoise act in the other chair, and he gave me the faintest of shrugs. Well, the guy was happy enough, and for an octogenarian with all the salient features of a reanimated Egyptian mummy he seemed to be thriving.

'Top that up for me while you're about it, little guy.' I passed him the jug. 'And another fruit juice for the mistress.'

'You drink too much, Marcus,' Mother said.

'First today.'

She looked at me - Mother's no fool, far from it - then turned to Perilla. 'How are the wedding preparations going?'

'Oh, we're getting there, Vipsania,' Perilla said. 'It's a bit awkward, with the ceremony being in Castrimoenium, but Marilla was insistent.'

'I think she's very sensible, myself.' Mother sniffed. 'The Alban Hills are much more picturesque than Rome. Besides, Clarus's family are all locals, aren't they?'

I stiffened slightly, but she didn't mean anything by it: Mother may be related to old Agrippa, who was Augustus's right-hand man, but she's no snob. And Marcus Agrippa had been provincial Italian himself. As, for that matter, had Augustus.

'Mmmaa!' Priscus said. Bleated. We all turned towards him. 'Before I forget, Marcus, and speaking of Clarus, I wanted to consult the

33

lad's father about a skull I came across recently. Pre-Etruscan, almost certainly Iapygian. Personally I think it shows Illyrian features, which of course would be most significant in determining the provenance of the Messapians. Although there again the features may be native Cretan, which in its turn would link them with Caria.'

There was a silence. Finally, Mother turned back to me. 'Yes. Well anyway, dear, the reason we dropped by was to ask you a favour.'

Oh, bugger. Mother's favours had a nasty habit of blowing up in your face, like one of these super-smart Greek experiments with steam hydraulics. 'Ah...what would that be, now?' I asked cautiously.

'It's to do with our wedding present. You know, the busts?'

Right: Mother and Priscus had wanted to commission a pair of portrait busts of Marilla and Clarus from a Greek sculptor rejoicing in the name of Archimenides. 'Yeah,' I said. 'Not a problem, is there?'

'Very much so, I'm afraid. We're back to square one now because yesterday the silly idiot got himself squashed by a marble block falling from a crane. And as I said Titus and I are off to Baiae tomorrow.'

'So you want me to find another sculptor.' Bugger. Double bugger.

'Oh, no. At least, we've got a name.'

'I did that,' Priscus said.

'In fact, you know him. Or at least you know someone who knows him.'

'Mother -' I said.

'Larcius Paullus.'

'I don't know anyone called Larcius Paullus.'

Mother sighed. 'Paullus is the sculptor, dear. You know, the trouble with you is that you never listen.'

'Young chap, totally brilliant.' That was Priscus. 'An Ostian native, if you'll believe it, but the family's Greek on the mother's side. He did a bust three months ago of my friend Septimius Gallus. Spitting image, peas in a pod. And he wasn't even dead at the time.'

Oh, gods. 'Look, Mother, can we start again? Please?'

'Certainly. You really shouldn't drink so much, dear, it rots the brain. Paullus is Agron's wife's nephew. We thought the Graeco-Roman connection on the sculptor's side would be quite a nice touch.

Very appropriate.'

Things were finally beginning to make sense. I'd known Agron almost as long as I'd known Perilla; in fact, he'd been mixed up in the Ovid business. He wasn't Greek himself - he was Illyrian, originally, an ex-legionary - but his wife Cass was. And, come to think of it, I knew Paullus as well, although I'd never met the kid: he was the young wizard with the charcoal-stick that I'd got to do me lightning sketches of the visitors to Publius Vitellius's house. Yeah, that'd be seven years back, so he'd be in his late teens now. Evidently the artistic kid had made good.

'Oh, thank you, Bathyllus.' The little guy had smarmed over with the loaded tray, and Mother took her chilled vervain mint. 'Lovely.'

'A pleasure, Madam.' Crawl, crawl. Sickening.

'So, Marcus, I can safely leave it in your hands, can I? We're not giving him much time, of course, especially since he'd have to go through to Castrimoenium to take their likenesses, but I'm sure he can manage and that we'll be delighted with the result. He seems a very capable boy, and as Titus said he really is quite brilliant.'

'Yeah,' I said, reaching for the fresh jug that Bathyllus had brought. 'Yeah, he is. No problem, Mother. I'll fix it.'

Damn right I would; in fact, the sooner I got over to Ostia the better, because I'd just realised how I could track down Dion.

Seven

I rode to Ostia the next morning, setting off at dawn before the heat started to bite: it's only fourteen miles, sure, down a good road, but with my expertise on a horse, or lack of it, it would take me three hours, easy.

Agron was doing well for himself these days. With Ostia's harbour silting up worse by the year and the local boat-building industry in consequent decline, he'd turned the boatyard he'd inherited through Cass over to making carts and furniture, which financially had been a very smart move. I saw him in Rome quite often - he came through on business once a month and stayed with us, or if it was a quick visit he and I would split a jug and a plate of cheese in Renatius's - but it was a good four years since I'd been to his place, a tenement building on the edge of town near the old Sullan Wall. He and Cass - Cassiopeia, she was Alexandrian Greek originally - owned the whole thing, from doorstep to tiles, which I reckoned was a sensible investment: his family was up to six now, and counting. By the time the kids reached the marrying stage he'd be able to fill the place, easy.

I parked the mare at a handy trough and went inside. Forget your picture of a tenement on the Aventine or in the Subura; Cass made sure this one was kept in good repair, and clean. The same went for the tenants. Me, I wouldn't be surprised if she held defaulters down in the horse trough and scrubbed them herself.

Agron's flat took up the whole first floor and I could hear the sound of kids running around screaming from the ground-floor lobby. I gritted my teeth, climbed the holystoned stairs, raised my fist and knocked; although with that racket going on whether anyone would hear anything hitting the door short of a sledgehammer was a moot point. Amazingly, it opened.

'Marcus?'

'Hey, Cass,' I said.

'What are you doing in Ostia?' Her broad face split into a grin as she hefted the grumpy-looking bobble-hatted gnome she was carrying further up against her hip. A big woman, Cass, almost as big as Agron, which was really saying something. Mind you, to control the bacchic rout of kids that she'd got she'd have to be.

'I'm -' I began, but I was drowned out by a prolonged scream from inside that froze my spine and turned my guts to jelly.

Cass turned round. '*Tertia!* Stop that! And if you make Quintus sick again, my girl, you'll be in real trouble!'

The screaming went down a notch. There wasn't all that much difference to the sound level, cosmically speaking, but it seemed to satisfy Cass because she was facing me again.

'Sorry about that,' she said. 'They've been on a high all morning.'

'Uh...that Septimus?' I said, meaning the grumpy gnome. Obviously a new addition to the scrum. At least he hadn't got the use of his legs yet.

'Septima.' The grin widened. 'Look, come on in. Agron won't be back for a while yet, but if you've ridden all the way from Rome you'll be -'

'Ah...that's okay, Cass, if you don't mind,' I said quickly. 'Not just now.' Absolutely no way was I crossing that threshold, not if the kids were on a high: they were bad enough at the best of times, and from the sound of things I'd probably be torn apart before I got the length of the living room, even with Cass there to provide the supporting muscle. 'It's business, and pretty pressing. A commission. In fact, two commissions.' There was a loud crash and another scream from beyond the door, followed by what sounded like a war-to-the-knife squabble between two blood-crazed maenads. I felt the sweat break out on my forehead, but Cass didn't even blink. 'For young Larcius Paullus.'

'Polyxene's boy?' She bounced Sprog Number Seven in the crook of her arm and the gnome burped. 'Two commissions? Marcus, that is *wonderful!* He'll be absolutely delighted! He's got a real talent.'

'Yeah, I remember.' There was another crash. Shit; time I was leaving. Past time. They'd be out here with us in a minute and it'd be Cannae all over again. 'Uh...where can I find him?'

'He works from home. One of the old houses beyond the seaside gate. I could send Tertia to show you, but you'd be better dropping in on Agron at the yard. It's practically next door.'

'Fine. Don't disturb Tertia. I'll just, ah, head on over there now.'

She laughed. 'Coward. Tell him dinner's two hours after noon, or it will be today now you're here. That'll give you plenty of time to see Paullus and have a cup of wine together. But don't be late, and come back sober or I'll skin the both of you.'

'Got you.' I had: the inevitable presence of homicidal sprogs or not, one of Cass's meals was not to be missed. She wasn't kidding about not being late, either: turn up when the sun was an inch past the mark and you were toast. 'Oh, by the way, you may as well have this now. It'll only get broken.' I handed her one of the two packages I'd brought carefully from Rome across the mare's crupper, a pistachio and almond-cream pastry the size of a paving slab. If Cass has one weakness - and it shows in her sideways spread - it's pastries. The other package was a Sarsina cheese. I hadn't had time to scour the cheese-market for a fresh Lesuran or a Gabalican, but Meton had come up trumps, and it was absolutely top grade. Cheese is Agron's thing. I'd give him that myself.

I left her sorting out whatever domestic crisis had been going on behind her back, beat a hasty retreat to the mare and headed towards the centre of town.

Ostia's an easy place to find your way around in; at least, easy compared with Rome. It's based around the old Republican fort, and although that's long gone the streets are laid out on the army's grid plan, parallel with the original ditches. The seaside gate's to the south-west, and beyond it the town straggles out along the shoreline, mostly warehousing and boat-builders' yards. Or what used to be the shoreline: the tidal changes that've been responsible for the silting up of the harbour are adding shallows and new land every year, and a lot of the builders' yards've been left high and dry. Agron's was one of these. He - or his father-in-law before him, rather - hadn't handled the big stuff, just small coastal fishing boats, but even so the old man had needed to dredge a channel and keep it clear to get them to and from the stocks. Since the changeover, though, Agron hadn't bothered. The cradles and pits had disappeared in favour of three or four large sheds. The place was certainly busy, with a dozen slaves working all out. Noisy, too, with sawing and hammering, but that sort of noise I could take.

I tied the mare to a handy cart and went inside. 'The boss around?' I asked the nearest slave.

'Corvinus! What the hell brings you here?' The man himself, coming over and wiping his hands on a rag. A bit older, like the rest of us, greying now at the temples, but he still looked like he could bend iron bars without breaking sweat. Which he could.

We shook.

'Business,' I said. 'You got half an hour?'

'Sure. More, if you want it.' He raised his voice. 'Decimus!' He did a mime-show of pointing at me and drinking. One of the slaves raised his hand in salute and grinned. 'We'll go to Vetus's place. He's got a decent Privernan in.'

'Maybe later. I was hoping you'd take me to your nephew Paullus.'

'What, Polyxene's Paullus? What do you want with him?'

'Commission from Mother of a couple of portrait busts for Marilla and Clarus. And something for me. Not another bust, just an idea.'

'No problem. And it's in the same direction.' He strode off towards the yard gates, and I followed. 'So how are you? Busy with the wedding?'

I laughed. 'Yeah. You could say that. Oh, and by the way, in case I forget Cass says to tell you dinner today's two hours after noon.'

'Fine. That'll give you plenty of time to get back to Rome. Unless you want to bunk down for the night in the living room, of course. We can manage that, easy.'

'Ah...no. Thanks anyway, pal, but I'll stick to the round trip.'

He grinned. 'Suit yourself.'

'And I brought you a cheese. Only Sarsinan, but it's a good one.' I handed the package over. 'I had to prise it out of Meton with a crow-bar.'

He stopped, unwrapped it and took a sniff. 'Beautiful! We'll have it with the Privernan. Vetus doesn't know a good cheese from old socks.' We carried on, back the way I'd come, towards the town proper.

'So. A couple of portrait busts, eh? Real upmarket stuff. Paullus'll be thrilled, and he could do with the work. He's a paint-on-wood guy, really, that's all people about here can afford, but he can handle a chisel with the best of them. Learned it from his great-uncle, and the old man really knew his marble. That's Vetus's, incidentally' - he pointed at a neat little wineshop with a trellised vine, that I'd noticed on my way out - 'and Polyxene's place is just down this alley. Couldn't be nearer. She lives alone now, apart from Paullus, since Larcius died a couple of years back.'

Like Cass had said, it was one of the old houses; probably it'd been a fisherman's cottage a hundred years or so back, when the coast was closer and Ostia hadn't spread out this far. There was a lean-to beside it, where the original fisherman would've hung his nets to dry and stored his gear.

'Hey, Polyxene!' Agron shouted. 'It's me! Anyone around?'

A tall, lanky kid came out of the lean-to, holding a paintbrush.

'Hi, Uncle Agron,' he said. 'Mum's gone to the market.'

'No problem. It was you I wanted to see.' Agron jerked his thumb at me. 'My friend Marcus Corvinus here's got a job for you. Two portrait busts.'

'*Two?*' The kid's eyes lit up. 'Wow! Great!' Despite his Latin name he was pure Greek, with tight-curled black hair, an oval face and olive skin.

'You did one for a friend of my stepfather's a few months ago,' I said. 'He was impressed.'

'That'd be Septimius Gallus,' Paullus said. 'Yeah, I was pleased with that myself. Luna marble.' He was examining my face. 'You want Luna as well, sir? Or something different? Black, maybe. Black's more unusual.'

'Luna'd be perfect. But they're not for me.' I explained, and quoted the price Mother had cleared with the terminally-flattened Archimenides. Paullus's eyes widened, and his jaw dropped.

'You've got it,' he said simply. 'Jupiter, have you got it! I'll have to go over to Castrimoenium and make a few sketches, naturally. That be okay?'

'Any time you like,' I said. 'We have a deal?'

'Absolutely.' We shook. Thrilled was right.

40

Well, that part of it was done. 'Actually, speaking of sketches,' I said, 'I've a job for you myself. Whether it's possible I don't know, but tell me what you think.'

'Sure.'

'There's this guy I want to find. I don't know his name, but I've met him and I could describe what he looks like. I thought maybe we could build up a sketch together.'

He looked blank. Then he snapped his fingers. 'Marcus Corvinus. You're the purple-striper that got me to draw these men visiting a house in Rome. Years ago.'

'That's me,' I said.

'Corvinus, what is this?' Agron was frowning.

'Just a bit of a problem I'm having at the moment, pal,' I said. 'I thought Paullus here might be able to help.' I looked at the kid. 'Possible?'

'We can try. Just let me get my stuff from inside. The light's better out here.'

And he disappeared into the lean-to.

'You in trouble?' Agron said quietly.

'No. Not really.'

'Because if you are, and you need some heavy back-up, you know where to come.'

I thought of the guy in the wineshop. Well, it was comforting to know, even if I did have Gaius's reassurance. 'Thanks,' I said. 'I'll remember.'

Paullus reappeared with a folding table, some sheets of paper and a charcoal stick. He set the table up.

'Okay,' he said. 'Go ahead.'

'He was early forties, Asian Greek, maybe Syrian.'

Paullus shook his head. 'No. You'll need to be more detailed than that. Start with the shape of his face. Long and narrow? Rounder, more moon-shaped? Square-cut?'

'Right. Sorry.' I closed my eyes for a moment and concentrated on my memory of Dion. 'Long. But jowly, a fair amount of padding over the bones.'

Paullus's hand with the charcoal stick moved over the paper, leaving a thin outline. 'Like this?'

41

'Broader in the forehead. No, a bit less than that. Rounder in the chin.' I watched as he changed the line. 'Yeah, that's about right. It'll do, anyway.'

'Eyes?'

'Sunk in over full cheekbones. Piggy; I said, he was fat. Heavy eyelids. The left one drooped a bit. Thin eyebrows, well apart.' The picture followed the words. Gods, the kid was good! His hand almost blurred, sketching the details in lightly as I gave them to him.

'Hairline?'

'High up. Receding. The guy was practically bald, and he was wearing a freedman's cap. Just the occasional strand of hair coming out from underneath.'

'Nose?'

'Big. Fleshy. And there was a mole at the side. A big one, with hairs sprouting.'

'Great! Which side?'

'The left. Low down, in the crease.'

Bit by bit, trial and error, we built up Dion's face. Finally, half an hour later, the man himself stared at me out of the page.

'Brilliant!' I said. I meant it, too. The kid was a genius.

'No problem. If you can wait a few minutes I'll do you a proper clean sketch without the rubbings-out and the faulty lines.'

'Can you do copies?'

'Sure. How many do you want?'

I did a quick calculation. 'Five. No, better make it six.'

'Give me an hour?'

I glanced at Agron. 'Vetus's?'

'Vetus's it is,' he said.

'Great. Thanks, Paullus.'

The kid smiled. 'No bother. Thank you. What I get for your two busts'll keep us for the next six months, easy. And I'll enjoy doing them, too.'

We headed for the wineshop.

'And meanwhile, you close-mouthed bastard,' Agron said as we went, 'you can tell me what's going on.'

Eight

I paid Paullus three gold pieces for the copies, which I reckoned was a bargain on my side, plus a down-payment on the busts, then went back with Agron to Sprogs' Castle for dinner. I was starving: I'd skipped breakfast in favour of an early start, and Agron had wolfed most of the cheese, which was fair enough since I'd accounted for most of the Privernan. Not a wine man, Agron, and it had nothing to do with Cass's threat: I suspected that had been directed more at me. Still, I managed to roll in sober and respectable. Or reasonably sober and not disreputable.

But there were no sprogs in evidence, barring Septima quietly asleep in her cradle, and I breathed a sigh of relief. That I'd been dreading.

'I fed them early and sent them outside,' Cass said as Agron kissed her and the sleeping gnome. 'I'm sorry to disappoint you, Corvinus. I know how much you like children.'

I grinned. 'Yeah.' They were probably even now spreading terror, havoc and despair for blocks around, and call me selfish if you like but I didn't mind. Ostia would survive it. Probably. 'What's for dinner?'

'Fish soup and oyster dumplings.' Hey, great! 'Did you see Paullus?'

'Yeah. All settled.' I'd told Agron about the Macro problem, but we'd agreed it was no business of Cass's. Mind you, she'd probably get most of the details after I'd gone anyway: the big Illyrian wasn't good at keeping secrets from his wife, and besides I'd arranged to hire half a dozen kids from among his collateral family and their friends for the next stage in the plan, so word would get back to her eventually.

'Sit down and I'll bring it through,' Cass said. 'Agron, would you cut the bread, please?'

Like I said, the flat wasn't your typical tenement's: there was

43

a kitchen with a charcoal range, small, sure, but it was there, and a dining room with a big table and benches. The table was ready-laid with earthenware bowls and iron spoons, plus - I was glad to see - winecups.

'Wine's over there on the dresser, Marcus,' Agron said as he divided up the poppy-seed loaf. 'Help yourself. Just you, Cass and I'll stick to water.'

I poured, sipped - it was Spanish mass-market, but not bad; Cass must've got it for me special that morning - and sat down while she brought in the soup pot and ladled out soup and dumplings.

'How're the wedding preparations going?' she said.

'Painfully.' I picked up my spoon. Cass's fish soup and dumplings were legendary. Mind you, I'd yet to have anything she cooked that wouldn't've got even our Meton's grudging approval. 'We've got a priest who might just turn up in his underwear, Marilla wants to invite the dog, the sheep and the donkey, and Perilla's tearing Rome apart for bridesmaids' dress material. Otherwise everything's fine.'

Agron laughed, sat down and passed me a piece of the bread. 'Perilla can't find dress material in *Rome?*'

'Not to suit.' I took a spoonful of soup. Delicious. 'Don't ask, pal, just don't ask. I don't know why not either.'

'Oh, *Marcus!*' Cass said.

'Tell her to try Alexandria.' Agron bit into a dumpling, still chuckling.

I set down my spoon. 'Now don't you start! And if you see Perilla in the near future don't you even *mention* the place. I'm serious.'

'Come on, boy! Joke!'

'You've never had a wife who was shopping for a wedding. They're not logical. Me, I think something snaps in the brain.'

'Eat your soup and shut up, Corvinus,' Cass said.

'Mind you,' Agron chewed on the dumpling, 'you get stuff there from the east that never gets this far. It makes sense. Second biggest city in the empire, huge sophisticated market and half of it's women. I mean, why bother to take the risk of shipping the goods any further when you can unload it at a decent profit there?'

'You shut up too, please, dear.'

Agron grinned. 'Yes, love.'

We ate in silence. Not that it was a hardship. The dumplings were beautiful.

'Besides,' Cass said after a bit, 'Alexandria isn't a place to visit at present.'

I looked up from my bowl. 'You heard something from Mika?' Mika was another of Cass's huge family of siblings, although she'd reversed the trend, married another Alexandrian Greek, and moved back to the old country. Her husband ran a barge on one of the city's canals.

'We had a letter just a few days ago,' Agron said. 'Mika's getting worried.'

'About what?' I scooped up a dumpling.

'What else? Trouble again between us and the damn Jews.'

Uh-oh. I held the dumpling poised. That had been Cass. I noticed the 'us'. And the 'damn'.

We'd hit serious cultural shoals here, or at least as close to them as the normally easy-going Cass - easy-going in that sense, anyway - ever went. To any reasonable person in the empire - certainly to any Roman - the Jews're a joke: they believe in and worship only one monomaniacally-bad-tempered god, they have dietary rules that make no practical sense, and they flatly refuse to burn incense to the Divine Augustus and the Spirit of Rome, which to any non-Jew is just plain bad manners. Still, as far as Rome herself's concerned if they choose to be stiff-necked, uncivilised, antisocial bastards then that's their business; so long as they don't get political and mess with the *pax romana* they can do whatever the hell they like, and we'll defend their right to do it against anyone who wants to object. Just like we would for the other guys, if the situation was reversed. That's what the *pax romana* means: you've the right to live as you like, believe what you want, so long as you keep the peace and don't meddle with the social and political status quo. Do that - even think of doing it - and Rome'll be on top of you like Archimenides's marble block, because the downside of all this is that you play the game by her rules or not at all.

Which was just the problem in Alexandria. Or potentially at least. And it had been simmering on for years. Greeks and Jews are cat and dog; put them together en masse in the one city and you've got a recipe for trouble that's inevitable. Two out of five of Alexandria's

45

population - and we're talking six hundred thousand here, more than half the size of Rome - are Jews; and that's a sizeable minority. Trouble is, with the exception of a handful of individuals from the oldest and richest families, they aren't citizens. Only the Greeks are. And the Jews don't like it. And the Greeks don't like the fact that the Jews don't like it.

The other important factor is that Rome rules Alexandria, not the Greeks who live there. We have done since Augustus beat Cleopatra and Antony at Actium sixty years back, and what we say goes, *nem. con.* The Greeks don't like that, either. And sixty years, in a Greek city whose history goes back almost three hundred to Alexander himself, is nothing.

Complicated, right?

Still, we weren't going to solve Alexandria's Roman/Jewish/ Greek problem in five minutes round an Ostian dinner table. It was time for a little tact. I put the spoon with its dumpling back down carefully on the plate. 'Oh, I'm sure it's nothing serious,' I said to Cass. 'Mika's always been a worry-monger.' That was certainly true enough: two years back, when a minor stomach bug had swept the city, Mika had sent a letter to Cass that read like it was a last desperate missive smuggled out before the plague wiped out all human life within the walls, and had her making offerings at every temple in Ostia. When a second letter arrived a month later to say it had only been a small dose of the gripes and enclosing a recipe for quince jelly she hadn't known whether to cry with relief or curse her sister black and blue for the worry she'd caused. According to Agron she'd done both.

'Not this time, Marcus,' Agron said. 'It's bad, or getting that way. And it's your fault.'

'*My* fault?' I'd been reaching for the wine cup. 'How the hell can it be *my* fault?'

'Come on, pal!' He chuckled. 'I mean the fault of you Romans. According to Mika, anyway. The governor's a guy by the name of Flaccus, Atillius Flaccus. You ever hear of him?'

'No.'

'He was a crony of the Wart's.' Yeah, well, I'd suppose he'd've had to be to make Egyptian Prefect: the job has always been a direct imperial appointment. 'Up to recently he was on the Jewish side, but now he's done a U-turn.'

'Not before time.' That was Cass again, and it was snapped.

Agron glanced at her. 'Maybe,' he said cautiously. 'But at least it kept the peace.'

'The *peace?*' Cass's spoon went down. 'We're not threatening the peace. All we're doing is protecting ourselves. Trying to, anyway. The Jews are parasites, they've all the perks of living in the city with none of the duties. They don't mix with us or anyone else if they can help it, they've their own assembly, their own courts, their own festivals -'

Uh-oh; this was a bad one, and when Cass got the bit between her teeth she was worse than Perilla. I lowered my head and concentrated on my soup.

'Cass, love.' Agron put a hand on her wrist. 'That's enough. Come on, settle down, eh? And what's this "us"? You were born here in Ostia. You've never even seen the place.'

It was touch and go for a moment, but then she took a deep breath, patted his hand and smiled. 'All right,' she said. 'I'm sorry. But it still makes me angry.'

Yeah, I could see that. And if someone like Cass could get so upset about conditions in Alexandria then there was trouble there right enough. None the less, I was interested. 'How do you mean, "done a U-turn"?'

'Flaccus used to support the Jewish community, like I said.' Agron dipped his bread in the soup. 'Stuck up for their rights to try purely Jewish cases, where only Jewish religious law was involved, in their own courts. Things like that.'

'Hang on, pal. No problem there. It's standard Roman policy anywhere a Jewish community's concerned. Their religious law's a minefield, even I know that. The governor would keep out of it, stay neutral. So long as no actual crimes or common issues were involved.'

'That's the point.' Agron put the piece of bread in his mouth and chewed. 'Oh, don't get me wrong, I'm no expert, I just know what Mika told us. But it looks like as governor he's not sitting on the fence any longer, and he's come down on the Greek side. Maybe it has something to do with what's happening in Judea. They've had trouble there in recent years, riots, that sort of thing. A few hothead Zealot

47

leaders crucified, and you know how these things spread, especially when religion and politics get mixed. My guess is he's stopping trouble before it starts, sending out a message to keep his own local Jewish hotheads' tails down.'

'Are there any?'

He shrugged. 'I'm only passing on what we get from the letters. Far as I can see, and reading between the lines, it seems like any hotheads there are're Greeks, and Flaccus isn't doing anything about them at all.'

'That's not fair,' Cass said.

'I'm sorry, love, but it is.' Agron could be firm when he wanted, and he was firm now. She frowned but said nothing. 'That guy Isidorus sounds a real troublemaker, for one.'

'Isidorus?' I paused, the wine cup half way to my mouth. 'I knew an Isidorus, a couple of years back. Here in Rome. He was one of the Wart's top men in the diplomatic corps.'

'Different person, then. This one's Alexandrian born and bred.'

Yeah, well, that wasn't surprising: Isidorus - Gift of Isis - is a pretty common Greek name, especially among Alexandrians. And I knew my Isidorus was an African, from Charax.

'Flaccus threw him out of the city for rabble-rousing two or three years ago.' Agron glanced at Cass again, but she was concentrating on her soup. 'Now it seems he's invited him back.'

I put the wine cup back down. 'That doesn't make sense. Unless the guy's changed his spots and promised to keep his head down in future.' Standard policy again: like I say, a governor's first job bar none is to keep the *pax romana*. Persistent troublemakers are either booted or chopped, and they stay that way.

Agron shook his head. 'He hasn't and he isn't. Not from what Mika says, although she's delighted. As far as she and the Greeks are concerned the sun shines out of his arse at midnight.'

'*Agron!*'

'Sorry, love. But it's true enough, Marcus. And he and Flaccus are bosom buddies now. Hence the threat of trouble. Oh, you're Roman, you'd be safe enough personally because this is purely a Greek and Jewish thing, but even so if Perilla's thinking at all of going over there now's not the time.'

Well, that was good to know, anyway, and I could always add it to my battery of arguments if the lady did raise the subject again. Still, it was odd about this guy Flaccus. Indulging a known troublemaker, especially one you'd previously sat down hard on, just wasn't something any competent Roman governor would do, even if there were other issues. And the guy would have to be competent, because the Egyptian governorship was one of the top imperial jobs.

'When exactly did Flaccus -?' I began; but Cass interrupted.

'I think we've had quite enough of the subject for one afternoon,' she said. 'Especially when the bad language starts to creep in.' I grinned. 'Now eat up your soup before it gets cold, Marcus. Then you can tell us more about the wedding. We're looking forward to it, Agron and I. We've never been up to the Alban Hills, and it'll be our first real holiday in years.'

So we talked about dresses, and catering, and the arrangements for the honeymoon - Mother had offered Clarus and Marilla the use of the villa she'd just bought at Baiae for a couple of months - and I finished the wine off. Then the marauding hordes came back and I thought maybe it was time to be heading home.

It had been a profitable day, all round. And tomorrow, or the next day, as soon as he could round them up and ferry them over, Agron had promised to let me have the kids.

Once they arrived we were in business.

Nine

They came after sunset, two days later, six of them, loaded in a cart with Agron driving, plus a big-boned woman I didn't know but who from the looks of her was another of Cass's many sisters.

'There you go, Marcus,' Agron said, climbing down. 'You get my message?'

'Yeah, everything's ready.'

'Fine. I've brought you the sharpest of the bunch.'

The kids - they were all boys, ten or eleven years old - jumped screaming from the tailgate. Bathyllus, who'd fetched me outside to say they'd arrived, blanched.

'*Now that's enough!*' the woman snapped. 'You've all been told! Behave properly!'

There was instant quiet.

'And this is Pausimache, one of my sisters-in-law.' Agron grinned. 'She'll be keeping an eye on them while they're here, if that's all right.'

I nodded to her. 'Hi, Pausimache,' I said. 'Glad to have you.' I was: the lads were typical Ostian kids and it would take an experienced Ostian mother to keep them in hand, which meant the female equivalent of a legion's First Spear. Pausimache clearly fitted the bill. Good name, too: Stay-the-Battle. 'Okay, boys,' I raised my voice. 'Listen a minute. We've put you in the east wing. This is Bathyllus. He'll see you're comfortable.'

Six pairs of eyes raked the little guy speculatively from head to toe and I saw him swallow. Me, normally I'd back Bathyllus against your crustiest senior senator or even a top-five-hundred dowager on a good day, but he was outclassed here and he knew it. With no Pausimache to ride shotgun on our guests he wouldn't last five minutes.

'Ground rules,' I said. 'The rest of the house is out of bounds. No chasing the chickens. No pissing in the fountain. No Bathyllus-baiting.

And no, absolutely *no* interference with next door. Even if their cat does come over the wall you leave it alone.' We'd trouble enough with our ongoing feud with the Petillius household without them finding that someone had lynched their Admetus, especially since the hellhound Placida had managed to nail his sister before she was dragged off in ignominy to Castrimoenium. 'Understood?'

They nodded. So did Pausimache. Grimly.

'Right, then.' I brought out Paullus's sketches. 'One each.' There was a scuffle as they surged forward. 'Don't grab, and anyone who tears or loses his goes straight home. This is the guy I want you to find. No flashing it around, no asking people, don't make it obvious, you keep a low profile and your mouths shut and just look at faces. We'll begin with the Palatine. There're six ways up there, so again that's one each. I'll get slaves to show you where these are. First thing in the morning and last thing in the afternoon when work starts and finishes're your best times, but hang around all day anyway and keep your eyes open. Pay's a silver piece each a day, plus ten to the one who finds him and tells me where *I* can find him without him or anyone else knowing that I know. Clear?' They all nodded again. There had been a lot of elbowing and grins when I mentioned the money, which was a good sign: these kids dealt in coppers, if they were lucky. A silver piece was a rarity, and ten of them was a fortune. 'Right. Any questions?' One hand went up. 'Yeah?'

'Where's the toilet?'

The rest sniggered. Pausimache glared at them and they stopped.

'Bathyllus'll show you in a minute. Any other questions?' No one spoke. 'Fine. Get settled in and then first thing in the morning off you go.'

They trooped off, with Bathyllus in the lead and Pausimache following behind.

'They'll do you a good job,' Agron said when they'd gone. 'What makes you think the guy's on the Palatine?'

'It's a fair bet,' I said. 'He'd professional clerk written all over him, and he knew too much about me and Macro for him to be private. So imperial civil service is my best guess, and that's where the main offices are. He won't live up there, of course, but that's all to the good because he'll be in and out every day. We've got all the entrances covered, and the chances are that if he's there we'll spot him. If we don't after two or three days we'll try the Market Square district. That's the other likely possibility.'

Agron shrugged. 'Seems a long shot to me, but you're the expert. And like I say they're good boys, they don't miss much. If he passes one of them then you'll know.' He grinned. 'Mind you, Bathyllus is going to have a hell of a time in the meanwhile, even with Pausimache around. So's Meton because they eat like horses.'

'Any special diet?'

'So long as you feed them plenty and often they're not particular. Food is food is food. They eat what they can get, when they can get it, and they can't afford to be picky.'

'When I knew you were coming I had Meton cook up a big pan of bean stew with meatballs. That do them for tonight?'

The grin widened. 'Meatballs? Marcus, they will *kill* for meatballs!'

'Fine. Okay. So come in yourself and have something to eat. What about Pausimache? She want to eat with us or with the lads?'

'Oh, she'll stay with them. Two are hers anyway, the twins.' Yeah, I'd noticed a couple of familiar-faced lookalikes in the bunch. 'Besides, like I said she's here to keep an eye on them and that's a full-time job because they're little devils. This business could be pretty hard on your furniture and fittings, Corvinus.'

'If it finds me Dion I can take it.'

'Don't say I didn't warn you.'

We sent them off the next morning after breakfast, with accompanying skivvies to show them which bit the Palatine was: none of the lads had ever been to Rome before, although I'd bet that wouldn't stop them from being completely at home inside of a day. Ostia's a hard training ground for kids, harder even than the Aventine or the Subura, and your average Ostian eleven-year-old is streetwise practically from when he can totter up to a fruit barrow and nick his first apple. It was a good breakfast, as well: Meton had worked his socks off filling them up with omelettes; things would be tough on the chickens, too, the next few days. Agron left at the same time for Ostia and Pausimache headed cheerfully in the direction of Cattlemarket Square on a big city shopping binge.

Okay; so it was in the hands of the gods now. All I could do was wait.

I was doing just that, in the shade of the portico with a half jug of Setinian, when Perilla got back from one of her literary outings and told me she'd wangled an invitation to a poetry reading the next day. For both of us.

'You've done *what?*' I stared at her in horror.

'Got you invited to a poetry reading, Marcus.' She was quite composed.

'Lady, you know me and poetry readings! I can't tell an ode from a fucking satire and I'm happy to keep it that way! Go yourself, sure, no problem, but leave me out of it!'

'You'll love this one, dear.' She sat down in the portico's other chair and took the fruit juice from the tray Bathyllus was holding. The little guy was looking definitely ragged, and I swear there was a twitch in his left eyelid. Less than a day, and our almost superhuman major-domo was feeling the pressure already. I hoped the kids found Dion quickly. 'It's Annaeus Seneca.'

'Who the bloody hell is Annaeus Seneca?'

'He's a Spaniard. From Corduba. He's also a rising orator.'

'I thought you said it was a poetry reading.'

'It is. He writes poetry as well. This is his first collection.'

'He any good?'

She sipped her fruit juice. 'Actually, he's absolutely dreadful.'

I did a double-take. 'What?'

'His poetry's complete drivel. And fawning, sick-making drivel at that.'

'So why do you want to go?'

'I don't. Not at all. But you do.'

'Perilla, I will kill you very slowly and painfully unless you -'

'Seneca,' she said, 'is a protégé of Gaius's sister Livilla. The reading's in her house on the Palatine.'

Oh, gods. 'You're kidding!'

'Certainly not. I bumped into Marcus Vinicius in the Pollio library - I told you I knew him - and he invited me himself. I asked if you could come too.'

'That surprise him?'

'No, of course not. You've never met, he doesn't know you're a complete literary boor, or at least I don't think he does. And he's a very nice man anyway, he'd never think of refusing.'

Jupiter Best and Greatest! It'd be worth sitting through an hour or so of guff if it meant I'd get a chance to talk to one of the imperial sisters and her husband face to face. And I would, too, I'd make sure of that. Oh, I'd go careful, sure, and it might not produce any results; probably wouldn't, in fact. But it was far too good an opportunity to pass up.

I kissed her. 'Brilliant!'

'I knew you'd be pleased. It's early evening, an hour before sunset, so we'll eat before we go.' Good idea; I didn't want to be sitting through a poetry recitation with a rumbling stomach. 'We can take the double litter.'

I skidded to a mental halt. Oh, hell! Of course we'd have to take the litter! No carriages inside Rome before sunset, so barring walking a litter was the only option. And I hate those bloody things. 'Ah... actually, come to think of it, Perilla,' I said, 'maybe it might be a better idea if we went separately and met up there.'

She blinked. 'Why on earth should we do that? You're not doing anything tomorrow afternoon, are you?'

'Just before sunset's when Agron's lads'd be reporting back. If none of them spots Dion today they might tomorrow, and seeing as we're on the Palatine anyway I could arrange for the kid to meet me somewhere there instead.' It sounded thin, but what the hell?

'Oh, Marcus, for goodness' sake don't be silly about this! The reading will only last a couple of hours at most. Surely you can wait for any news until we get back? Or if you absolutely insist on knowing straight away you can come with me in the litter as far as the Pollio and then I'll drop you off and go on ahead.'

'Ah...' Bugger; she was right, going separately didn't make any logical sense. It would have to be the plain unvarnished truth. 'I'd rather walk it, lady. Honestly.'

'Marcus Valerius Corvinus, you are *not* turning up at an imperial poetry reading in a crumpled, sweaty mantle, even if you do hate travelling in litters!'

54

I grinned; she's no fool, Perilla, and after almost twenty years of marriage she knows my quirks inside out. Just like I know hers. 'Yeah, okay,' I said. 'Fair cop. But I was dead serious about the kids: I wouldn't be able to concentrate on anything else all evening for wondering whether one of them had seen the guy. Besides, it's not all that far to the Palatine, I'd get just as hot in a closed litter that time of day, if not hotter, and on foot I could take the short cut up the Staurian Stairs. I'd probably get to Livilla's place before you did, and in far better shape.'

'Hmm.'

'Plus, I'll be careful with the mantle. Pristine condition, I promise. Bargain?'

She frowned, then kissed me. 'Oh, very well, bargain. But turn up looking like you've been dragged through a hedge backwards and I will personally kill you. Understood?'

'Understood.'

Excellent!

Ten

There'd been no word of Dion that day, so the next I saw Perilla off in the litter in plenty of time for the reading and set off for the Palatine myself. I hadn't been kidding when I'd said that, even if one of the kids did turn up with news outside the Pollio as arranged, I'd probably be there before her: she'd be taking the long way round, whereas the more direct route along Staurus Street and up the Staurian Stairs might be knackering on the legs but it was a good twenty minutes shorter. Besides, our litter team were lardballs with all the pace of arthritic tortoises. I could give them half an hour's start and still beat them to the finish.

Arrive fresher, too. The heat was off the day and there was a cool breeze blowing. Perfect walking weather.

I came down off the Caelian with its more upmarket houses into the tenement area that fills the dip between it and the Palatine, cutting off the view you get from the higher ground of the definitely-upmarket private and public buildings along its eastern ridge. Me, I like the tenement areas. Oh, sure, your average tenement is a crumbling, overcrowded, smelly eyesore with poky rooms that're hell to live in, but then most families only use them for sleeping: which means that unless the weather's really bad they spend their spare time - what they have of it - on the pavements outside. The last couple of hours before sunset, when work's finished for the day, is traditionally family mealtime, and so what you get is a succession of ad-hoc street-parties, with chairs and folding tables and portable cooking stoves crammed into most of the space between the buildings, the blue haze of burning charcoal, the smell of soup and bean stew and grilling sausages, and people by the hundred: mothers dishing up or gossiping with each other, men sitting around shooting the breeze, beefing about their bosses or arguing racing form while they drink their after-work wine, and kids weaving in and out playing tag or screaming that they hate cabbage. Quiet it isn't, but then Rome isn't a quiet place, most of it, any hour of the day or night. If you want peace and quiet, try the Alban Hills, but for me you can keep them. I'll take the street parties. I'm happy here.

I walked along Staurian Street to its end where the Stairs lead up the back of the Palatine Hill. It's a long, hard climb: they're steep and narrow, wide enough for two people to pass abreast but not much more, and closed in either side for most of their length. This time of day they were deserted, although even at busy times that didn't vary much: the Palatine's definitely upper-class ground, your ordinary punter, unless he's a slave or a workman, has no reason to go there, and the more well-heeled wouldn't be slogging up a long flight of stairs on foot in any case. It's only stupid eccentrics like me that don't like litters who do silly things like that.

I started to climb.

I'd got about three-quarters the way up, and I'd stopped for a breather, when I noticed the cart at the top of the flight. It was piled high with stones - probably a mason's cart; they'd be doing some road repairs - and it was parked tail-end-on, so that it practically blocked the exit. Bugger! Well, there was just enough room to squeeze past on either side. Stupid place to leave the thing, though: there was plenty of space in the open ground beyond.

Then, as I watched, the cart began to move. Backwards. Its rear wheels dropped down the first of the steps, and the sudden tilt sent part of its cargo rattling over the tailgate while the weight of the rest pulled the front wheels over the lip. I stared in horror as the thing started to bounce and jolt down the flight towards me, gathering speed as it went.

Oh, shit!

There was nowhere I could run. If I tried back the way I'd come I hadn't a hope in hell of reaching the bottom before the cart caught up with me, even if I didn't trip in the first few steps and break my neck tumbling down the stairs, which I probably would. And even if that didn't happen I'd be crushed where I lay under the wheels. On the other hand, to stay where I was would be suicide: there wasn't a hand's breadth of clearance either side, and unless the damn thing stuck on the way, which didn't seem likely with the momentum it was building up, it'd squash me against the wall like a bug.

Bloody, bloody shit! Think, Corvinus!

Up was the only way out. Twenty yards ahead, if I remembered rightly, there was a break in the wall where the masonry had crumbled, leaving a hole. It wasn't much, sure, but it was the best I'd got.

If I was right. If it was big and deep enough. And if I could reach it in time.

Too many ifs. Fuck!

I started running up the steps towards the oncoming cart, breathing hard with pure terror. Shit, where was it? Blank wall, blank wall all the way. They'd fucking repaired it! Just when I needed the fucking City Works department to be their fucking inefficient selves they'd fixed the fucking thing!

Stones rattled past me, bouncing up like slingshots, shattering themselves against the side walls. One caught me on the shoulder, and I winced. The cart was no more than a dozen yards away now, and coming like a bat out of hell.

And then I saw it. Sweet Jupiter, I'd almost missed the thing in the shadows! I raced up the last few yards, lungs bursting, and dived sideways...

The cart's wooden side scraped my back as I pressed myself as far as I could go into the hole, hard up against the crumbling masonry, and it was gone, thundering down the steps behind me. I stayed where I was, shaking and gasping for breath.

From far below came a shattering crash. Then there was silence.

Somewhere a bird sang. I don't know what the hell kind it was, but at that moment it was the sweetest sound in the world.

Gods!

I didn't bother with the rendezvous in front of the Pollio; like Perilla had said, if any of the kids had spotted Dion then I'd know soon enough, and I was far too shaken at present to care about little things like that. I went straight to Vinicius and Livilla's place, next to the palace.

The front door was open, and there was an expensive-looking slave on duty outside. He was wearing a smart red tunic with silver trimmings, which made him a hell of a lot better-dressed than I was, currently.

'I've come for the poetry reading,' I said.

He gave me the once-over and his eyes widened; but then he just said, 'Yes, sir,' and led me inside and through what looked like a major art gallery to one of the big public rooms.

It was packed to the gunnels with Rome's brightest and best, tucking in to the pre-show drinks and nibbles. I'm not absolutely sure what a cynosure of all eyes is, but when I stepped across the threshold I was it. In spades. As an equivalent conversation-stopper, a fart at a funeral comes to mind.

Perilla was there already, talking to a woman who I recognised as one of her literary cronies. When she saw me she came over like a bolt from a catapult.

'Marcus!' she hissed. 'I told you! What the *hell* do you think you're - ?' She stopped when she saw the cuts and bruises, and her face went pale under her makeup. 'What happened?'

'An accident with a cart,' I said.

'A *cart*? It's not sunset yet! There aren't any carts!'

'It's complicated. I'll explain later.'

A dapper-looking guy in his mid-forties was coming towards us. 'You must be Valerius Corvinus,' he said, holding out his hand. We shook. 'We haven't met. I'm Marcus Vinicius.'

'Uh...yeah,' I said. 'Pleased to meet you, sir.'

'I'm sorry, but -' He gestured delicately at what was left of my mantle, which wasn't much. 'Did you have a problem on the way here?'

I grinned; I felt like laughing, but I knew that was just hysteria. 'Yeah. You could say that. A bit of an accident on the Staurian Stairs.'

'Good gods!' He'd noticed the blood and the bruising too, now. 'Are you all right? No, don't answer that.' He looked round and signalled to a slave, who came over. 'Tynnias. Fetch Theodorides. Now, man! Do it quickly!' He turned back. 'Theodorides is my doctor. He'll take a look at you. Meanwhile, get this down you.' He held out the winecup he was holding.

Thank Jupiter for a man who had his priorities right. I took it and drank. Caecuban. Beautiful, and just what I needed.

'You fell?' he said.

'Uh-uh. Runaway mason's cart.' Beside me, Perilla gasped, but she didn't say anything. 'Almost got me.'

'On the *Stairs?*'

'Yeah. Some idiot had left it parked off the brake at the top and it must've rolled backwards somehow and gone down the steps.'

'Good gods!' he said again. 'They're only a few feet wide! You're lucky to be alive, man!'

'Yeah. Yeah, I know.' A slave was passing with a jug. I grabbed his arm, got him to refill the cup and downed that one too.

A thin-faced Greek in a plain mantle was hurrying over, with the slave Tynnias in tow. The doctor, obviously. Well, that's imperials for you: they even have their own medical staff on the household roll.

'Theodorides,' Vinicius said. 'Take Valerius Corvinus to the bath suite and patch him up.' Then, when I started to protest: 'No, I won't hear of it, Corvinus! And Tynnias, fetch a clean tunic and mantle!' He turned back to me. 'Take your time. We'll talk later, when Theodorides has finished with you and you've had a chance to freshen up. Meanwhile I think Seneca's about ready to start, so I'm afraid I must...if you'll excuse me?'

'Sure. Thanks.'

He left in the direction of a fat, jowly purple-striper who was moving purposefully towards the podium at the end of the room clutching a thick book-roll.

'This way, sir,' the doctor said, plucking at my sleeve.

'You're all right, Marcus?' Perilla said anxiously. 'Really?'

'Yeah, I'm fine, lady,' I said. 'All surface, no bones broken. Go and enjoy.'

I let myself be led off. Well, you had to look on the bright side. At least I'd miss the bloody recitation.

Eleven

I did, but not by much, despite the fact that I was away for a good hour and a half, which was what it took for the doctor to sponge my cuts and examine the bruise on my shoulder, and for me to wash off the mortar from the Staurian wall in Vinicius's bath suite and change into the fresh tunic and mantle that Tynnias had brought me. Also to sink another half pint of Caecuban while all this was happening.

When I rejoined the party I was feeling almost human again. They were applauding, but not very enthusiastically, which suggested that Seneca's poetry had been the pulp-factory-fodder that Perilla had said it was. Mind you, if I'd had to choose in advance I'd still've taken it in preference to being almost squashed flat by a stonemason's cart. But then maybe I'm just getting old.

'Marcus?' Perilla was there, beside me. 'How are you feeling?'

I was looking around the room; Rome's brightest and best was right, if you kept your tongue firmly in your cheek while applying the phrase, with a generous sprinkling of four-star imperials. Not counting Vinicius I could spot three of these straight off, even if I didn't know them personally. First, the nondescript, middle-aged guy in the plain mantle, who twitched while he talked like he had the palsy and favoured his right leg whenever he moved: Gaius's uncle, the idiot Claudius, who the imperial family had kept under almost permanent wraps since he was born, and quite rightly so from the looks of him. The broad-striper he was talking to was smiling and nodding like he wished he was a million miles away, but at a party you can't flatline a gabby imperial, even although he is a no-brainer who's boring your socks off, and the poor guy was stuck for the duration. Second, Livilla, Vinicius's wife, Gaius's sister, about six feet to our left, against the wall behind the Marsyas statue, talking to the fat would-be star of the show who was lapping up her compliments like a cat at a cream-bowl. Livilla was fairly hefty herself, thick in the body but pretty enough in the face.

Not, from reports, that there was very much going on behind those heavily-made-up eyes. To distinguish between Gaius's youngest sister and a brick, intellectually speaking, would be a decision that went to the wire.

Third was Agrippina...

Agrippina. I'd never met her either, but I recognised her as soon as I saw her. An Imperial with a capital 'I', straight from the Livia mould, and that bitch I'd remember even if I made ninety. She and her sister were chalk and cheese, with Livilla being the cheese, and a full-fat one at that. There was none of her sister's flab about Agrippina. Early twenties or not, she was bone-dry, angular and hard, more flint than chalk, and by the gods the lady had presence and she knew it. She was talking to a young man with a squeaky-clean broad-striper mantle. I suddenly thought of female spiders, and the hairs rose on my neck.

There was no sign of her husband Domitius Ahenobarbus. Him I'd've spotted anywhere.

'Marcus?'

'Hmm?'

'I asked you a question. How are you feeling?'

'I'm okay, lady. I told you, no bones broken. Just scratches.' I fielded a cup of wine from a passing slave's tray. 'Where's Ahenobarbus?'

'He's dying.'

'*What?*' I nearly dropped the cup.

'Or the next thing to it.'

Well, I wouldn't grieve for the bastard, nor would many other people. Still, it was a facer. 'You're sure?'

'Absolutely. I asked Vinicius. Oh, very discreetly, but I thought you'd want to know. A combination of dropsy and alcohol. His doctors don't think he'll last the year.'

Bloody hell! 'Does Agrippina know?'

'Of course she does.'

'Ah, Corvinus.' It was Vinicius himself, coming up on my blind side. 'Suitably restored?'

'Yeah. Yeah, thanks. I'm fine.'

'You missed a treat.' I glanced at him suspiciously, but his face was bland. 'Annaeus Seneca was in marvellous form. As usual. A true showman.'

'I'm not into poetry myself, sir,' I said. 'Can't tell bad from good, I'm afraid.'

'That can be an advantage. Certainly a blessing, in some circumstances.' He turned to Perilla. 'Your stepfather, now, Rufia Perilla, *he* was a poet. I'm sorry I was too young ever to meet him. His Metamorphoses are a lovely idea; Circe the enchantress changing men into swine is such a telling comment on the morality of our times, isn't it?'

'I, ah, don't think my stepfather meant it like that.'

'Poets can say more than they intend, or even what they know, my dear. It's one way of telling good from bad. And speaking of your stepfather, there's someone who'd be delighted to meet you.' He raised his voice. 'Anteius! Over here, please!'

The young guy talking to Agrippina said a few final words to her and came across. He was big-built, with a florid complexion and reddish hair: Northern Italian, probably, maybe even with more recent Gallic blood.

'Gaius Anteius, Rufia Perilla and her husband Valerius Corvinus,' Vinicius said. 'Anteius is a fellow-poet, Perilla. A close friend of Seneca's. He's one of our new quaestors.'

That explained the squeaky-clean mantle. 'Pleased to meet you,' I said. We shook.

'You're in distinguished company, Anteius.' Vinicius patted his arm. 'Rufia Perilla is Ovid's stepdaughter, and an excellent poet in her own right. Now if you'll excuse me I must just go and check on the wine supplies. Glad to see you're little the worse for your experience, Corvinus. I'll have my carriage take you back, even so.'

'Hey, no, that's okay,' I said. 'We can manage in the litter.'

'I insist. It'll be waiting for you outside whenever you're ready. In the meantime, enjoy yourselves.' He smiled, and was gone.

'You're from the north?' Perilla said to Anteius.

'Yes. My father has estates near Mantua.' The guy was blushing; one of nature's ingénus. Well, the family must be rolling right enough: even these days, a Cisalpine Italian his age didn't make the first rung on the senatorial ladder easily, not with so many youngsters from the top Roman families in contention. 'What was he like? Your stepfather?'

'You enjoy his work?'

'It's brilliant,' he said simply. 'I've read every line a hundred times. He's even better than Virgil, and as a Mantuan myself I shouldn't say that.'

Perilla laughed. 'Well, he wasn't at all like you might imagine from his poetry. A very quiet family man. If you'd met him you might have been disappointed.'

'Oh, no! He was a genius, everyone says so. I was talking to Cornelius Gaetulicus a couple of months ago, and he said Ovidius Naso was the greatest lyricist Rome had ever produced, streets ahead of Catullus. He models his own style on your stepfather, although he says he'll never be a fraction as good.'

'Gaetulicus?' I said.

He stared at me. 'The erotic poet, of course.'

'Ah,' I said. 'Right. Right.'

'He knew your stepfather, you know.' He turned back to Perilla. 'Not well; he was only my age when Ovid was exiled. In fact, I think he only met him twice. But he said he was the most intelligent man in Rome. Not the cleverest, but the most intelligent. And, of course, an absolutely brilliant poet. His banishment was a tragedy.'

'Yes,' Perilla said quietly. 'Yes, it was.'

'Why did Augustus do it? Do you know?'

'Yes. But it's a long story.'

'Where did you - ?' I began; but I was interrupted.

'Gaius, dear, Seneca would like a quick word.' Agrippina. Her hand was on Anteius's arm. 'I'm sorry to drag him away,' she said to me, 'but you know these sensitive artists. Everything has to be done now.'

'Uh...yeah. Yeah, no problem.' I frowned. 'Another time, Anteius.'

'A pleasure to meet you,' Perilla said.

'Me too,' the youngster said. Agrippina gave us a brittle smile and led him off.

'Well!' Perilla watched them go. 'That was incredibly rude, even if she is the emperor's sister.'

'Goes with the job,' I said absently. Now what the hell had happened there?

Now that the reading had been over by a decent interval people were beginning to leave: I couldn't see any of the imperials, barring Vinicius who was talking to a camel-faced senator's wife while her husband hovered, obviously eager to get away, and wherever Agrippina had taken Anteius it must've been through to one of the private rooms, because there was no sign of the jowly would-be poet, either. Ah, well, I'd be happy to call it an evening myself. Like I'd told Perilla, there'd been no bones broken, but my shoulder hurt like hell, the cuts on my face were still stinging and my muscles were stiffening up fast. I hoped the bath-suite furnace was still on at home: I could do with a long steam before bedtime.

Besides, there might be news about Dion.

'Jack it in, lady?' I said.

Perilla smiled. 'If you like. You've seen all you want to see?'

'Yeah. If you can call it that.' Not much in the way of information, but a couple of points to ponder.

Definitely that. The evening hadn't been a complete waste of time, not by a long chalk. And so far it certainly hadn't been uneventful.

We went home in Vinicius's carriage.

'Now, Marcus.' Perilla rounded on me as soon as we'd hit the lamb's-wool-stuffed cushions. 'Tell me exactly what happened. And don't lie, because I'll know.'

So I told her. She was quiet for a long time. Then she said:

'Could it have been an accident? A real one?'

'It's possible. Just.'

'But you don't think it was?'

'No. The top of the steps is level ground. I checked. The only way that cart could've moved was if it was pushed.'

'Did you see anyone?'

I shook my head. 'Trouble is, lady, if it wasn't an accident it complicates matters.'

'How do you mean?'

'Look. If you want to murder someone you don't have your perp park a mason's cart at the top of the Staurian Stairs just in the hope that the victim'll come up them, right? Not unless you think there's a fair chance he might do it. And the only way you might think that is if you know beforehand exactly where he's going, and where he's coming from, and what time he's liable to be there.'

She was staring at me wide-eyed. 'Oh, Marcus! *No!*'

'You got a better explanation?'

'You mean it was someone at the reading?'

'Come on, lady! You can do better than that! Who gave me the invite in the first place?'

'*Vinicius?* You're not serious!'

'I wish to hell I wasn't, because you're right: as a villain the guy just doesn't make any kind of sense. That's what I meant by complications. But if we ignore them and go for the obvious solution then he's it in spades, no question. He knew I was coming and he knew when. I'll bet you you even mentioned to him at some time or other that your husband preferred walking to litters, so the odds that I'd take the Stairs from the Caelian was practically a dead cert.'

She looked shifty. 'I may have done. In the past. We do see each other socially on occasion, and the topic may have come up in conversation. But Marcus! Vinicius is totally impossible!'

'Uh-uh.' I shook my head again. 'Improbable, sure, because he's not the type and he's got no form. But not impossible, not any more, far from it. We agreed: the only people who could benefit from the fake Gemellus plot are the three imperial pairs, sisters plus husbands. Vinicius and Livilla were rank outsiders because he's an apolitical bookworm with zero ambition and she hasn't got the brains to organise a honey wine klatsch. Livilla might've known I'd be coming to the reading, fine, because Seneca's her protégé, it was her show and Vinicius is her husband, but there's no logical reason to think any of the other three surviving ones did, not that much ahead of time. Lepidus wasn't even there, for a start. And if they didn't know then they wouldn't've had time to organise the business with the cart. Livilla on her own hasn't got the nous for that, so it must've been Vinicius. QED.'

'What about Agrippina? I thought she was the most likely candidate?'

'Perilla, you told me yourself: her husband's dying. Oh, sure, if Ahenobarbus had still been a viable option then I'd go for that pair of beauties any time, whatever the objections. But he is, so all she's got in the bank, or will have soon, is her son Nero, and he isn't even on solids yet. Unless you think she has something going with Vinicius and they're in it together.'

'Don't be silly, dear! Marcus Vinicius isn't the philandering type. And I know for a fact that he can't stand Agrippina.'

'There you are, then.' I settled back into the cushions, frowning. 'And like I say after the business of the cart Vinicius has to be involved. Bugger! I quite liked the guy! Why does it always have to be the wrong one?'

'Perhaps it was just a simple accident after all.'

'Yeah, and Cleopatra was my grandmother.'

'All right, but why go to all these lengths? If Marcus Vinicius is the villain you make him out to be - and I don't accept that for one minute - and wanted you stopped then why didn't he just arrange for you to be stabbed in an alley or something? It would be easy enough. He's no fool, and if you can work out the implications then he certainly could as well.'

'For a start, because I wouldn't be around to work anything out. Let's face it, lady: by rights I should be a smear on the Stairs by now. It's only luck that I'm not.' She shuddered, but didn't say anything. 'Besides, it had to be an accident, and a credible one, because I've got the emperor on my team, and you don't get better than that. He knows the situation, he's put the word around - or at least he said he would - , Gaius isn't an idiot and if I were found knifed in an alley he'd make it his business to find out whodunit and why. And if he did, or even suspected who was responsible, chummie would be hamburger before the sun set. Me, I reckon whoever the perp was, Vinicius or not, he did pretty well.'

We travelled on in silence.

'There's only one thing that's nagging at me,' I said finally. 'Although it could be just coincidence. These things happen.'

'What's that, dear?' Perilla turned away from the window.

'Gaetulicus. The erotic poet that young Anteius mentioned?'

'Yes? What about him?'

'He used the name in Agrippina's hearing. She was only a few yards off, and she came over as fast as if she'd been greased. Gaetulicus may be an erotic poet with a crush on your stepfather, lady, but he's also currently military governor in Germany.'

We got back home ten minutes later. One of the kids had left word that they'd found Dion.

   The steam-bath could wait.

Twelve

Dion's real name, it transpired, was Tiberius Claudius Etruscus. He was a top civil service freedman with an office in Augustus House.

I went round there the next day, without bothering to make a prior appointment: if Etruscus had been chary about giving me his name in the first place he wouldn't exactly break his neck to talk to me at work. Not that that concerned me. If there was any neck-breaking to be done I'd do it myself, and whistle while I did it.

'Good morning, sir.' The slave on the front desk gave me a big professional smile. 'Can I help you?'

'Yeah. I'd like to speak to Claudius Etruscus.'

He pulled over a set of wax tablets. 'Your name, sir? You have an appointment?'

'No. No appointment. And it's, uh, Gaius Anteius.'

'Your business?'

'A private matter.'

The slave hesitated. 'Well, I'll see, sir,' he said. 'But Claudius Etruscus is rather busy this morning. If you could possibly come back later, or better still arrange a time for another day -'

'No. It has to be now. And it's urgent.'

'I'll ask. If you'd like to wait.'

'Sure. No problem.' There was a bench against the wall. I went over and sat on it while he disappeared down a corridor.

He was back in two minutes. 'This way, sir.'

He led me down the corridor to a door, opened it and stood back. I went in.

Etruscus, aka Dion, was sitting behind a desk loaded with paperwork and wax tablets, dictating to a secretary. His eyes widened when he saw me, but he stretched out a hand.

'Ah, Anteius, wasn't it?' he said. 'I'm pleased to meet you.' We

69

shook. 'Do have a seat. It'll be about the tenders for the repairs to the temple of Venus Erycina, no doubt.'

'Uh...yeah,' I said, pulling up the guest chair and sitting on it. *What?*

'You're a bit premature, I'm afraid. We've only got the raw figures at present, and we need to compare them with the materials specifications which Public Works still have. But I can certainly show you those.' He turned to the secretary. 'Stephanus, go and fetch them, please. Oh, and while you're about it look out the bills for the Octavian Porch work and the new Augustan Marketplace bronzes. You know the ones I mean. I'll need to refer to them later.'

'Yes, sir.' The secretary left, closing the door behind him.

Etruscus was on his feet like a rocketing pheasant. 'Corvinus, what the *hell* are you doing here?' he snapped. 'How did you find me?'

I shrugged. 'It wasn't all that difficult, pal. And I think you owe me an explanation. Plus telling me a lot more about what's going on than the shovelful of garbage you handed me the last time we met.'

'If I could do that I would've done it in the first place!' He sat down, pulled a handkerchief from his tunic-sleeve and mopped his forehead. 'I had good reason not to then, and I still have. As it is, you've now seriously compromised the pair of us and may have caused far more damage than you can imagine.' He did a double-take and looked at me more closely. 'What've you done to your face?'

'An accident with a runaway cart.'

'Good gods!' He put the handkerchief down. 'What happened?'

'That's not important.' I leaned forwards. 'The explanation is. Now just exactly what is going on here?'

'I said: I can't tell you.'

'Bugger that, sunshine. I want an answer. Now.'

'Then you can want it. Look, Corvinus, I'm sorry, but this is exactly the situation I was trying to avoid. I know it's difficult for you but believe me, I cannot get involved. Not directly. If I did it would ruin everything. They'd find out, and that would be the end of both of us.'

Yeah, well: judging by chummie at the wine shop and the business with the cart, we'd already gone past that point. As far as I was concerned, at least. Still, there was no reason to panic the guy any further than he was evidently panicking already. 'Who's "they"? The imperials? Vinicius? Agrippina?'

He looked blank. 'What? *No!* What've the imperials got to do with it?'

The surprise was genuine; nobody was that good an actor. I sat back again. Bloody hell! 'All right,' I said. 'Then who?'

'*I can't tell you!* That is *final!*' He mopped his forehead again. 'Oh, good sweet Jupiter, I'm trying to...' He stopped, put the handkerchief down and took a deep breath. 'Corvinus, listen to me. Please. I've done the best I could, but I dare not go any further. I dare not! You're on your own, completely, and I have total confidence in your abilities. All I will say is that it is vital for Rome that you find out the truth behind Macro's death. I swear it. Now just go away, leave me alone and don't come back.'

'Now hang on, pal! That's not -'

'You've already done both of us possibly irreparable damage by coming here. Fortunately I've never met the real Anteius, and luckily neither has Stephanus, nor Euthias on the desk, but I do know he's one of the new finance officers. Using his name to get in to see me was sheer stupidity, and asking for trouble. Good gods, man, you're not even wearing a senatorial mantle!' Oops; the guy had a point. I hadn't thought of that, and Anteius's name had been the first to spring to mind. Well, it was too late to worry about spilt milk. 'Now, Stephanus will be back in a moment. We'll play a small charade which hopefully should get me at least out of this nonsense. Where it will leave you with your half-baked impersonation of a quaestor is your own concern, but that's your own stupid fault.'

I'd had about enough of this. 'Look, sunshine,' I said. 'No charade. Not unless you give me something tangible in exchange, because at present I'm floundering. So when your Stephanus walks through that door I'm going to get up, thank you nice as pie for delivering Sertorius Macro's letter to me the other day and call you Dion when I leave.'

'You wouldn't!' His face was grey. 'This is a nightmare! Corvinus, you absolute bloody *fool!*'

'Your choice, pal.' I crossed my arms.

There was the sound of footsteps coming along the corridor.

71

Etruscus licked his lips. The footsteps slowed.

'All right,' he said quickly. 'Two names. Flaccus and Isidorus. That's all I can give you.'

My brain went numb. Oh, Jupiter! *'Who?'*

'Corvinus, for the gods' sake! *Please!'*

The door opened and the secretary came in with an armful of documents. I recovered enough to smile at him as he put them down on Etruscus's desk.

'Are you all right, sir?' he said.

'Yes. Yes, of course. I'm fine.' Etruscus took a deep breath; I could see the reason for the guy's question because he was visibly shaking. 'Thank you, Stephanus.' He fumbled through the documents, pulled out three and handed them to me. 'There you are, Anteius. As I said, only the raw figures, but I hope they help.'

I unrolled them one by one, scanned the meaningless columns of numbers for a minute or two for effect and to give both of us time to settle, then gave them back. 'That's marvellous,' I said. 'Just what I needed.' I stood up. 'Thanks, Etruscus. We'll be in touch.'

I could feel his eyes on my back all the way to the door.

I left the building and walked in the direction of the Staurian Stairs, brain churning. Well, that had been a facer. Two facers. Whatever the hell this was about, the imperials had to be involved, they just had to be. Only seemingly they weren't; I'd given Etruscus my best shot, point-blank, and he'd scotched the idea in no uncertain terms. And if anyone knew what was going on here then Etruscus did. So scratch the imperials theory completely; in which case floundering was right. He was scared, too, deathly scared: whoever his 'they' were carried clout, and I didn't like the sound of this 'vital to Rome' business at all.

It didn't make sense. Any of it.

The second facer, of course, and it was a real whammy, was the two names, Flaccus and Isidorus. That combination couldn't be coincidence, no way, they had to be Agron and Cass's Egyptian governor Atillius Flaccus and his new pal the Alexandrian Greek rabble-rouser. I'd had Etruscus over a barrel, and he'd known it; he wouldn't've given me chicken-feed, not at that point, not the way he was sweating. Which meant that however the hell Flaccus and Isidorus fitted in they were important. Vitally important. Maybe even crucial. The real bummer was that both of them were currently more than a thousand miles away, in Alexandria, and if I wanted to follow the lead through then...

Hell. If the bastard thought I would just jump on a ship and sail to Egypt he was whistling through his ears.

On the other hand, like I say, he hadn't given me the information lightly. And whatever the ins and outs of it, Etruscus wasn't faking; he wanted the case solved even more than I did. He wouldn't be interested in sending me on wild goose chases, and if he was pointing me at Alexandria then he'd a good reason to do it. The best. That meant I'd be a fool not at least to think about going there if I wanted hard answers; and *that* meant I was more than half committed before I started. Especially since as far as ideas and leads at the Roman end were concerned I was totally screwed.

Bugger; it was a conspiracy. First Perilla, now Etruscus. But when you find yourself fighting the gods then all you can do is roll with the punches.

By the time I reached home I'd made my decision.

'I've changed my mind, lady,' I said. 'We're going to Alexandria after all.'

She stared at me and put her book-roll down on the atrium pool's rim. 'We are *what?*'

'Pack your smalls and draw up your shopping list. I'll send Alexis over to Ostia to make enquiries at the shipping offices first thing tomorrow.'

'Marcus, have you taken complete leave of your senses? We can't just drop everything and go to Alexandria! What about the wedding arrangements? What about the -?' Perilla stopped. 'This has something to do with your investigation, doesn't it?'

'Ah...could have. Could have.'

'You've seen Etruscus and he's said that for some reason you've got to be in Alexandria.'

'Not in so many words.'

'Marcus Valerius Corvinus!'

Shit. Nothing for it. I settled down on my usual couch and told

73

her the whole story. 'I thought you'd be pleased,' I finished.

'Oh, I am! And forget what I said. It's just that I would've liked to be going for other reasons than to have you furkling about in the dirty linen basket of politics.'

'I don't furkle,' I said. Mind you, the image started up a certain train of thought that I might chase when I had more time. 'Besides, while we're there you could do what you like. See the sights. Shop till you drop.'

'I'll have to let Marilla and Clarus know.' She swung her legs over the edge of the couch. 'We can send Lysias on the mare. If he leaves now he can be in Castrimoenium before midnight.'

'Hang on, Perilla,' I said. 'You and me, fine, but I'm not sure about the kids. Cass's Mika said there might be trouble there shortly.'

She paused. 'You never told me that. What kind of trouble?'

Bugger. Well done, Corvinus. Marvellous. Mouth open and foot straight in as usual. 'Ah...between Greeks and Jews.'

'Marcus...'

I backtracked, desperately. 'Oh, I'm sure it'll be okay. Agron said himself, we're Romans, we won't be involved. And you know Mika. Exaggerate, exaggerate, doom and gloom, everything's a crisis. Besides, the two communities've been at loggerheads with no real harm done for years.'

'In that case Marilla and Clarus are definitely coming.' She was sitting on the couch. 'It's their wedding. Marilla can help me look for dress material, she can even get her wedding dress made there. And Clarus has never been further than Bovillae. It'll let him see a bit of the world. At least we should give them the opportunity to refuse.' She got up, crossed the space between the two couches, and kissed me. 'I think it's a marvellous idea, dear. Whatever your reasons are. And old Stratocles will be delighted to see us. Now, I'll just go and talk to Lysias.'

She went out.

I took a swig from the winecup that Bathyllus had handed me as per usual when I'd arrived back. Well, barring the slight wobble at the end that'd gone okay. Not that I'd had any doubts that it would, mind, because it'd been the lady's idea in the first place. And, like she'd said on the earlier occasion, there were plenty of sailings from Brindisi this time of year. The crossing would only take twelve days, max, which meant that including the trip down to Brindisi in the sleeping carriage we could be there in about half a month. All the major arrangements for the wedding were already made; we were just at the fine-tuning stage. A round trip was possible inside the time, despite what I'd said before.

Meanwhile, I wanted to think about the business with the imperials. Oh, sure, Etruscus had put the lid on that good and proper, but after mature consideration I wasn't convinced that there wasn't something there, maybe an angle that the guy himself wasn't aware of; although they hate to admit it, civil servants don't know everything. What it was, and how it connected, I had no idea; but the implications of the Gemellus plot, plus the stage-managed accident with the cart, suggested that it fitted in somewhere along the line. Besides, I'd got that itch at the back of my neck that always comes when things're slightly out of kilter, even if the how isn't immediately obvious, and that I'd learned to trust over the years. Etruscus wasn't infallible, he could make mistakes like the rest of us, and he couldn't know everything. Certainly the angle was too promising just to let it drop. And I might as well do something while we were waiting for our Alexandrian boat.

Which meant dirty linen.

Caelius Crispus.

Thirteen

I packed Alexis off to Ostia first thing in the morning and then walked over to the city judges' offices on the Capitol where Crispus worked. To use the verb loosely.

Mind you, maybe that wasn't altogether fair any more. When I'd last seen him about eighteen months previously the erstwhile professional rumour-merchant and all-round slug had been well on the way to becoming a born-again conscientious civil servant. Not that it had seemed to blunt his appetite for insalubrious gossip, fortunately, or his sense of smell for sniffing it out, which was what I was interested in. If anyone could help me in the dirty-linen-furkling business then it was Crispus, the ace dirty-linen-furkler. All he needed was a little persuasion.

I got the slave to show me up to his snazzy office: Crispus might not be a praetor himself, but he'd wormed his way so deep into the infrastructure that he'd somehow managed to bag a room which was top of the range. When I went in he was sitting behind a desk that could've been filched from the palace. Knowing Crispus it probably had been.

'Oh, bugger,' he said.

'Morning, Crispus.' I gave him my best smile. 'And what a lovely morning it is. Not too hot, nice fresh breeze -'

'I'm busy, Corvinus. As usual. What is it this time?'

Well, there was no point in beating about the bush. 'You know the imperials? Agrippina, Livilla, Vinicius? I was wondering if -'

He was on his feet. '*Out!*'

'Oh, come on, pal!' I went over to the desk, pulled up a chair and sat on it. 'I've got the emperor's blessing.'

'And I'm the bloody King of Parthia. *Out!*'

'It's true. I talked to him myself and he's given me carte blanche. You wouldn't like to upset the emperor, now, would you?'

That one went home, as I knew it would. He frowned. 'Corvinus, if you're pissing me about -'

'Cross my heart, hope to die. Private interview at the palace, just me and him, face to face.'

'He actually gave you permission to investigate his sisters?'

'Any questions I liked. Told me to follow my nose, enjoy myself.'

'You swear it?'

'Carte blanche.' I held up my hand. 'All his own words. I so swear.'

'Good gods!' He sat down again. I'd never seen Crispus really, really fazed. I saw it now. 'Why the hell would he do that?'

I shrugged. 'He has his reasons.' Well fudged, Corvinus. That'd been close. Crispus knew I wouldn't lie under oath, but being the product of twenty generations of slippery politicians comes in handy sometimes.

'All right. What do you want to know?'

'Anything and everything that they might not want me to, pal. Let's take Vinicius first.'

'*Vinicius?*' His eyes widened. 'Why're you interested in him?'

'You mean I shouldn't be?'

'There's no reason I know of. He's squeaky-clean. Totally above board. Not a peccadillo out of place.'

'He isn't having an affair with Agrippina?'

Crispus laughed. 'Corvinus! Please! Venus herself could parade past that guy stark naked and making beckoning signs and he wouldn't look twice. He hasn't got an adulterous bone in his body. Besides, he can't stand the woman and it's mutual.'

Yeah, that'd been Perilla's assessment too. Still, it was nice to have it confirmed by an expert. 'And he wouldn't be interested in, uh, taking over if Gaius left off?'

He gave me a sharp look. 'That what this is about? Conspiracies? Treason?'

'Could be,' I said cautiously. 'It's one angle, anyway.'

'Bloody hell!' He licked his lips nervously. 'Look, Marcus -'

'Gaius's blessing, remember? What about Livilla?'

'Forget her too. Thick as two short planks, and not the ambitious

77

type. She's screwing Annaeus Seneca, mind, but -'

'Livilla's having an affair with Seneca?' I stared at him.

'Very discreetly. It started a couple of months ago.'

'Does Vinicius know?'

Crispus chuckled. 'Not unless they've been having it off in the reading room of the Pollio, dear. And even then he probably wouldn't notice unless they were doing it on top of a book he was using at the time. As a husband he's an adulterer's dream.'

Gods! 'Okay. The big one. Agrippina.'

'Oh, now!' He licked his lips again, but this time not from nervousness: Crispus was the scandal-monger's scandal-monger, and he was beginning to enjoy himself. As I'd known he would if I could get him going. 'Where do I start? *She* has picked up with a lovely young North Italian boy. Quite dewy and virginal. One of the new quaestors. In fact, that's the reason he *is* one of the new quaestors.'

'Gaius Anteius?'

'You know him?'

'Yeah, we've met.' Jupiter!

'Of course, he's just a passing interest. I'm not sure if they're even sleeping together, but the innocent lamb is certainly besotted. And Ahenobarbus is at death's door anyway, so he's out of it.' He hesitated. 'The really juicy gossip, though - and keep this to yourself, because it's top-grade and definitely *not* common knowledge - is that she's currently consoling the young widower. Aemilius Lepidus.'

'*What?*'

'Fact.' He beamed. 'His wife so recently dead, too. Quite convenient, that, isn't it? Mind you, Agrippina never could stand Drusilla, especially since she was Gaius's favourite sister. But she's always had a soft spot for Lepidus. Particularly after the emperor fell ill and named Lepidus as his heir.'

My stomach had gone cold. 'Hang on, pal. That was Gemellus.'

Crispus shook his head. 'Oh, no. Gemellus was the heir on paper, naturally. But when Gaius fell sick he passed his signet ring to Lepidus and Drusilla.'

Bloody hell! I sat back. 'You're sure?'

'Absolutely certain.'

Oh, joy in the morning!

'I've cracked it,' I said.

Perilla looked up, startled, from her book. 'I'm sorry, dear?'

'The case.' I set the wine jug and cup on the folding table between us - we were out in the garden again - and dropped into the wicker chair. 'It's cracked. Wide open, top to bottom. Lepidus and Agrippina are plotting to replace Gaius.'

'Oh, Marcus!' Not a gasp of appalled horror or congratulations, more of a heard-it-all-before sigh. Hell.

'Come on!' I said. 'We knew it had to be something like that. Given the fake Gemellus conspiracy it was obvious. The only question was which of the imperials was responsible.'

'All right.' She put the book aside. 'Why Lepidus and Agrippina? In combination, I mean?'

'Because they each have something the other needs, and together they fit the bill perfectly. And they're definitely an item. Crispus was sure about that.'

'Caelius Crispus is a dirty-minded degenerate muck-raker.'

'True. Only he's a *professional* dirty-minded -'

'Marcus. Please.'

'All I'm saying is he takes a pride in his work, and he's been living successfully off muck-raking for years. He knows what he's talking about. And when he's sure he's sure. That's the thing about Crispus: the guy's hundred-per-cent reliable.'

She sighed again. 'Very well. Explain.'

'Fine. We're assuming Gaius is dead, right?'

'How does he get that way?'

I frowned. 'They kill him, of course. Jupiter!'

'Marcus, it is *not* easy to kill an emperor. You have to be very sure he doesn't suspect you in advance, you have to be certain that no one can stop you doing it when it happens, and assuming you do succeed you have to know that you're safe and will profit from the crime. Unless you can tick all these boxes you're a fool to try. You think Agrippina and Lepidus are fools? Agrippina especially? Or perhaps Gaius himself is?'

'Ah...no, but -'

'There you are, then. So I'll ask you again: how do they kill Gaius?'

Gods! 'Come on, lady!' I said. 'I don't know! That's a detail! Just give me a chance, okay?'

She sniffed. 'Very well, dear. Carry on. We'll assume that the emperor is dead.'

'Thank you.' I took a swig of the wine. 'Right, then. Let's take Lepidus first. There's no direct heir, so with his family and imperial connections he has as good a claim as any, and better than most. Plus Gaius has already designated him as his successor.'

She looked startled. '*What?*'

'Yeah,' I said smugly. 'That was something else Crispus told me. When the emperor was ill he handed his ring to him and Drusilla. In front of witnesses."

'Wait a moment.' She was twisting her hair: a good sign because it showed she was moving onto the defensive. 'Drusilla was Gaius's favourite sister, yes?'

'So?'

'But, Marcus, surely that makes all the difference! Gaius wasn't appointing Lepidus as his successor because he was Lepidus, only because he was Drusilla's husband. And now Drusilla's dead that connection's gone. Don't you think that would weaken his claim just a little now?'

'That's the nub of the thing. I told you, lady: give me a chance. It all works out, believe me.'

'Very well. You still have the floor.'

I topped up my winecup. 'So. To sum up for Lepidus. He's from a good family with imperial ties that go back to Augustus, he's already been marked de facto as a successor, and as far as the senate is concerned - and they're the ones who'll be making the choice of emperor - the only other candidates with a claim to the job are Marcus Vinicius, who's a political non-starter, and Claudius, who's an idiot. The drawback - the *only* one - is that with Drusilla dead he has no direct link with the imperial family any more.'

'Oh, Marcus!' A different *Oh, Marcus!* this time. She was beginning to see where I was heading.

'Agrippina, now. She's a full-blown five-star imperial. She

already has a son, the only one of the sisters who does, so the dynastic line's already assured. She's married at present, yes, but she'll be a widow before the year's out. And she's an ambitious, ruthless, smart-as-paint bitch. You getting there, lady?'

She'd stopped twisting her hair. 'They do complement each other, don't they?'

'Like fish-pickle sauce on radishes.'

'And Crispus is sure? That they're having an affair?'

'Absolutely.'

'So the idea would be for Lepidus to become emperor, marry Agrippina, adopt young Nero and make him his heir?'

'Right. He gets the immediate kudos but Agrippina gets to play Livia to his Augustus, which she'd do to perfection. And eventually her son makes it to the purple.'

'You don't think they -?' She stopped. 'I mean, Drusilla's death was convenient, agreed, but a husband and a sister! They wouldn't!'

'Of course they would. They'd have to. Things don't make sense otherwise.'

She frowned. 'Why not?'

'Okay. Gemellus and Silanus died when?'

'The end of last year.'

'And Macro and Ennia?'

'About two months later. What has that got to do with -?' Her hand went to her mouth. 'Oh.'

'Right. It all has to do with timing. Drusilla died less than a month ago, by which time the fake Gemellus plot, which cleared the ground, had been dead and buried along with its protagonists for almost half a year. Unless Agrippina and Lepidus - or one of them, at least - was pretty hot in the prediction business, that was fairly fortuitous, now, wasn't it? Crispus obviously believes Drusilla's death wasn't natural, but there again the guy's a dirty-minded degenerate muck-raker, isn't he? That type'll believe anything.' I took another swig of the wine. Perilla said nothing. 'So. Crunch time. You think the scenario's valid?'

She was quiet for a long time. Finally she said: 'Oh, yes. It makes perfect sense.'

Hey! 'You're sure?'

81

'No criticisms at all. Barring what I said about the problems of killing Gaius, as a theory it hangs together perfectly. It might even be true.' Ouch! 'Only -'

'Only what?'

'Well, several things, really.'

A cold wind blew: *several* things? 'Such as what?'

'First, where does Etruscus fit in? After all, if what he wanted you to bring to light by investigating Macro's death was a plot against the emperor the broad details of which he already knew, then why should he be so shocked and surprised when you mentioned the imperials? That makes no sense at all. And what about these two men Flaccus and Isidorus? He obviously thinks they're vitally important, but in your theory they play no role at all.'

Bugger; she was right. In all the excitement I'd forgotten all about Etruscus. 'Yeah, well...'

'Secondly, what about this "accident" of yours? You said yourself: Agrippina couldn't have known you were going to be on the Stairs in time to arrange that, and for the same reasons nor could Lepidus.'

I was on firmer ground there. 'Yeah, they could,' I said. 'I've thought about that. Livilla would know, and she's having an affair with Seneca. Crispus told me that as well. Her husband isn't aware of it, and more to the point I'd bet Gaius isn't either. My guess is Agrippina and Lepidus have got her on the team - at least marginally - by threatening to tell the emperor. Gaius wouldn't take kindly to his sister committing adultery with a no-account hack poet from Spain. They'd both be heading for their respective fly-speck islands before you can say "Pandateria"'.

'Hmm. Which brings me to the last point. Even if you're right about this plot, what can you do?'

'Jupiter, Perilla! Tell the -' I stopped. Fuck! She was right again! Even though Gaius was accommodating, it was only a theory: I'd no proof, none whatsoever. And without it the emperor wasn't going to take kindly to being told that practically the entire imperial family wanted to put him in an urn. 'Ah.'

'Quite.'

At which moment Alexis came in.

'I've booked the passage, sir,' he said. 'A passenger-carrying merchantman sailing from Brindisi in seventeen days' time.'

'Perfect!' Well, at least that was done. And we could pick up Clarus and Marilla on the way.

Rome, for the present, was played out. We'd have to see what Etruscus's Alexandria had to offer.

Fourteen

We set out five days later, in the big sleeping carriage plus one cart for the supernumeraries and another for the luggage: twelve days would be enough to get us to Brindisi, sure, with good roads all the way, but you don't take chances where sailing times're involved. Or pickups: I'd sent a skivvy haring down to Castrimoenium to tell Clarus and Marilla that we'd meet them at the Appian crossroads near Bovillae on the evening of the first day, but delays happen and it was best to be careful.

Where the supernumeraries were concerned we were travelling light. Bathyllus was staying behind to look after the house: the little guy was an even worse sailor than I was, and I doubted if when we got to Alexandria our fingers-crossed-host Stratocles's major-domo, whoever he was, would welcome the little guy butting in with helpful suggestions on running the household. Which, as inevitably as night follows day, he would. That hassle I could do without. The same went for Meton the chef. In spades. He'd packed us a huge hamper of the sort of goodies that would keep best on the trip, and that plus what the young sous-chef we were taking along could rustle up would have to do us. If the choice was living on salami and cheese for the duration and being the cause of a full-scale turf war in Stratocles's kitchen I'd take the sausage any day. So we were down to Alexis, three more assorted skivvies, including the sous-chef, and Perilla's maid Procne, who'd do for Marilla as well. Lysias and his co-drivers would come as far as Brindisi and then take the vehicles back.

Me, I hate travelling, although if you've got to do it and have the time to spare a sleeping carriage is the best way because at least the thing's comfortable. We were both well-equipped. Perilla had brought along a couple of large book-boxes filled with what looked like half the Pollio, and I'd laid in a decent supply of Setinian plus a Robbers board and pieces: I'm no games player, normally, but Clarus was, and you have to do something to pass the time besides watching the scenery. Scenery you can keep.

We made the pickup no bother. Clarus and Marilla were waiting outside the roadside wineshop at the crossroads.

'Everything okay, Princess?' I hugged her.

'Oh, yes. No problems.' She was looking as bright as a button as usual, and excited as hell. 'Corvinus, this is great! Thanks for asking us.'

'Pleasure. Hi, Clarus.' We shook. 'How's it going?'

'Fine.' He'd filled out in the few months since I'd seen him. Grown, too: he'd be as big as I was, easy. A lot more serious, though, but then that was no bad thing.

'What's that?' I pointed at the case he was carrying. It had thin wooden sides covered with leather, like a book-box, but it was rectangular rather than round and there was a clasp under the handle.

'Basic medical kit.' He grinned. 'Dad put it together for me. We thought it might come in useful.'

'You got anything for sea-sickness? Because, pal, I'll tell you now that I'm going to need it, for one.'

'Oh, yes. There isn't much call for sea-sickness pills up here, but Dad made them specially and he says they should work. Not that I've ever tried them out on anyone personally.'

'Always a first, boy, always a first.' The slaves were transferring luggage from Marilla and Clarus's carriage to our cart, and changing the horses for the fresh ones they'd brought from Bovillae: we'd be travelling through the night to pick up a bit of distance, with Alexis and the two skivvies spelling Lysias and the cart-drivers. 'Quick cup of wine while we're waiting?'

'Sure, if you like.' He's no wine-drinker, Clarus - that's another difference between us - but he's quite happy to sit and sip. Besides, Perilla and the Princess were talking wedding business, which I'd had up to the ears.

We went inside. Inns out in the sticks are pretty hit-and-miss - you wouldn't want to spend the night in one, for a start - but the Bovillae crossroads is fairly major, and of course there's a lot of passing traffic. The place wasn't crowded, by any means, but there were a few punters at the bar counter and sitting around the tables, which is always a good sign. It was clean, too, and that's not something you take for granted. I had a look at the board: not a bad list, but then this close to the Alban Hills it shouldn't be.

All in all, a pretty good place.

'Half a jug of the Fundanan, pal,' I said to the innkeeper. 'You serve meals, by the way? Not to eat in; to take out.' We didn't have time to stop for dinner, but some hot food would be welcome

'Sure.' The guy reached for an empty half jug and filled it from the jar. 'Hare stew. Lentils with leeks. Or I can grill you some sausages.'

I poured the Fundanan into the cups he set in front of us and sipped. Not bad. Not bad at all. Always judge a place by its wine. 'Make it all three, I said. 'Enough for twelve. No, that's thirteen with the carriage-driver. Can you manage that?'

'No bother, sir. Ready in twenty minutes.'

'Fine.' That's another thing about inns next to major roads, they're geared up to takeaways and really fast food. I turned back to Clarus. 'Incidentally, the sketches for those busts. Did Paullus manage to get them done in time?'

'Oh, yes. He came through four or five days ago and was finished in an hour. Perfect likenesses. He's good, isn't he?'

'Yeah. Quite a find, young Paullus.'

'He said he'd have the busts themselves done by mid-September.'

'Great.' Well, that was a relief. If there'd been a hitch with her wedding present Mother would've killed me. 'Everything okay otherwise?'

'No problems.' He hesitated. 'Paullus said you'd got him to do some sketches yourself. Or one, anyway. Of someone you were trying to find.'

I took a swig of the wine. 'That's right.'

'You find him?'

'Yes.'

'Corvinus, are you on a case here? I mean, this sudden trip to Alexandria. It's not just for pleasure, is it?'

Bugger: he's sharp, is Clarus. Still, he'd've got to know sooner or later anyway. 'No, it isn't. And yeah, I suppose you could call it a case if you wanted to.'

'Fantastic!' He beamed. 'Marilla was wondering. She'll be delighted.'

Oh, hell. Time for some ground rules. 'Look, pal,' I said, 'we've been through this before. Whatever I'm doing, as far as you and the Princess are concerned you're on holiday. Especially the Princess. See the sights, shop, have a good time, let me faff around how I like. That is final, okay?'

'You want to tell me what it's about?'

'No.'

He shrugged. 'Please yourself. But unless you can arrange to go deaf for the duration you're going to have a hard time of it between now and Alexandria. The girl is no pushover, believe me, and she is very, very persistent.'

'Tell me something I don't know, pal. Even so, it's no business of yours.'

'We'll see,' Clarus said.

'That we will. Just don't mention it to her, right?'

'I won't have to. She'll find out anyway.'

'Alexis, stop the carriage! *Stop the bloody carriage!*'

'Oh, Marcus, not again! That's the fifth time tonight!'

'Bloody, bloody hare stew!'

'No one else has had any problems with it, dear. Drink some more of Clarus's stomach mixture.'

'Fuck the stomach mixture! Just move over so I can get out of the fucking door!'

'*Marcus!*'

Ah, the joys of travelling.

Fifteen

We reached Brindisi on the afternoon of the eleventh day. The boat would be loading the next morning and sailing at noon, so I booked us into a suite at one of the big guest houses along the coast from the harbour itself: being the main port for Greece and the east, with a fair-sized slice of its population from March to November in transit to elsewhere, Brindisi has these rarities, and they're not bad, catering as they do for the middle class bracket of the market who don't have friends to stay with locally but wouldn't go near the fleapits which are the traveller's only usual alternative. Certainly it'd do for one night, and after the carriage, comfortable as it was, I was looking forward to a real bed for a change. Especially since it'd be the last real bed I'd get until we landed.

Perilla was opening the doors of the three rooms that led off a common sitting area with couches and a table.

'But it's lovely, Marcus!' she said. 'So compact! There're even window-boxes with flowers. Which one do you want, Marilla?'

'Oh, I don't mind.'

'Then Marcus and I will take the one on the end. They've all got the same view, so you're right, it doesn't really matter. Just put our trunk in there,' she said to the slaves with the luggage. 'Marcus, did you ask about dinner?'

'Yeah,' I said. 'There's a big communal dining room downstairs. Or we can have it up here.'

'Oh, I think the dining room would be quite fun. We can have a look at it anyway, and decide later.'

'There's a bath suite as well.'

'Fantastic! I would *kill* for a bath.' She grinned. 'This place really is marvellous, isn't it, dear? Much more the east than Italy. Why don't they have them more often?'

Good question. Well, like I said, being the major port for Greece

Brindisi works to different standards from the usual Italian towns. We could be back in Antioch.

'So what do you want to do?' I said. 'Dinner's towards sunset and we've got practically the whole afternoon to play with.'

'Marilla?' she said.

'A bath sounds great. After ten days in the carriage I stink.'

'Fine, dear. Then we can go out and have a look at the town. There must be something to see, and it's not too hot. Marcus?'

'I'd rather stretch my legs first. I thought I might go along to the harbour, check where the *Erytheis* is berthed.' The *Erytheis* was the ship we'd be travelling on. 'Clarus?'

'I'll go with you,' Clarus said. 'Have the bath later.'

'Okay. Rendezvous back here in time for dinner. Where have they put you, pal?' I said to Alexis, who was supervising the luggage-slaves.

'In the attics, sir. Very comfortable. And there's even a servants' dining hall, too.'

All mod cons. I was impressed with this place, they thought of everything: put up in your usual Italian flop-house and the bought help slept and ate where they could. Bathyllus would still've been miffed, mind. The little guy's wants were few and simple, but a bed under the tiles just didn't square with them.

'Fine,' I said. 'We'll get off. See you later.'

It was good to have real pavement under my sandals again. And like Perilla had said it wasn't too hot: the north-easterly breeze that'd take us direct to Alexandria kept the air moving. We walked along the corniche past the other guest houses and upmarket private properties towards the harbour complex proper.

'It's huge,' Clarus said. 'Much bigger than I'd expected.'

'Yeah.' I'd just been thinking that myself. Brindisi's harbour - harbours, rather - fills both sides of the long branching inlet that stretches in from the coast proper towards the heart of the town. It isn't just a mercantile port - that would make it big enough - but a naval one as well, and there're broad no-go areas where the warships are berthed, filled with government offices, warehouses and shipyards, plus barracks for the crews. I knew the *Erytheis* sailed from pier forty-seven, but it'd be like finding a needle in a haystack. 'Still, we can ask someone.'

No problems on that score, mind. Once we were into the port complex the place was heaving with people and carts, making it difficult to move at all. I stopped a slave carrying a bale of cloth bigger than he was on his shoulder. 'Excuse me, pal,' I said. 'We're looking for pier forty-seven.'

'Don't know, sir. Try the harbour-master's office. Straight ahead, small square on your right with the fountain outside.'

'Thanks.' We went on, pushing our way through the crowds. Jupiter, it was a good job I'd thought to check in advance. How the hell we'd manage to get the luggage cart through this lot the next day I didn't know. As for the sleeping carriage, forget it. We could hire litters, of course, but it'd probably be easier to walk.

We found the office, though, no bother, and got directions: Pier forty-seven was in the inner harbour, half way along the northerly inlet, which was good news because it meant we could take the cart further round the edge towards the town centre and come in that way. Still, when we found it I'd walk the route just to make sure.

The piers themselves, when we reached them, weren't nearly so crowded: plenty of boats, sure, but only a few were actually being loaded. Even so, if they were you had to watch out for cranes: the bigger, heavier stuff has to be swung aboard mechanically rather than carried, and a pillar-drum or a twenty-gallon wine jar can make a real mess of your head if you don't see it coming. And with their sailing schedules to think of the guys doing the loading don't have much regard for unauthorised pedestrians.

I asked another slave for directions and he pointed me another fifty yards or so along.

'There she is,' I said.

The *Erytheis* was a lot bigger than your usual merchantman, which would be because of the extra cabin space: cargo ships per se carry passengers, sure, but they're not equipped for them, and unless you have the clout to rate a share of the deckhouse it means bunking down in the hold along with the cargo and probably some of the crew as well, or in the open under an awning. I reckoned Alexis had done us proud. If I was going to spend the next ten days throwing my guts up - which I was - then I'd rather do it in private. She looked fairly new, too, and sleeker than the normal round-bellied washtub. Again, good news: we might be sailing at the best time of year, but on anything other than a flat sea with a stiff wind behind to keep them going these bastards wallow like a pig in muck.

I called, but there was no one aboard, which since the gangplank was missing added up.

'Okay, Clarus,' I said. 'She's there and we've seen her. Onwards and upwards, pal. Carry on into town, maybe find a wineshop for a quick half jug on the way back home. Then a slow bath. Suit you?'

'Sure.'

We walked along the pier in the direction we'd been going, past the cargo stacks and the warehouses behind them, me in front, Clarus behind. I turned round. 'It should be easy enough to -'

'*Down!*' Clarus yelled.

Something moved in the corner of my eye, coming at me fast from the side, head height. I threw myself flat. The crane hook hissed past above me like a sigh, stopped, then swung back, its heavy iron block shattering one of the big terracotta pots in the cargo stack to my right. Pottery fragments tinkled on the concrete.

'Shit!' I got up and looked round. The guy was off and running, back the way between the cargo and the warehouses. 'After him!'

We piled in, neck and neck. Gods, I wasn't up to this any more! Two lung-bursting sprints inside of a month was too many; my calf muscles hadn't recovered from the last one yet, and I'd just spent eleven days sitting on my backside in a carriage. Even so, I was damned if the bastard was going to get away. Not this time.

And it was the same man who'd almost killed me with the cart, I could see that even from the back when he veered onto the pier access road proper about fifty yards ahead of us. Or at least it was the same man as the one who'd threatened me in the Augustus Market wineshop, which I'd bet was the same thing. Fuck! He'd followed us all the way to Brindisi!

We were gaining; or Clarus was, because he was pulling ahead, dodging round the punters going about their lawful business or more likely stopped and staring at whatever the hell could be going on here. I gritted my teeth and put my hand to my aching side.

And then the guy made his mistake. It was easy enough: the

91

access road forked at a big warehouse, with the left fork taking you round the back but meeting up again with the line of the inlet and leading, eventually, to the main drag we'd come in by. The right-hand fork simply led onto one of the projecting piers. And it was a dead end.

Chummie went the wrong way.

I didn't realise it myself at first; there was nothing to show, and because the fork followed the water's edge it was the more likely of the two. But then I saw the clear water at the end of the road and on either side, and I knew we'd got the bastard after all.

He realised it too. He stopped, turned, drew a knife from his belt and waited. Yeah, it was the guy from the wineshop, right enough.

'*Clarus, be careful!*' I shouted. Bugger; this I didn't need.

Clarus slowed to a walk. He was about twenty yards ahead of me, ten from the guy with the knife. The pier was empty, and there was only one boat moored there, right where they were standing, lines holding it fore and aft.

Clarus stooped, and his hand came up holding an iron bar; maybe the axle of a winch or a marline-spike or whatever you call these bits of recherché nautical equipment. He moved forward slowly.

'Don't be a fool! Leave him!' I was almost up to them now.

The guy grinned, spread his arms wide, the knife held low, and took a step backwards...

And then his heel must've caught against the moored ship's bow-rope, because he went arse over tip over the side of the pier. There was a splash.

'Oh, shit!' I covered the last few feet between me and Clarus, and we looked down.

There was at least eight feet between us and the surface of the water. He was floundering, scrabbling desperately at the pier wall and the bows of the boat, but there were no handholds there. And he couldn't swim. That was obvious, from his gaping mouth and the terror in his eyes as he stared up at us.

'Oh, *fuck!*' I said. 'Find something that'll float! Anything!'

But there wasn't anything. There were no ropes, either, apart from the hawsers holding the ship, and to my landlubber's eye they looked pretty solidly tied.

Clarus was tugging at the end of the bow-rope. The knot unravelled, but the ship pulled away as the rope slackened off, tightening the coils wrapped around the stone bollard so quickly that it stopped them from slipping free. I grabbed the taut ship-side length and heaved, trying to bring the bows around again and give Clarus some slack. It was like shifting a rhino, but finally the ship moved, its wooden side thumping against the pier. Clarus freed the rope from the bollard and turned towards the edge, ready to throw...

But the guy had gone. There was just a dark shape in the scummy water below, about three feet down and sinking fast, with a white blob on top which was his upturned face, and a burst of bubbles trailing up from the open mouth.

Then there wasn't even that.

Sixteen

Clarus and I agreed not to mention what had happened to the ladies. Whoever he'd been, and whoever he'd been working for, the guy was dead, and there was an end of it.

We sailed on schedule the next day.

As sea trips go, I've had worse. Far worse. Like I said, the *Erytheis* was a big boat, built with passengers as well as cargo in mind - we weren't the only ones, by any means - and although we just had the one cabin, with four bunk beds, it wasn't the poky hell-hole I'd expected. Not luxury standard, sure, but a whole lot better than you can reasonably hope for unless your bank balance runs to owning a blue-water yacht. I wasn't seasick, either, or no more than a little queasy towards the start: whatever Clarus's father had put into his anti-seasickness pills it was the stuff of miracle. Not that I could complain about the weather: the sea was flat as an atrium pool all the way, the Etesian winds didn't let up, and exactly ten days out from Brindisi we were sailing past the lighthouse into Alexandria's eastern harbour.

Me, I'm not one for gawping at buildings and monuments. Even so, I challenge anyone not to gawp, the first time. The Greeks may be smarmy oversophisticated buggers who're too clever for their own good, but by the gods they can build cities. And when you arrive by sea - which almost everyone does - your first sight of Alexandria hits you between the eyes like a meat cleaver. The guy who designed the city made sure that it would.

Start with the lighthouse. Forget your end-of-the-breakwater-at-Ostia tat with the smoky lamp. The lighthouse is two hundred and fifty feet high, built in three storeys, sheeted top to bottom with coloured marble and set in its own massive colonnaded courtyard. Facing you at its base when you sail past are six forty foot high seated statues of three royal couples, with the Ptolemies as pharaohs and their wives as

94

the goddess Isis. The beacon at the top is kept lit all day every day, three hundred and sixty-five days a year, and you can see it shining from a hundred miles out.

On your left, stretching all the way along the shore on the higher ground above it, are the Caesareum and the old palaces. The Caesareum isn't a single building; it's a huge complex of libraries, porticoes, basilicas and gardens behind a wall - marble-faced again - eleven feet thick, centring around the temple commemorating Augustus's arrival in the city after Actium. In front of the sea-side entrance, flanking it, are two huge rose-granite obelisks that the Egyptians say date to four hundred years before Troy...

Yeah. I know, I know: straight out of a tour guide, all of it, and not my usual style at all. Still, no apologies: Alexandria's special. Unique. Beautiful. Even I can see that. And when you get your first sight of it the city is totally, *totally* gobsmacking. There is nowhere in the world that comes close, even Rome. That's got to be said and understood, right at the start.

They still dicker like hell over transporting you and your stuff to where you want to go after you've landed, mind. Alexandrians are Greeks, after all, most of them, and life without a good dicker wouldn't be worth living to a Greek. It cost us an arm and a leg, even with Perilla on the team.

Stratocles's house was in the best of the residential districts immediately south-east of the city centre between the Mouseion and the Park of Pan. It filled practically half the length of the tree-lined side street, and the marble-faced wall around it would've done justice to a temple precinct.

'The master's resting at present,' the door-slave said, 'but I'm sure he won't mind being disturbed. If you wouldn't mind waiting, sir, I'll tell him you're here.'

We left Alexis in charge of the baggage and followed the guy through a set of marble-pillared and mosaic-floored rooms like something off the Palatine. Successful businessman was right: for an ex-slave to work his way up to this inside twenty-odd years, the paper trade had to be a real gold mine. And it was tastefully done, too. If I've got one criticism of the Alexandrians, it's that their ideas of decoration can be too garish for my liking. Marble's all very well, but they tend to take the colour mix a bit too far.

'Is this all right, sir?' The slave had led us out through a portico into a broad courtyard garden with a fountain in the centre. There was a trellised grape arbour with a wrought-iron table and cushioned chairs. 'You can wait inside, if you'd prefer.'

'No, this is lovely!' Perilla said. 'And look, Marcus! Peacocks!'

'I'll have some drinks and fruit brought out. Wine for the gentlemen? And fruit juice for the ladies?'

'Just water for me, please,' Clarus said.

'A cup of wine'd be nice, pal.' I sat down on one of the chairs and stretched out my legs. The breeze from the coast together with the spray from the fountain made the air in the garden deliciously cool. Birds were singing in the trees all around us, and Perilla's peacock was spreading its tail. Beautiful. Maybe coming to Alexandria - the case aside - had been a good move after all: I could do with a holiday, and I hadn't seen Perilla looking this relaxed for months. 'You wouldn't have Mareotis, by any chance?'

'But of course, sir.'

Hey, great! Better and better, perfect, in fact. I'd been looking forward to trying that again on its home ground.

'Corvinus, this is *amazing!*' Marilla said when the guy had bowed and left. Her mouth hadn't closed properly since we'd crossed the harbour bar: like I say, gawping at your first sight of Alexandria is par for the course.

'Yeah. Let's just hope we don't get thrown out on our ears.'

'Oh, Stratocles is a dear,' Perilla said. 'He was very fond of Uncle Paullus and Aunt Marcia. There'll be no problems, I'm sure.'

Five minutes later, the slaves came out with the drinks and fruit, together with a tall, rake-thin old guy with white hair and an impressive Greek-style beard.

'Well, well,' he said. 'Rufia Perilla.'

'Hello, Stratocles.' Perilla got up. 'How are you?'

'I'm fine, of course. And all the better for seeing you again, ma'am.' The old man hugged her. 'Why didn't you tell me you were coming? Or did the message go astray?'

'It was a last-minute decision,' Perilla said. 'We didn't know ourselves until a few days before we sailed.'

'Indeed?' He smiled. 'Well, you always were impulsive, even as a girl.' *What?* 'And this must be your husband.'

'Marcus Corvinus,' I said. I stood, and we shook. Stratocles had to be seventy, at least, but he was spry enough, and he had a strong handshake. 'Ah..."impulsive"?'

'Oh, yes. The master - that was Fabius Maximus, Corvinus, rest his bones - always said he never knew what young Rufia Perilla would be up to next. How is the mistress, by the way? The Lady Marcia?'

'I'm afraid Aunt Marcia died late last year,' Perilla said. 'No, nothing to be sorry about, Stratocles, she was very old and she didn't mind going. But she would have wanted me to give you her greetings. This is Valeria Marilla, my stepdaughter, and her fiancé Publius Cornelius Clarus.'

'Delighted.' Stratocles shook their hands. '"Cornelius"?' You're a relative of Cornelius Gallus, perhaps, young man? A great poet, and of course an Egyptian governor himself. Such a tragedy, his death.'

'No relation I'm afraid, sir,' Clarus said. 'My father's a doctor.'

Stratocles's eyes widened. He was too polite to make the obvious comment, but I could see what he was thinking: there was only one way a doctor's son could have one of the best middle names in Rome.

'Clarus's family've been citizens for over two hundred years,' I said. 'They came over from Greece with Africanus. He and Marilla are inheriting Aunt Marcia's villa.'

'Really?' The old man smoothed his beard. 'I knew a Cornelius Polymedes many years ago. A fine man, a fine doctor, and a good friend. He brought me through the fever the year after I had my freedom.'

'My grandfather.'

'You don't say! Was he, indeed?' Stratocles beamed. 'Then you're doubly welcome, my boy!'

I grinned to myself. That's how things work; have family or a friend in common and you're in. I was glad that Clarus had a connection of his own.

'Stratocles, we were hoping you might put us up,' Perilla said. 'I know it's an imposition, but -'

'Nonsense! Of *course* you can stay, my dear, there's plenty of room, as you can see. In fact, you can have the whole east wing.

97

Cleonicos!' The guy who'd been supervising the slaves as they laid the drinks and plates of fruit on the table looked up. 'Take care of it, will you? Your baggage is at the harbour, is it, Corvinus? I'll have my slaves -'

'Actually, it's outside.' Perilla had gone red. 'I'm sorry. We brought it with us.'

Stratocles laughed. 'Don't apologise! It's a compliment; I'm delighted that you could be so sure of your welcome. Cleonicos?' The major-domo bowed and left. 'Now. Sit back down, all of you, and tell me how things are in Rome. I have my news, of course, but it's never the same. And most of it's to do with business.'

So we talked, about Rome and the crossing and the wedding and old times. Finally:

'Stratocles,' Perilla said. 'I really am sorry, but would you mind if I went inside and lay down for a while?'

I glanced at her suspiciously. Oh, sure, we'd all hit post-travel relaxation mode - I was getting very pleasantly stewed on the Mareotis - but the lady isn't normally one for an afternoon siesta, and once she gets herself out of bed in the morning she's got more staying power than I have. The sudden wilting-violet act didn't seem to fit, somehow.

Even so, it worked with Stratocles. The old guy stopped in mid-flow - he'd been in the middle of a story about the teenage Perilla hiding a piglet in her bedroom for a month, which I just didn't *believe* - and was all apologies.

'Of course not, my dear,' he said. 'I'm being a very poor host, and very selfish. Clemens,' - to the hovering slave - 'show the Lady Rufia Perilla to the guest wing. And go by the bath suite on the way, tell them to light the furnace if it isn't lit already. Dinner's an hour before sunset, Perilla, but don't feel you must be prompt, it'll do my chef good to wait for a change.' I grinned: shades of Meton. I was glad we hadn't brought the bugger. 'Marilla, dear. Clarus. Corvinus. You may want time to freshen up too.'

'Oh, no, I'm sure Marcus is fine here for the present,' Perilla said. I sent her another suspicious look. 'You are, aren't you, Marcus?'

'Uh...yeah,' I said. 'Yeah, no problem.'

'Clarus and I might take a walk,' Marilla said. 'If that's all right.'

'Of course it is.' Stratocles smiled. 'Off you go, my dear. Enjoy yourselves. I'll send a slave with you in case you get lost.'

'Oh, that's okay,' Marilla said, getting up. 'We're used to wandering on our own. Come on, Clarus.'

A conspiracy; *definitely* a conspiracy. Still, the pair of them knew why we were here: as Clarus had predicted, the Princess had got that out of me before we cleared Sicily. And I should be grateful: leaving me alone with Stratocles gave me the perfect first opportunity to get my bearings where the Alexandrian side of the case was concerned.

Which, I supposed, was the idea.

Seventeen

When they'd gone we settled to our wine.

'Actually, Corvinus,' Stratocles said quietly, 'I'm glad of the opportunity for a word in private without the Lady Perilla or the youngsters. Oh, it's nothing to worry about, I'm sure, especially where Roman citizens are concerned, but you've arrived at a difficult time and it's as well you're forewarned.'

'You mean the Jewish business?' I said.

'You knew already?'

I shrugged. 'Not the details. But a friend of mine back home has family here. He said there might be trouble between the Jews and the Greeks.'

'Let's hope it doesn't come to actual trouble.' Stratocles reached for the jug and filled our cups. 'But it may do, now that Herod Agrippa's here.'

I stared at him. Agrippa was one of the imperial inner circle, a protégé of Gaius's grandmother Antonia and a long-time friend of the emperor's: he'd just been made, I knew, king of a large swatch of the eastern client-kingdoms that for the last few years had been under direct Roman rule. And being a Jew himself he was a shit-hot supporter of Jewish rights. I was with Stratocles on this one: if Herod Agrippa was in Alexandria then the likelikood of trouble had taken an appreciable hike.

'When did he arrive?' I said.

'Yesterday. And very publicly. He's brought an armed escort with him.'

Gods. 'It's an official visit? I mean, Roman-official?'

'No, not at all. At least, so he said. Seemingly he only called in in passing on his way to Judea.'

'From *Rome?*'

'Indeed.' Stratocles's voice was dry. Alexandria isn't on the way to Judea, not from Rome. 'Oh, yes, it had to be quite deliberate, and Alexandrians, whether they be Greeks or Jews, aren't fools; we can all see the implications. The only question, and it's crucial, is who is he representing, himself or Rome?'

Yeah, right. The obvious answer was 'himself', sure: he'd been careful to stress that the visit wasn't pre-planned or official, and from all I'd heard of Agrippa he wasn't the sort to play things down; if he'd come as Gaius's personal rep then he'd've made sure that everyone knew it and treated him accordingly. On the other hand, it was a delicate situation: Herod Agrippa, emperor's bosom pal or not, king of Judea or not, was still technically only a private citizen in Roman terms, and for Gaius to clap a rep's hat on him and send him into an official head-to-head with his own appointed governor would've been downright stupid and really have blown the lid off things. An unofficial carpeting on the emperor's behalf, now, or even a covert investigation of whatever the hell Flaccus was up to...

'It means trouble all the same, whichever it is,' Stratocles said. 'Agrippa's no stranger here, far from it, and he's not popular at all, not with the Greeks.'

I took a sip of my wine. 'Yeah? And why's that?'

Stratocles smiled slightly. 'Because - not to mince words, Corvinus, and meaning no disrespect to Gaius Caesar regarding his choice of friends - he's what you would call a chancer. When he was last here a couple of years ago he borrowed a large sum of money which he has failed to pay back. Nor does he seem likely to, especially now he's so far in the emperor's favour. In this city reneging on a debt is something that isn't easily forgotten or forgiven, especially when it's obvious that the man can fully afford to repay it, as Herod Agrippa now can. No, I'm afraid that if he takes up cudgels on the part of the Jews he'll find the Greeks here are more than willing to give as good as they get.'

'You, ah, including yourself in that?' I said.

'No, I am not. Most definitely I am not. Oh, I'm as much an Alexandrian as any. I was born here originally and after the master freed me I moved straight back and I've lived here ever since. But although I can understand my fellow Greeks' feelings and sympathise with them to some degree I like to think I've more sense than to take it further, especially at my age. Unfortunately I'm in the minority.'

'That friend in Rome I mentioned. He said something about a guy named Isidorus.'

'Ah, yes.' Stratocles touched his wine cup but didn't lift it. 'Isidorus is quite a different matter. If he had his way there would be no Jews in Alexandria at all, or since that's clearly impossible that they should be confined to their original quarter in the east part of the city. Herod Agrippa is a godsend to Isidorus. If he needed a spark to light the tinder then I'm much afraid he has it.'

A spark to light the tinder. Shit; that I didn't like the sound of at all. Well, we'd just have to see what happened. 'I understand the governor threw him out a couple of years ago. How long has he been back?'

Stratocles looked at me in surprise. 'You're remarkably well informed about Alexandrian affairs, aren't you?' I didn't reply. 'For about four months. Since late April.'

'And he and Flaccus are quite close these days, aren't they?'

'Yes, they are. Oddly so, perhaps, and unfortunately so in my view, but there it is.'

'You have any idea why?'

The look I was getting now was definitely suspicious. 'No. How should I have? My business is with paper, not politics, and my interests don't lie in that direction either. There are rumours, of course, but only a fool trusts to them.'

'Rumours such as?'

'Corvinus, I'm sorry, but what precisely is this about? We seem to have moved from discussing the likelihood of trouble during your stay, which I grant is something you have every right to be interested in, to bar-room gossip concerning the murkier side of local politics. Or pseudo-politics, rather, because the topic has no basis either in fact or reason. And in that subject I can see no logical cause for you to have an interest at all. Or do you?'

Bugger, the guy was smart! Still, like I said, you don't work your way up from ex-slave to millionaire without having a smart head on your shoulders, and self-confessed apolitical or not Stratocles could tell how many beans made five. Even so, I couldn't let him in on the real reason for me coming to Alexandria. It would've complicated things, and it wouldn't be fair. Or possibly, for that matter, safe for the old guy.

'No,' I said. 'Not as such. Just straight curiosity. Perilla's always telling me I'm too damn nosey for my own good.'

The suspicious look cleared, and he laughed. 'The Lady Perilla's not the one to lay that charge, young man! Not unless she's changed a great deal herself over the past twenty-odd years. Very well. It's probably arrant nonsense, of course, or if it isn't then there's nothing to be done about it, but people are saying that it's by no desire of Flaccus that the two are so hand-in-glove; that Isidorus has some hold over the man he's using to advance Greek interests.'

My neck prickled. Shit! 'Uh...what kind of hold would that be?' I said casually.

Stratocles laughed again. 'My dear Corvinus, if the gossip-mongers knew that, or even had a reasonable suggestion to offer, then no doubt they'd've added it in. Which to my knowledge they haven't. It's yet another indication that the whole thing's no more than the usual baseless wineshop calumny. Now' - he got slowly to his feet - 'you must forgive me. I don't consider myself particularly old, but my body disagrees, and sometimes, as now, I have to listen to it. If you don't mind, I'll follow your wife's lead and rest for a while. Dinner, as I said, is an hour before sunset or thereabouts, and I'll see you then. Meanwhile this house is your own. Treat it as such, please.'

I watched him go and sat for ten minutes or so, finishing off the wine in the jug and thinking. Then I whistled up a slave and got him to take me to Perilla.

She wasn't asleep in our room; which came as no surprise given that I knew the wilting-violet act had been a ploy from the start. The east wing of the house which Stratocles had turned over to us was practically a self-contained property in its own right, and the lady was sitting in a small shaded courtyard with flower beds and a fountain, with one of her book-rolls in her lap.

'Isn't this marvellous, dear?' she said. 'Much cooler than Rome, and the flowers are beautiful. Did you have a look round?'

'Mmm.' I leaned down, planted the hello kiss, and stretched out in the chair opposite. 'Very nice.'

'How was your talk with Stratocles?'

'Isidorus has his hooks into Governor Flaccus. Whatever

he's got on him is major, and six gets you ten it's something involving Macro.'

Her eyes widened. 'You're sure of that?'

'About the hooks, yes. It had to be something along those lines, sure, because no governor worth his salt would give a troublemaker like that house room, and otherwise the turnaround makes no sense. About Macro...well, Etruscus bracketed the pair of them, and Etruscus's one and only interest is Macro, so it's a logical assumption. As to what the details are your guess is as good as mine.'

'Could he have been involved in the false Gemellus plot? Flaccus, I mean.'

'It's a possibility, lady. But the fact that he's still breathing, and still the Egyptian governor, argues against it. If Lepidus and Agrippina had included him in their plans for some reason - although why they should bother I don't know - then they'd've been careful to arrange for him to be chopped with the rest. And Gaius had already appointed Macro to replace him.' Something tickled at my brain. Shit!

'Unless the proof was missing somehow,' Perilla said.

'Hmm? How do you mean?'

'They'd have to have something concrete to give to the emperor, wouldn't they? And if that was no longer to hand the suspicion might be there - enough, say, for Gaius to have Flaccus recalled - but now with nothing to back it. You see?'

'Yeah.' I frowned. 'What you're saying is that Flaccus had been living on borrowed time. Oh, sure, he wouldn't know it himself because the conspiracy was a complete fake, but that'd make no difference to the result. Somehow Isidorus gets his greasy hands on this "proof" of yours and presents Flaccus with it, scaring the guy's wollocks off enough to get him back into Alexandria with a seat at the top table thrown in. I'd go for that, lady. There's only one problem.'

'What's that?'

'Like I said, why would Lepidus and Agrippina bother to set him up in the first place? Oh, sure, as Egyptian governor he's one of the top men in the empire, but in their terms, as far as their succession plans go, he's a nonentity. Put him alongside Silanus, Gemellus and Macro and he just doesn't fit. He might, because of the grain supply, if they were planning a military coup but they aren't: if they manage to stiff Gaius then they can do things legitimately. Targeting Flaccus makes no sense, and if they didn't target him then there can be no concocted proof. If Isidorus is blackmailing the guy - and he is - it must be for something else.'

Perilla sighed. 'Yes, dear. I agree completely. Damn.'

'Never mind, lady. Early days yet. We'll get there eventually. Oh, by the way, Stratocles told me something else. Herod Agrippa's in the city.'

'*What?*'

'Yeah. He arrived yesterday. Not an official visit, or so he claims, but the guy's here all the same. The Jews're over the moon about it and the Greeks are spitting blood.'

'But that's dreadful!'

'It's not good, no. It may cramp your shopping plans for a start if you have to climb over the barricades.'

'Be serious, Marcus. I mean it. Oh, I know we wouldn't be directly threatened, not as Romans, but if there is a danger of rioting then here is not the place to be. Particularly for Clarus and Marilla.'

'Lady, there's the best part of a legion camped outside the city, plus the local force. And under Isidorus's thumb or not it's more than Flaccus's neck is worth to let a riot start. They know that on both sides. The first to cause any real trouble - Jews or Greeks - will find themselves smacked silly and taxed to the eyeballs for the next ten years.'

'Well, if you say so. All the same, if Herod Agrippa's -'

'What I was wondering was whether he'd been sent deliberately. To investigate Flaccus and report back.'

That stopped her. 'By the emperor? You think that's possible?'

'Sure. It's even likely. Remember, technically the guy'd already been recalled. The only reason he's still around is that his replacement was chopped before he could take up the post.' Bugger! There was that itch again! 'And if he is playing favourites against standard policy - which he is - then Gaius will want to know why. Agrippa could just be carrying a private rap over the knuckles, or he could be up to something more serious, but I'd guess it's one of the two. And I'll bet that either way Flaccus is currently sweating. Even if he wasn't implicated in the fake Gemellus plot -' I stopped. 'Shit!'

'Marcus? *Marcus!*'

I waved her down. Sweet and holy Jupiter!

'Marcus! What is it?'

'Flaccus was involved. Only he was on the other side, with Lepidus and Agrippina. Why he should be, and how the hell the mechanics of it work out I don't know, but it'd make sense. It'd certainly explain Isidorus's hold over him. Just exchange involvement in one plot for another, the only difference being that this one's genuine and Flaccus is genuinely in it past his eyebrows. Added to which, it's still running. If Isidorus peaches then the whole thing's blown sky-high.'

'That's sheer speculation, dear. All of it.'

'Yeah. Yeah, I know. But it's a working theory. And it explains the Macro connection.'

'How so?'

'Flaccus had been recalled, with Macro as his replacement. Say that for some reason it's important, vitally important, that Flaccus stays governor. Lepidus and Agrippina can't put their oar in with Gaius on his behalf; what excuse could they give, and it might only make Gaius suspicious. What they can do, though, is take out Macro - with Flaccus's knowledge and possible help - and the problem'll solve itself. As it has done.'

'But, Marcus, we already have a reason for Lepidus and Agrippina getting rid of Macro. He was too close to the emperor and too influential. You can't use the man twice.'

'I don't see why not, lady. Both reasons could be valid and reinforce one another. Killing two birds with one stone's a pretty effective way of doing business.'

'Also, if Isidorus presents such a danger, why hasn't Flaccus just had him killed? Surreptitiously or otherwise? I mean, he's governor here, he's in complete charge, answering to no one except the emperor himself, and Isidorus is a comparative nobody; certainly where Rome is concerned. He could manage it easily.'

'Perilla, I told you: I haven't worked out the mechanics and I've got nothing in the way of fact to go on. But the guy's not stupid. He'll've thought of that and have safeguards in place. Besides, like you say he's a comparative nobody, which means the likelihood is that he's just a middleman acting for someone else. Someone in Rome, high enough up to have access to whatever information he's using to burn Flaccus.

Getting rid of him'd probably do more harm than good.'

'Someone in Rome? Such as who? And what's their interest?'

'Search me.'

'All right. Change the subject. If Flaccus is involved with Lepidus and Agrippina then what's his role?'

I sighed. 'Pass. Pass completely. Look, lady, give it a break, now, will you? It's an idea, sure, but right or wrong we can't take it any further. File for reference, agreed?'

'Agreed.' She got up and laid the book-roll down on the chair. I glanced at the title: Philo's 'Guide to Alexandria'; what else? 'Now. After travelling for the best part of a month I itch like mad and probably smell. I would kill for a bath, and the furnace should be hot enough by this time.'

I grinned, and got up too. 'Fair enough.' I'd've imitated Marilla and Clarus and gone out to stretch my legs for an hour or so - it was still only late morning - but a long steam and a bit of pampering from Stratocles's bath slaves, followed by a quiet afternoon in the garden with some more of the Mareotis to keep me company, seemed a much better deal.

Alexandria could wait. After all, we were on holiday.

Eighteen

Next morning Perilla went out on the first leg of her shopping binge, taking the kids with her. I felt a bit sorry for Clarus; the guy has as much clothes sense as I have, and no man should be subjected for hours on end to the company of women in pursuit of the perfect dress material, not sober, anyway. Still, he's an easy-going lad, Clarus, and he didn't seem too put out. Besides, if he was getting married then the sooner he learned to take the rough with the smooth the better.

Me, I'd no definite plans, barring to get out and around. Something would suggest itself eventually, sure, and in the meantime, like I preferred to do first off when I was in a new town, I could get the general feel of the place and an idea of where things were. Not that that would be difficult, given the layout: Stratocles's house lay more or less in the geographical middle, south-east of the actual centre, and if I went due north I'd hit the Canopic Way which ran roughly east and west from one side of the city to the other. Then if I took a left towards the Mouseion crossroads I'd pick up the other main drag, the Street of the Soma, which would take me north again towards the sea, through the market square and on to the harbour where we'd arrived. After that I thought I might follow the coast round to the Lochias peninsula, the old Palace area where Flaccus had his offices, then head back south through the Bruchium quarter and so home, completing the circle. Not that I was in any hurry, mind. There was bound to be a convenient wineshop or two on the way, and whereas Perilla's bag is monuments mine is wineshops. They should be pretty good in Alexandria, if the quality of the local wine was anything to go by.

It was a perfect day for walking - warm, rather than hot, with that sea breeze that must've attracted the original city-builders to the site keeping the air moving - and after ten days at sea and a dozen before that in a closed carriage it was nice just to be on foot on dry land again. I covered the quarter mile or so to the Canopic Way past the upmarket properties in their own grounds almost without noticing it.

I'd got about half way when I heard the noise. I thought at first it was one of those processions you get in Rome sometimes but are a lot more common in places where they go more for the mystery cults: the ones in honour of Cybele, or Isis, or maybe the Great Goddess, not that it matters, because these foreign ladies're all of a piece anyway, and they all seem to be into loud chanting and percussion that'll have your eardrums out. Only that wasn't quite right. There was percussion and chanting, sure, but it was rough stuff, like whoever the celebrants were they were banging together any odd bits of metal that came to hand without trying to keep to a rhythm and shouting their lungs out. Shouting just two words, repeated over and over.

Then I got closer and was able to make the words out:

'*Basileus...karabas...basileus...karabas...basileus...karabas...*'

King cabbage? What the hell kind of religious chant was king cabbage?

When I got to it, the end of the street was blocked four or five deep across its width with people, all with their backs to me and rubbernecking at whatever was happening on the main drag beyond. I pushed through as far as I was able and did a bit of rubber-necking myself...

There's nothing like the Canopic Way in Rome, or anywhere else, for that matter. It's dead straight, almost three miles long, paved in stone and a hundred feet wide. And the procession filled it to bursting, side to side and end to end; at least, from where I was standing, all of its length that I could see. I'd been just in time to catch the main part. Oh, sure, it was a procession, all right, but forget your orgiastic rites of Cybele or our tame Roman version with the fluteplayers, the poker-faced senators and the bulls. This was a parody, and the people making it up were a rabble. I'd been right about the bits of metal. The guys doing the processing - and there must've been hundreds, if not thousands of them - were banging together anything from tin trays to kebab-spits.

I pulled at my nearest fellow rubber-necker's sleeve and he turned round. 'Hey, pal,' I shouted. 'What's this all about?'

He held his hand to his ear and I tried again, louder. No luck. He shrugged, scowled, and turned away again. Shit, maybe he was naturally deaf. Practically the whole Alexandrian population to choose

109

from and I had to pick this one. Then the guy on my other side tugged at my tunic. I turned round myself and he put his mouth to my ear and yelled:

'*Herod!!!...Agrippa!!!*'

King Herod. King cabbage. Oh, fuck; they'd lynched one of the emperor's closest buddies and the ruler of Rome's biggest client kingdom, or they were on their way to do it. I put my hands on the shoulders of my pals either side, heaved myself up higher and goggled around at as much of the procession as I could. Yeah; there was a litter there to my left, an open litter, more of a chair on sticks, being carried shoulder-high, with a man in it. On it. Whatever. He was wearing the robes and headband of an eastern king, and swaying about as if he were drunk or had been knocked silly. Gods, trouble was right. When this got back to Gaius he'd send in enough legions to stamp the city flat and nail the entire Greek population to crosses. The fools. The bloody, *bloody* fools.

Then I looked again. The litter - chair - was getting closer and I could see the man more clearly over the heads of the crowd around him. I'd never met Agrippa, sure, but whoever he was this guy wasn't him. He was a dwarf, for a start, and he had a face that looked like one of these lanterns the kids make from turnips for the Lemuria to scare away the ghosts. He was grinning like one of them, too, and the grin was slack and empty. I could see the spittle glistening on his jaw. I breathed again: not Agrippa, just some poor idiot dressed up to look like him.

Bad enough, mind. Not quite *lèse-majesté* as far as the Roman side of things went, but easily within the definition of the term. And Gaius, when he got to hear of it, wouldn't be amused. Not one bit. Whatever excuse Flaccus could make, the guy had -

I stopped.

Where were the troops? Where the hell were the troops?

The simple fact was that anywhere under Rome's jurisdiction nothing like this should be happening; and if it did look like happening then the authorities - Flaccus, in this case - would see that it was stopped pretty damn quickly before things got out of hand, as they'd evidently done here. Rome's pretty strong on nipping civil demonstrations in the bud - she can't afford not to be - and any official who doesn't have a shit-hot system in place to provide early warning of a disturbance is just asking to be booted off the payroll. The procession wasn't a riot, sure, but it was the next thing to it, and it certainly constituted an incitement: most of the crowd, from what I could see, were Greeks, and cheering like my erstwhile informant, but some of the heads wore skull-caps, and the faces underneath them were looking seriously unchuffed. In fact, as the last of the procession passed and the crowd began breaking up there were scuffles and one or two outright fist-fights. As under the circumstances there would be. So where the fuck were the guys in armour whose job was keeping the *pax romana*?

The Way was clearing fast now; a lot of the gawpers had headed east in the wake of the procession, leaving the pillar-fringed pavement a lot emptier than it probably was usually. I carried on in the direction I'd originally intended, towards the main crossroads. Gods! That had been something, and I just hoped that Perilla and the kids hadn't got mixed up in it. Not that, probably, they had: they'd be a good half mile off, in the centre proper where the upmarket shops were.

I'd got to within about a hundred yards of the Mouseion when I saw the loungers on the pavement ahead. They were drunk: obviously drunk, two slumped against the inside wall and a third with his back to the facing pillar, passing a wine jar between them. Bugger; this I didn't need, not on top of everything else. I stepped off the pavement onto the street and began to cross over, keeping an eye out for chariots. That's one thing you don't have to worry about in Rome: wheeled traffic isn't allowed within the city boundaries during daylight hours, sure, but even if it was the streets are far too narrow and crowded for anyone in a chariot to get up a decent speed. Like I said, the Canopic Way's a hundred feet wide, dead straight and well-surfaced, the local wide-boys treat it like a racetrack, and crossing it means you take your life in your hands. Today it was deserted, obviously because everyone in the city with the notable exception of the governor had known about the procession in advance and had either joined in or were keeping clear of the whole boiling.

The three drunks unpeeled themselves from their respective wall and pillar and wove their unsteady way towards me, cutting me off. The guy with the wine jug brandished it.

'Hey, Roman!' he yelled. 'Have a drink on us! Celebrate King

Cabbage Day!'

Hell. Still, they looked harmless enough. Certainly cheerful.

'Thanks anyway, lads,' I said; they were only about a dozen yards off now. 'But maybe another time. I've places to go and things to do.'

'Oh, come on, you poncy Roman bastard! It's King Cabbage Day, and one drink won't kill you!' The drunk with the wine jug spread his arms. Wine spilled...

And then he'd dropped the jug, which smashed on the flagstones, and he and his pals were rushing forward, not stumbling-drunk, not drunk at all. I caught the gleam of a knife in the lead-man's hand as his arm went back...

Oh, shit.

I'd no time to defend myself as the knife drove at my gut, but I managed to twist sideways and grab him round the shoulders, hugging him close. I felt the knife tear through the loose part of my tunic and brought my knee up hard. He grunted and doubled over.

The other two came in either side, pinning my arms as he pulled himself free.

'Hold him steady!' he snapped. I struggled, but they had a good grip and there wasn't much I could do. He straightened, drew back his knife arm again and...

There was a dull thud. The guy jerked forwards like someone had shoved him smartly from behind. His mouth and eyes opened, and he was suddenly toppling towards me, the knife slipping from his fingers to clatter on the stone paving.

Which was when I saw the javelin in his back.

The others saw it too. They glanced up. One of them said, softly, 'Fuck.'

Then they turned and ran. For about three yards, before the other two javelins got them.

I'd twisted round to watch them go. There was the sound of running hobnail sandals behind me and I looked back.

Yeah, well, maybe Rome was there when you needed her after all. I took a deep breath, held it and let it out. Gods, that'd been close!

'You all right, sir?' The officer commanding the batch of squaddies was hurrying over as the three legionaries went to recover their weapons and check the bodies for signs of life. Not from the looks of things that there was much chance of that.

'Yeah.' I examined my tunic. A tear as long as my hand, but I hadn't been so much as scratched. 'Yeah, I'm fine.' I registered his insignia. 'No permanent damage, tribune. Thanks.'

'Then you're bloody lucky. If we'd come out of that side street a heartbeat later you'd've been dead.'

I grinned. 'You don't have to tell me that, pal. And thanks especially to you three buggers.' I gave the three returning squaddies my best sloppy military salute. 'Nice throws.'

The nearest guy chuckled and spat on the roadway. 'Our pleasure, sir. Keeps us in practice.'

'Care to tell me what happened?' the tribune said.

'I saw them up ahead, started crossing the road to avoid them and they came after me. Then they went for me and you and the lads turned up. That's all I know.'

He shook his head. 'Then it makes no sense. It's broad daylight, a public place, you're obviously a Roman. No knifeman in the city would dare. They didn't even threaten you first? Ask for your purse?'

'No. They were drunk, mind.' They hadn't been, of course, but I wasn't telling him that, however grateful I was. I wanted to think about it first.

'It's still crazy. That sort of thing just doesn't happen in Alexandria.' I said nothing. 'Your name, sir? Just for the record.'

'Marcus Valerius Corvinus.'

'Fine.' He held out a hand. 'Marcus Gallius, tribune with the twenty-second. Pleased to meet you.'

'Likewise. Obviously.' We shook. 'Uh, you have time for a cup of wine somewhere, pal, or are you seriously on duty? I owe you that, at least. I owe you the jar. Oh, and speaking of which' - I reached into my purse and brought out the three gold pieces that were among the silver and copper - 'perhaps your lads will accept a small contribution to the Javelin-Hefters' Benevolent Fund. With my gratitude and congratulations.'

Gallius took them and sucked on a tooth. 'Well, now,' he said. 'Regarding the wine, I'm not actually on duty at all as such, Corvinus. And interviewing the victim of an attempted murder, especially if he's from one of the oldest families in Rome, would be a reasonable cause for coming off it if I was. Wouldn't it? So you're on.' He turned to the squaddies, who were taking a lounging break. 'Hey, Quintus!'

'Yes, sir.' The first javelin man came over and saluted.

'Take over. See that this mess is cleared up.'

'Sir.' The guy grinned.

'Oh, and these are compliments of Valerius Corvinus here.' He handed over the three gold pieces. 'I've given him my word that you and your mates won't spend them on loose women and drink.'

The grin widened. 'Sir!' He saluted and went back to his troop. They began to drag the bodies back towards the portico.

'You care to recommend a wineshop?' I said. 'We only arrived yesterday and I don't know the place yet.'

'Jupiter!' Gallius chuckled. 'You've only been here two days and someone tries to knife you?'

'So it would appear. Maybe I'm just unlucky.' Yeah; sure I was. But that aspect of things wanted mature consideration, and I hadn't got the time at present. Besides, this fresh-faced kid didn't need the complication.

'We'll go to Hagnon's. It's not far, and he serves good Mareotis. Not the best in the city, but close.'

'Fine by me, pal,' I said. 'Lead on.'

Nineteen

It wasn't far; back a bit the way I'd come and down one of the side streets. Yeah; this'd do: a wineshop with a courtyard garden at the rear, tables and wickerwork chairs under a spreading vine cover. We settled down, the waiter came over and I ordered half a jug of the Mareotis.

'So,' Gallius said, 'what're you doing in Alex, Corvinus? Business or pleasure?'

'Bit of both.' I told him about Perilla and the bridesmaids' dress material.

He shook his head. 'You came all this way just to buy *cloth?*'

'So it seems.'

'Jupiter, how the other half live!'

'Yeah, well. How about you? You been here long?'

'Long enough. Just short of a year now. My uncle - my mother's brother - got me the posting. You know him? Crispus Passienus?'

'Uh-uh. I don't get out much.' I knew the name, though. The lad - he couldn't've been any older than early twenties, twenty-five absolute max - had impressive connections: Sallustius Crispus Passienus, I remembered, had held the consulship about ten years back, and he was still well up on the military side. 'You enjoying it?'

'It's okay.' He took a sip of the wine. It was good stuff: not great, in comparison with Stratocles's, but more than passible, like he'd said. The guy knew his wine. 'Quiet. Saving occasional visiting purple-stripers from knife attacks aside.'

'Yeah. Right.'

'I still can't get over that, Corvinus. It really does make no sense at all. Maybe it's just something in the air just now.'

'Like the King Cabbage procession.'

'You get caught up in that?'

'I saw it, sure.' I took a careful swallow of wine. 'Not that I

115

could miss it if I was in the area. Where were the troops, incidentally? Or did it take the authorities that much by surprise?'

'Oh, we knew it was going to happen. Only we'd orders from the governor not to interfere.'

I kept my voice neutral. 'Is that so, now?'

'Strictly hands off.' Gallius was bitter, and it showed; still, he wouldn't bad-mouth his commanding officer to a civilian, especially one he'd just met. That was standard army etiquette.

'So what were you and the lads doing on the street? Besides saving my skin for me?'

That got me a weak smile. 'I told you. I wasn't on duty. I thought I'd just ask for a few volunteers and take a stroll through the city.' Yeah; right. I'd been wondering what a tribune was doing out on patrol with a scant dozen squaddies. That was a centurion's job, if it rated even that highly. We'd got a man who took his responsibilities seriously here, even in the face of orders. 'And the gratitude needn't go all the one way. For what it was worth that was the first action I've seen since I arrived. So far it's been the highlight of the posting.'

'Quiet as that, eh?' Me, I'd settle for the easy life any day, but it wasn't an unfamiliar complaint, especially coming from youngsters like Gallius: I'd heard it a dozen times in the past from friends of mine who'd done their compulsory stint with the Eagles before getting their foot on the first rung of the political ladder. They expected battle and excitement on the frontiers, and what they got, nine times out of ten, was boring routine and mind-numbing admin. Mind you, the tenth time could leave them dead or scarred for life, but they didn't think of that. Nor would it've stopped them if they had.

Gallius took another swallow of wine. 'Oh, I'm not complaining,' he said. 'I was lucky to get my tribuneship at all, the twenty-second's a good bunch, and there're far worse places to be than Alex.'

'Like the Rhine,' I said. 'I've never been there myself, but I've a good friend in Rome who was with Varus in the Teutoburg. He said it still gives him nightmares, even thirty years on.'

Gallius set his cup down slowly and stared at me. 'You know someone who was with *Varus?*'

'Sure. He was his orderly, in fact.'

'I thought they were all killed. Massacred. All three legions.'

116

'He was lucky. He escaped.'

'Gods!' He took a swallow of wine. 'Did he ever meet Germanicus?'

'Uh-uh. That was after his time.' It never fails: mention the Rhine in Augustus's day to anyone who's army and that bastard's name comes up like a twitch. And with that same starry-eyed look and reverent tone of voice. It makes me want to throw up. 'You're better off here, pal. Believe me.'

'Corvinus, I'd trade places with any guy in one of the Rhine legions like a shot, and hand him six months' pay into the bargain. Especially now.'

'Yeah?' He meant it, too. Jupiter! 'And what's so special about now?'

That got me another stare, right across the army/civilian divide. 'You don't know?'

'Uh-uh. Why should I?'

'There's going to be another push to the north, a big one, chances are a crossing-over into Britain. Next year, so my uncle says.'

Shit. I'd've thought Gaius would've had more sense: pushing the empire's boundaries beyond the Rhine has always proved a mistake in the long run, a costly mistake too. That's why, after he learned better, Augustus didn't do it, nor - more significantly - did the Wart: Tiberius had been a hands-on soldier himself. And Germany was bad enough, but Britain! That was opening a whole new can of worms.

'So the Rhine's the place to be, or will be soon,' Gallius was saying. 'Only me, unless I can persuade my uncle somehow to get me a transfer, I'll be stuck here in bloody Alex.' He took another swallow of wine and grinned. 'Never mind. Like I say, it isn't a bad place to be, all round.'

I topped up our cups. 'You think there'll be more trouble? Between the Jews and Greeks?'

'Could be. Feelings're running pretty high, especially on the Greek side. If Governor Flaccus doesn't -' He stopped and drank; yeah, we'd got onto sensitive ground again there. 'I might get my bit of excitement after all, not that I'd be glad to have it at that price. Herod bloody Agrippa being here isn't helping matters much, either. The most constructive thing that interfering bastard can do is sail for Judea

117

tomorrow and let things settle down a bit.'

Yeah, right, I was with him on that. *A spark to the tinder*, Stratocles had said, and that just summed him up. Problem was, once tinder has caught alight it's difficult to put out. 'Has he, uh, seen the governor at all?'

'Sure. He went straight to the Palace from his ship, didn't even wait for an invite. Not just him; his entire fucking bodyguard as well, like he was some sort of visiting royalty. Which he is, of course, but you know what I mean. Like he was the one calling the shots. That was another thing that put the Greeks' backs up.' He drank again. 'Have you arranged to see Flaccus yet yourself, by the way?'

I felt my pulse quicken. 'Uh-uh. No reason to. I said: we're just holidaymakers, more or less.'

'You've got a reason now. Roman purple-stripers don't get attacked in the street without the governor wanting to know about it. I'll be putting in a report, naturally, but you might like to give him the circumstances first hand, if you can spare the time.'

'Yeah.' Jupiter! 'Yeah, I can do that. Sure.'

'No problem, then. I'll set up an appointment with his aide and let you know. Where're you staying?'

'With Fabius Stratocles. You know him?'

'The paper merchant? Sure. He's a big man here in business circles. You connected in any way?'

'Not me, not directly. He's a freedman of my wife's late uncle.'

Gallius chuckled. 'Then he's done pretty well for himself. Better than I'll ever do, certainly. Fine. I'll make the arrangements and send to let you know. It should be within the next couple of days.'

'Great!' I indicated the wine jug. 'You want the second half?'

'No, I'd best be getting back. I'm on duty at sunset.' He drank what was left in his cup and stood up. 'A pleasure to meet you, Corvinus. Despite the circumstances. Enjoy your stay in Alex.'

We shook. 'Look, pal,' I said. 'It's not our house, but I'm sure Stratocles wouldn't mind. You fancy coming round to dinner some evening?'

He smiled. 'Yeah. Yeah, thanks, I'd like that. I'm tied up most of the time but we could arrange something, I'm sure.'

'You like to suggest a date?'

118

'When the messenger arrives with a time for your interview with the governor you can give him three or four possible ones and we'll take it from there.'

'Sounds okay to me. Oh, and one big favour. As far as my wife's concerned we met here in the wineshop, right?' I wouldn't be telling Perilla about the attempted knifing: no *way* would I be telling Perilla! A casual wineshop crony she'd believe. 'The interview with Flaccus is just a courtesy call.'

'Understood. I won't forget. I'll see you later.'

He left.

There was another cupful in the jug, so I poured it and settled back to think. The whole knife attack thing was odd; crazy, to use Gallius's word. If it had been a coincidence, that was. But it couldn't've been coincidence, not in a million years, not the way it happened: I'd been deliberately targeted. Someone in Alex wanted me not just discouraged but dead.

Only that made no sense either. We'd just arrived, literally. I hadn't even begun poking around. So if the attack was connected with the case - and it was - then how the hell had whoever had set it up known who I was and why I was here? That quick, it just couldn't happen.

Shit, it was a mystery. And turning it over and over in my head wouldn't get me anywhere in any case. Leave it for now. The fact remained that I was blown before I'd started, and from here on in I'd better go careful.

Gallius had been a lucky break, though, and in more senses than one: I might have sharked up an interview with Flaccus, sure, but like I'd said I had no real reason to. Now I was having the job done for me. And it would be interesting to see how the guy reacted. If he had, somehow, been behind the attempted stabbing there might be some mileage there. Also, dinner with a tribune on the inside of things might be informative: he might be a little less close-mouthed in the family setting. Not that that was my only reason for the invite: he was a very nice guy, Gallius.

Well, I couldn't complain that my first proper day hadn't been eventful, or that I hadn't made full use of it. And I could chalk up the location of a good wineshop, too, which was an added bonus. I finished the Mareotis, stood up and nodded to the waiter. Time to resume the walk. Only now I'd be sure to stop off at a decent cutler's somewhere and buy myself a knife of my own.

If the buggers tried again then I'd need it.

Twenty

The shopping binge had been a great success: Perilla hadn't found her perfect material yet, sure - after only one day trying and maybe only a dozen or so shops that would've taken a stroke of luck on the scale of being hit by a bag of emeralds dropped from a flying pig - but she'd come pretty close at times, and in the process her wedding-supplies hit list otherwise had got a lot smaller than it was when we'd arrived. So the pressure in that direction was definitely off. Now she meant to combine business with pleasure by fitting in some sightseeing.

Which under normal circumstances would've been bad, bad news: wedding fever's temporary, but artwork, temples and monuments are her ongoing obsessions. Perilla's approach to them is ruthlessly efficient. The lady ticks boxes. And as far as thoroughness goes, the nearest parallel would be old Africanus's reduction of Carthage to an empty field ploughed with salt. She doesn't like doing the rounds alone, either, and that's the point. Usually if I want to miss out on even so much as a footnote in her most detailed guidebook I have to dicker like hell.

Not this time. Bringing Clarus and Marilla had been a stroke of genius. If the choice was between practically having to haul me round the city on a rope and doing the tourist thing *sans* grizzling with the kids then for once she was happy to let me wallow in philistine sloth. It got the youngsters out of my hair, too, because they'd only've wanted to get involved with the case. Me, I don't mind risking being knifed or having my head beaten in in a good cause, but putting anyone else in the way of trouble's different, especially family: Clarus'd given me enough of a fright in Brindisi.

Gallius's note arrived the next day to say he'd booked me for an appointment with Flaccus for the late morning of the day after. Great; so things were moving. I reckoned the next step was up to the other side in any case, whoever the other side were, and the best I could do was keep rattling the bars and hope something would jump. Going and talking to Flaccus, whether he was a villain or not, was pretty effective bar-rattling in anyone's book: it'd show that I knew he was involved somewhere along the line, and that might just prompt a little panicky reaction that would open up an avenue or two. Those I definitely needed.

Like I said, I'd checked out the exact location of the Palace on my walkabout. It was on the Lochias peninsula to the east of the two harbours, the focus of a huge complex of public and private-official buildings and gardens that the Ptolemies'd spent over two and a half centuries putting together and that sprawled beyond the peninsula itself part-way along the coast either side. Whether it was the normal arrangement or not - possibly not, because somewhere in this gobsmacking marble rabbit-warren would be where Herod Agrippa was staying while he was in Alex, and given recent events Flaccus would want to be careful over his health - the place was heaving with legionary guards; there weren't exactly formal military checkpoints, but the lads in the iron lobster suits were obviously keeping a close eye on incoming traffic. I got precise directions from one of them and found my way to the governor's suite of offices.

The entrance lobby was what a top-notch Janiculan villa's would like to be when it died and went to heaven: the width and length of a small basilica, floored in different-coloured marble, with original bronzes that would've had Perilla squeaking with delight and, forty feet up, a coffered ceiling in cedar-wood with gold filigree and inlaid paintings of gods, nymphs and assorted members of the old royal family looking smugly down at the plebs beneath. Yeah, well; I'm no culture buff, as you know, but the thought that I was standing on the same spot where, perhaps, Cleopatra had greeted Antony gave me goosebumps.

There was a secretary's desk at the centre. I went over, my sandals clicking on the marble and sending the echoes round the panelled and picture-hung walls.

'Yes, sir.' The secretary was waiting for me.

'Marcus Valerius Corvinus,' I said. 'I've an appointment with the governor.'

He checked a list. 'Yes, of course.' There were two or three slaves hanging about in identical red tunics. The secretary beckoned one over. 'Take Valerius Corvinus upstairs. To the governor's office.'

'Follow me, sir,' the slave said.

There was a broad staircase behind the secretary's desk, flanked by a couple of equestrian statues in white marble that wouldn't've been too big for a major square in Rome. The staircase was built to match. We went up.

In the palace as it was originally, we would've been in the private apartments. Or at least a tiny bit of them. The staircase gave out onto an octagonal hall built on the same scale, with doors leading off, more bronzes and paintings, and two or three couches against the walls: sitting couches, not reclining ones. Sitting on one of them was Marcus Gallius.

'Hey, Corvinus.' He stood up. 'The governor asked me to come as well, to fill in any details. You mind?'

'Not at all. Good to see you again.' We shook.

'I'll just tell the governor you're here, sir,' the slave said. 'Then if you'd like to wait until he's ready for you.'

'Sure. No problem.' I sat down on one of the couches, and Gallius did the same, while he knocked on one of the doors and disappeared inside.

'So, how are you feeling after your adventure?' Gallius said.

'Oh, I'm fine. No ill effects.'

'That's great.' Just then one of the other doors opened and a man came out. He was Greek, plump and balding, in his fifties, with the pouchy look of a worried hamster. He nodded to us as he passed, then did a small double-take when his eyes met mine. He looked away at once and speeded up, pattering off down the staircase. 'It can't be -'

'Hang on, pal. Sorry.' I was frowning. If it hadn't been for that double-take I wouldn't've given the guy a second thought. Now I did, and he'd looked vaguely familiar. 'You happen to know who that was?'

Before he could answer, the governor's door opened and the slave came back out. 'If you'd like to come through, gentlemen.'

Well, the hamster could wait. We went in.

The room was all of a piece with the rest of the place so far, in scale and everything else: big enough almost for a formal reception hall and kitted out with furniture and artwork that would've put any urban villa's in Rome to shame. Flaccus was sitting behind a big scrollworked desk at the end, his back to a set of windows that looked out towards the harbour and Pharos Island beyond. He stood up: a big man in his late fifties, florid faced, dressed in a formal narrow-striper mantle; yeah, being the Egyptian governor he would be an equestrian rather than a senatorial.

'Valerius Corvinus. Delighted to meet you. Please sit down. Gallius?' The tribune had stopped at the door and was standing at attention. 'You too, my boy. This is quite informal. Pull up another chair.'

I went over, shook, and sat down. The chair had a back to it, and it was made of inlaid cedar.

'Well,' Flaccus said when we were all settled. 'Gallius here tells me you've been in the wars.'

'Yeah. It was only thanks to him and his lads that I came out the other end of them.'

'I'd like to apologise first.' Flaccus frowned. 'We have our share of knifemen and street-thieves, yes, of course we do, every city does. But for a Roman citizen to be attacked on the Way in broad daylight... well, if it hadn't happened I would've said it was impossible. Have you any explanation yourself? Besides the fact that they were drunk.'

'They weren't drunk.' Gallius made a movement, and I glanced at him. 'Sorry, pal, that part wasn't true. They acted it, sure, at first, but they were as sober as I was.'

'Then -' The governor's frown deepened. 'You said they didn't demand your purse? That they simply tried to kill you?'

'Yeah. That's right.'

'And you hadn't provoked them in any way?'

'Uh-uh. Quite the reverse. I was heading across the street to avoid them at the time.'

'But that's incredible. You have no explanation for their behaviour? None at all?'

'Not that I'd care to offer.' I paused. 'You have one yourself, maybe?'

'No, Corvinus. Absolutely none. It makes no sense whatsoever.' Well, his puzzlement seemed genuine enough, but then he'd had plenty of time to prepare. 'Still, all's well that ends well, I suppose. I hope it won't spoil your stay in Alexandria. You're here for long?'

'We haven't got any fixed plans. Just as long as it takes.'

'As long as what takes?'

'My adopted daughter's getting married. My wife wanted to find material for the bridesmaids' dresses.'

He laughed. 'You've come all the way for that?'

'Plus the holiday. And a bit of personal business.'

'Oh, yes? And what would that be?' There was a knock on the door, and it opened. 'Excuse me. Yes, Sextus, what is it?'

I turned round as the guy came over. He was Roman, wearing a formal striped mantle of his own.

'I'm sorry, sir, but if I could have your signature on this, please? If you remember, you wanted it sent as soon as possible, and the courier's ready to leave.'

'Let me see.' Flaccus took the sheet he was holding out and read it. 'Oh, yes. Quite right. Thank you.' He reached for the pen on his desk and dipped it in the ink-pot. 'Valerius Corvinus, this is my aide, Acilius Glabrio.' He signed the sheet at the bottom, sanded it and gave it back.

'Thank you, sir.' The guy took the letter. 'I'm sorry to have interrupted. Pleased to meet you, Valerius Corvinus. Tribune.' He nodded to Gallius and left.

'Now.' Flaccus looked back to me. 'You were saying. Some personal business.'

'Yeah. A favour to a freedman. Not one of mine, one of Naevius Sertorius Macro's.' I was watching his face closely. He managed pretty well, but he couldn't stop the giveaway blink and the slight freezing of his expression. Got you, you bastard! 'Did you know him at all?'

'Macro? Of course. As an acquaintance rather than a friend, but certainly I knew him. I was sorry to hear of his death. He was a very...able man.' Interesting choice of adjective. 'Which freedman, as a matter of interest?'

'His name was Dion. He used to be Macro's secretary.'

'Did he? Then I never met him. But then Macro was only an acquaintance of mine, not a friend.' Odd; that was the second time he'd said it: deliberately? And if so, was it just the usual career man's knee-jerk reaction of distancing himself from someone who'd been chopped?

125

But then, what about that *I was sorry to hear of his death*? 'And the business itself? If you don't mind telling me.'

'Nothing important. Just finding out something he was anxious to know.'

'Really? In Alexandria?' Another blink, and the face too controlled. I didn't answer. 'Well, I won't press you further. It's none of my concern, but I wish you luck.' He got to his feet. The interview, obviously, was over. 'Thank you for coming, and my apologies again for your unfortunate introduction to the city. Gallius, thank you for coming too.'

'Sir.' Gallius stood up and saluted.

We let ourselves out.

'I might as well've saved myself the bother.' Gallius grinned as we headed for the stairs. 'I'm busy enough today already.'

'Sorry, pal. And for throwing you a wobbler over that drunk business.'

He stopped. 'Yeah. Why did you do that, by the way?'

'I'll explain another time. It's complicated.' Then I remembered the worried hamster. 'Incidentally. That guy who passed us before we went in. You know him?'

'Cineas? Sure.' He carried on down the stairs.

'He work here?'

'No, he's one of the big local merchants.' He stopped again. 'Now there's a point. He deals mainly in textiles. Wholesale, import and export. If your wife hasn't found the material she's after yet then maybe I should've introduced you. I might've got a commission out of it.'

Hey! 'You have an address for him?'

'Sure. His place is easy to find. One of the big warehouses just off Market Square, between it and the Eunostos Harbour.'

Bugger; centre of town. The chances were that Perilla had been there already. But there again, if he was a wholesaler perhaps not; it was worth a try, anyway. 'So what was he doing in the Palace?'

'He's in and out. He's one of the main government suppliers.'

'And the room he came out of?'

'Oh, that was Glabrio's office. The guy you met. The governor's aide. Now I'm sorry, Corvinus, but I've got to rush. Pick you up again?'

'Sure.' My brain was buzzing. 'Oh. The dinner. I checked with Stratocles; any evening's fine, you choose. Just give us a day's warning and turn up an hour before sunset with your party slippers.'

'Will do. See you.' He rushed off, and I followed him down more slowly.

Well, I'd certainly rattled a few bars, and the result had been interesting. Plus there had been the unexpected bonus of seeing hamster-face. I remembered him now, sure I did.

He'd been one of our fellow passengers on board the *Erytheis*.

Twenty-One

Next morning after breakfast I bundled the whole family into Stratocles's coach and we headed for Soma Street and - ultimately - Cineas's warehouse.

'But I still don't understand why you want to come, dear,' Perilla said. 'I mean, the suggestion may've come from your wineshop friend, but Marilla, Clarus and I are perfectly capable of looking at material by ourselves.' She sniffed. 'You certainly haven't shown any interest so far.'

Bugger; this is what you get for trying to hide things from your wife. I couldn't give her my real reason for tagging along because that'd mean telling her about the knife attack: if the finger pointed at anyone for blowing the whistle on me in Alex with Flaccus or whoever so quickly then it was our fellow traveller in ladies' dresses. And I wanted to face him myself with a reasonable excuse to back me and see whether he jumped. As cover, Perilla's bridesmaids quest was perfect, because it was genuine. If the guy was straight - and I'd bet a jar of Mareotis to one of pickles that he wasn't - he wouldn't turn a hair.

'Yeah, well,' I said. 'Maybe I'm just feeling a little guilty about that.'

She sniffed again. 'The guilty part I can believe. You're certainly guilty about something, dear. But I don't think it's a failure to look at dress material.'

Shit. 'Look, lady -'

'This Cineas is connected with the case, isn't he?' Marilla said.

'Obviously.' That was Clarus.

Bugger, this was a conspiracy! The three of them were ganging up on me and they were too bloody smart by half! 'Uh...maybe. Could be. It's a possibility.'

Clarus grinned.

'Well, you haven't been beaten up since we got here,' Perilla said. 'That's the usual reason for you looking shifty and being reticent. I'd've noticed the cuts and bruises. The fresh ones, on top of those you got dodging that cart.' Ouch. 'And you haven't come back from your walks with your clothes in a -' She stopped. 'That big rip in your tunic the other day. How did you get that? I meant to ask and I forgot.'

'Ah...'

'*Marcus Valerius Corvinus!*'

Oh, fuck. She'd nailed me. Well, lying would just lead to more complications, and I doubted she'd believe anything I said now anyway. So I told her.

'Someone tried to kill you? When we'd only just arrived?' She was looking at me aghast. 'How did they know?'

Yeah, well; I suppose the fact that it'd been three days ago, I hadn't been damaged, and I was still alive and breathing had sweated some of the drama out of it, but the lady had taken the news a lot more calmly than I'd expected. Not that I was ungrateful. Or maybe it was happening so often these days that she was getting blasé about it. 'That's the point,' I said. 'I bumped into this Cineas guy outside Flaccus's office yesterday. He was with us on the ship and yet he went past me like greased lightning without letting on.'

'Perhaps he didn't recognise you.'

'Sure he did. I said: when he saw me he slipped past like he'd been greased. And him being in the governor's offices is too much of a coincidence to swallow.'

'Hmm.' She looked out of the window. We were almost up to Soma Street now: the main north/south drag, if you remember, that crosses the Canopic Way and takes you to the harbour. The Soma was the big tomb near the crossroads where Alexander and the Ptolemies were buried. Fortunately the lady had already ticked that particular box, so we wouldn't be stopping.

'You think the governor was behind the attack, Corvinus?' Clarus said.

Oh, bugger. I sighed. Well, sometimes you just had to go with the flow. 'Yeah. I'd say that was pretty certain. He handled that part of the interview well, but he'd already had a full report and plenty of time to get his act together. But he wasn't expecting me to bring up the Macro angle, and when I did it rocked him,. He's got something cooking he doesn't want found out, that's a hundred per cent definite.'

'But Marcus, that's dreadful!' Perilla said. 'We've been through this before when you were talking about Isidorus. Flaccus is the governor. If he wants rid of you, even if he does it clandestinely, he has the authority to smother any investigation before it starts. I'm sorry, but again this is getting too dangerous. Give it up. We don't need to go straight back to Rome, all it takes is for you to treat this like an ordinary holiday and he'll leave you alone.'

'Uh-uh.' I shook my head. 'Pride aside, I'm safe enough.' Or at least I hoped so. 'I'm a purple-striper after all. He's got one senseless attack on official record already, and thanks to my tribune pal it didn't come off. Two of them'd be too much of a coincidence to cover up, especially if the second were successful. And if I were found dead in an alley tomorrow, lady, what would you do?'

'Go back to Rome and demand to see the emperor, of course. Tell him the whole thing. But Marcus -'

'Right. Flaccus can't risk that, not in his shoes. He's in a shaky enough position in any case. And getting rid of you too would be just plain stupid.'

'Then what can he do?'

'Me, I'd keep my head down and just hope to hell the nosey purple-striper didn't lift the lid off the pot. Which is what I mean to do.' I glanced out of the window. We'd turned into Soma Street and were heading down the broad tree-lined avenue towards the market square. 'Okay. So we play this straight, right? Forget the case. We're ordinary customers, full stop. And if you do happen to get your material, lady, then it's a bonus.'

'Very well, Marcus. But I hope you know what you're doing.'

Yeah; so did I.

Cineas's warehouse was one of several in the back streets between the agora and the two main harbours: a big, solid building fronting on the street and covering almost half a block. We stopped the carriage by the front door and got out. There were some slaves outside loading bales of cloth onto a wagon. I went up to them.

'The master around, pal?' I said to the one in charge. 'Cineas?'

'Yes, sir. In the office on the left. You can't miss it.'

'Fine.' I led the way.

Wholesale was right: the place was full of bolts and bales, but not laid out like they would be in a shop so the customers could examine them. The office was built out from the main wall, and the door was open. I went in.

A clerks' room, lined with docketed pigeon-holes, with three or four desks and the usual complement of admin slaves. Hamster-face was talking to one of them, his back to me.

'Uh...excuse me,' I said. 'Your name Cineas?'

He turned round. Bull's-eye! From the look on his face I could've been Medusa on a bad hair-day. Whatever the guy said now wouldn't matter, because I'd already got what I'd come for in spades.

He recovered, said a word to the slave, and came over. Forget worried; this particular hamster looked sick as a dog. 'Yes,' he said. 'Can I help you?'

'Yeah. My wife here's looking for -' I pretended to do a double-take. 'Well, well, small world!' I held out my hand. 'You came over with us from Rome, didn't you? A few days ago, on the *Erytheis?* Valerius Corvinus.'

'I -' The guy looked ghastly. He swallowed. 'Oh, yes. Yes, of course, I didn't recognise you at first, sir.' We shook. It was like holding a boned fish. 'Welcome to Alexandria. Now, how can I help?'

'Perilla?' I said, turning to her.

'I was looking for dress material,' Perilla said. 'Very light-weight, suitable for bridesmaids' dresses. Smart but not too showy. As far as colour's concerned -'

I left her in shopping mode, drifted over to an empty desk and played with the abacus. Well, I'd got my whistle-blower, no doubt about that; and I'd got my contact between Flaccus in Alexandria and his imperial pals in Rome, too. As an unofficial courier, a merchant would be perfect: these guys are back and forward all the time during the sailing season, and if he was a major government contractor, like Gallius had said, then no one would be surprised if he were a frequent visitor to the governor's offices. And if ever bars were rattled then I'd rattled Cineas's. The guy was running scared already. I glanced back at him. Perilla was doing well: slaves were scurrying about, the desk in front of her was covered with swatches of material, and she and the Princess were deep in a three-way conversation about the relative merits of cotton and silk, and whether he could manage that one in a slightly paler colour. Clarus, like me, had edged off to the sidelines. I grinned: the poor bastard had had three days of this already, and his brain must've been leaking through his ears. Still, like I say, if he insisted on getting hitched then it was a necessary learning experience. He'd just have to work out his own avoidance strategies like the rest of us.

'Marcus!' Perilla said. She sounded excited.

'Hmm?'

'Come and see this!'

Oh, bugger. I went over. She was holding up two swatches.

'These are good. Really good. In fact, I think one of them would do very nicely. Which do you think? Marilla says the one on the left, but I prefer the other one.'

They both looked the same to me. Blue. 'Ah...I'm with the Princess.'

She frowned. 'You're sure?'

'Absolutely certain. No comparison.'

'Oh, well...' She turned round. 'Clarus?'

Clarus agreed with me. The kid was learning fast.

'Then that's settled, I suppose.' She sniffed. 'Three against one. We'll have to take them out into the light to make sure, of course. Do you mind?' she said to Cineas.

The guy was looking distinctly chewed, which with Perilla is par for the course. I almost felt sorry for him. 'No, of course not, madam. Carry on.'

'I'll stay here,' I said. 'I've made my mind up already. The one on the right's perfect.'

'You said the one on the left.'

'Yeah. Yeah, that's what I meant. Slip of the tongue.'

She gave me a suspicious look. 'Fine. Marilla? Clarus?'

They left.

'So, uh, what were you doing in Rome, pal?' I said to Cineas when they'd gone.

'Business, Valerius Corvinus,' he said. He was still looking

132

nervous as hell, and having been thoroughly Perilla'd for the past twenty minutes or so obviously hadn't relaxed him any. 'Naturally. I try to get over there two or three times a year to discuss things with my agents. Rome is my biggest overseas market.'

'Yeah. Yeah, I'd expect it would be. Ah...material the only thing you handle? Business-wise?'

'Yes. What else would there be?'

I shrugged. 'I don't know. Favours for friends, perhaps. Packages they want delivered, in one direction or another. Confidential documents too sensitive to trust to strangers. Letters. That sort of thing. It must be pretty handy, in some quarters, to have a pal who shuttles between Alex and Rome on a fairly regular basis.'

His face was grey. 'No doubt it is. And of course yes, I do carry things for friends, when I can. It's the way things are done.'

'Friends like the governor?'

I thought he'd peg out; he put one hand on the desk to steady himself, and two or three of the swatches slid to the floor. 'No, of course not,' he said. 'I don't know Avillius Flaccus. Not personally. I meant business friends, naturally.'

'Right. Right.' I picked the swatches up and put them back. We were getting covert glances now from the bought help, and they were being too busy with their styluses. 'And your friends at the Rome end. They wouldn't have connections with the ex-Praetorian prefect, would they? Sertorius Macro?'

'I don't...Valerius Corvinus, what's this...I'm sorry, but I don't understand what...' He was stuttering, and grey as old porridge. 'If you're trying to...'

'Marilla's quite correct, Marcus. The darker shade's much better.' Perilla, back from her sunshine test. Bugger! 'It'll do perfectly. Cineas, we'll take -' She stopped, her eyes darting between us. 'Is everything all right?'

'Yeah. Yeah, lady, everything's fine,' I said. 'We were just having a quiet chat, that's all, only he was taken over dizzy. Seems he has these spells now and again, right, pal?'

Cineas nodded weakly. You could've used the guy as the before picture for a health spa advert and the punters would've come flocking.

133

'Oh, dear,' Perilla said. 'You're all right now? Should I tell one of your slaves to bring you a cup of water?'

'He's okay as he is,' I said.

'Well, then.' The lady shot me a look. 'As I was saying, we'll take twenty yards.' Bloody hell! I couldn't remember exactly who the bridesmaids were going to be, but they must be hefty girls. 'Can you deliver it, please? We're staying with Fabius Stratocles, in the Bruchium district.'

'Ah...yes, madam. Certainly.' Cineas wasn't looking at me. He didn't look at me all through the negotiation of the price, either. The guy looked as if he was sleepwalking, and walking through a nightmare at that. Perilla paid, and we left.

'You could've given me a few more minutes, lady,' I murmured as we got into the carriage. 'When you came breezing back I had him on the ropes.'

'Oh, I'm sorry, Marcus.' She looked stricken. 'In all the excitement I didn't think.'

'"Excitement"?'

'Of finding the material, of course. We couldn't've done better. It really is absolutely perfect.'

Jupiter. I'd never understand women. Still, I couldn't complain; I'd got what in practical terms amounted to an admission of guilt, and no doubt once Cineas had got over his funk he'd be up at the Palace passing on the glad news that I was well down in the pile of dirty smalls. Before the Roman admin service put the shutters up for the night I reckoned Flaccus would be a very worried man indeed.

I didn't think I could've done much better either.

Twenty-Two

The next day we left the kids to their own devices and, like I'd promised Agron we would at some stage, paid a courtesy call on Cass's sister Mika. She and her husband Nikos lived in the south-western district of Rhakotis, not far from the big Temple of Serapis. Not a very upmarket quarter - it's where most of the native Egyptians live, and in Alexandria's ethnically-stratified society these poor buggers're the absolute lowest of the low - but within spitting distance of the main canal which joins the northern harbours with Lake Mareotis to the south. Nikos ran a barge between the Mareotis quays where the goods that come down the Nile from Egypt proper are landed and what the locals call the Box, the square artificial harbour off the Eunostos, and living close to the canal was handy.

I'd got detailed directions from Cass, so we found the house easily: a big, rambling place built of mud-brick that Mika and Nikos shared with three other families, and that looked like it'd already been there when Alexander's architects were laying out their grid. As, maybe, it had, because Rhakotis was the original Egyptian town, before the Greeks built Alexandria proper around and on top of it. I had Frontis, Stratocles's coachman, park on a bit of waste ground so he wasn't blocking the road; streets were a lot narrower and more haphazard in this part of the city, and barring the style of the buildings and the nodding date-palms behind the courtyard walls we could almost have been back in Rome. We left Frontis to fight off the local kids, who'd been clambering all over the carriage practically from the moment it slowed, and went up to the door.

There was a gaggle of women outside, sitting on stools and shooting the breeze as they worked on whatever the family were having for dinner, only they'd stopped when we'd pulled up and were eyeing us suspiciously like we had designs on their stuffed vegetables. Mika I recognised straight off from her resemblance to Cass: they bred them big and distinctive in that family, and she would've made two of any of the others, easy.

'Hi, Mika,' I said. 'Valerius Corvinus, from Rome. This is my wife Perilla. And Cass and Agron told me to say hi from them.' She'd know our names, sure, from Cass's letters, but we'd never met. And of course she wouldn't've known we were coming to Alex.

'Corvinus?' The suspicious look vanished, replaced by a broad grin. She got up and laid the bowl of beans she'd been shelling on the stool behind her. Big was right, in all directions, but she hadn't got Cass's looks. *Homely* just about fitted, although the home in question would have ten rooms and an annexe. A pretty sizeable balcony, too. 'Goodness! Come in! Welcome!' The other ladies were rubber-necking now and the suspicion had changed to lively interest: see the exotic foreigners. 'We'll go up to the roof.'

'The roof?'

'It's not too hot yet, and there's a nice breeze.' She led the way inside. 'Well, this is a surprise.'

'Excuse us, ladies.' I edged through the gaping vine-leaf-stuffing and chickpea-rissole-rolling klatsch, with Perilla behind me.

The door opened onto a tiny courtyard with a steep flight of open-air steps curving up from it. 'Just go on up and make yourselves comfortable while I get you something to drink,' Mika said. 'I won't be a minute.'

She disappeared through one of the doors leading off the courtyard.

'Okay, lady,' I said to Perilla. 'Roof-climbing time. Onward and upward.'

The steps gave out eventually onto a flat roof-space a dozen or so yards long by half that wide, with chairs and a table under a trellised vine and a low parapet wall running round its edge.

'Marcus, it's beautiful!' Perilla said. 'And what a marvellous view!'

It was. There're only two areas of high ground in Alex, the wooded Park of Pan to the east and this bit, with the Serapion at its peak, to the west. The rest of the city's more or less flat. Which meant that from where we were we could see all the way to to Pharos Island in one direction and across to Lake Mareotis in the other. Mika'd been right about the breeze, too: you got it in the streets, of course, but it was stronger up here, and it smelled of the sea.

We parked ourselves on two of the chairs looking towards the Island. Mika was far longer than the minute she'd promised, but the laden tray she was balancing on one hand explained that.

'Mika, you shouldn't have gone to all that trouble,' Perilla said as she set out cups, a flask of wine and one of fruit juice, and various trays of pastries and fresh and dried fruits. 'This is lovely.'

'It's nothing. You should've warned me you were coming.' But the lady was pleased all the same. She poured two cups of the fruit juice. 'Help yourself to the wine, Corvinus. It won't be what you're used to in Rome, but Nikos says it isn't bad. He gets it from a friend with a vineyard near Therapeutae.'

I did, and sipped. Mareotis again, and Mika's husband knew his wines: as good as the one I'd had at Hagnon's, if not better.

'This is delicious.' Perilla had taken a sip from her own cup. 'What is it?'

'Barley water with lemon, honey and mint. You haven't had it before?'

'No. You must give me the recipe.'

I unpacked the bag I'd brought with me - a long letter from Cass, plus a few things we'd brought as presents from Rome - and we did the social chat bit while the plates emptied, particularly the pastry plates: where pastries were concerned, anyway, Mika was as good a cook as her sister. Which explained the spread. Finally, she said: 'So what brings you to Alex?'

Perilla told her about the wedding - and the material - at length, while I sipped my wine and looked at the view. 'Perhaps, though, it wasn't the ideal time to come,' she said at last. 'Not if there's going to be trouble.'

Mika frowned. 'If there is then it'll be none of our making, originally,' she said. 'Those Jews've needed putting in their place for years.'

I felt a chill touch my neck that had nothing to do with the breeze: if Mika was representative of grass-roots Greek feeling in Alex, and she probably was, then we'd just heard the *vox populi* in no uncertain terms, and it wasn't encouraging. 'That what this guy Isidorus is saying?' I said.

'He's a good man, Isidorus. He talks a lot of sense.'

'Yeah, right.' I took another sip of wine. 'He seems to have the support of the governor now, too.'

'Maybe the governor's just seeing the Jews for what they are at long last and treating them accordingly. They don't fit in, they never have and never will, from what I hear they've been causing no end of trouble in their own country and now they want to bring it over here as well. We should pack them all off home and be rid of them, let them sulk on their own midden. That's what my Nikos says. What a lot of people are saying.'

'Uhuh.' Shit, here we went again.

'And that Herod Agrippa. He's a slimy piece of work, that one. They say he's a friend of the new emperor, but I don't believe it for a minute. Anyone'd see him for the crook he is as soon as look. Him and the local Jews, they're just made for each other, one piece of scum helping the other. The governor should throw him out of the city on his ear, send him back where he belongs, and tell him to take all his Jewish sweepings with him.'

Perilla was looking at her wide-eyed, a pistachio-stuffed pastry half way to her lips. Bugger, we'd ripped a scab off here, and no mistake. I'd half-expected it after Cass's reaction, but even so -

'Ah...Flaccus seems a sensible enough guy, certainly,' I said.

That stopped her. 'You've met him?' she said. Obviously impressed.

'Yeah, a couple of days back. Only for about ten minutes, but we had quite a friendly little chat.'

'Nikos says he's on his way out, more's the pity.'

I looked at her in surprise. Her husband was a Greek, of course, and the Greek never breathed who wasn't interested in politics and didn't consider himself an expert on the subject. Still, you didn't expect a bargee to be up on internal Roman affairs. 'What makes him think that?' I said.

'He says he's losing his grip. And that fuss over the Jews' message wouldn't've done him any good with the emperor, either, even if he was completely right to ignore it. The mud-stirrers'll've seen to that.' She sniffed. 'What business did they have sending their own anyway? As if we had two city councils, not just the proper one. I'm telling you, Corvinus, you have to watch those Jews like a hawk. Give them an inch and they'll take a yard.'

'I'm sorry, Mika, but you've lost me,' I said. 'What message was this?

'You mean you hadn't heard about it?' She looked incredulous, but then she shrugged. 'Well, no reason why you should, in Rome, but it was all over Alexandria at the time. When word came that old Tiberius was dead and Gaius had been made emperor the Jews drafted their own message of congratulations and gave it to Flaccus to pass on. They said he'd said he would, but in the event he didn't, he only sent our one. They were livid.' She chuckled. 'Served the pushy so-and-so's right.'

'We haven't seen your children yet, Mika,' Perilla said. 'Aren't they around?'

'No, they're out playing with friends. I've got too much to do to have them under my feet in the mornings, so I'm not complaining.'

'How many do you have?'

'Four alive and one on the way.' Mika patted her stomach and smiled. Yeah, well; at least she was back in housewife mode again: Perilla had done it deliberately, and I was grateful. 'The eldest's ten and the youngest is three. All boys. Nikos says -'

I settled down to my wine and left them to women's chat. Jupiter, things had really started to get hairy there for a minute. I reckoned that unless matters improved Alexandria in another month or so would not be the place to be. We'd have to be setting off home before that, sure, but it still wasn't a comforting thought.

Finally, half an hour or so later, Perilla glanced across at me. 'We really should be going, Marcus,' she said. 'We've kept Mika back long enough.'

'Oh, I've enjoyed the company,' Mika said. 'Nikos will be sorry he's missed you. He won't mind dinner being a bit late for once. And thank you for bringing me Cass's letter. It's always a worry when you write to someone and give the letter to a stranger that it won't arrive safely.'

'You're welcome,' I said, getting up. 'It was nice to - *Shit!*'
'*Marcus!*' Perilla stared at me.

'Uh...sorry, lady. A cramp in my right foot.' I banged it on the ground two or three times. 'That's fixed it. Mika, thanks for the hospitality. We'll see you again before we leave in case you want us to take anything back for you. Give my regards to Nikos and tell him to hang on to that vineyard friend of his.'

We left. On the way back Perilla insisted on ticking the box with the Temple of Serapis in it. You do not want to know. Believe me.

Not that I was paying much attention to what she told me Philo had to say about the place, because that last exchange with Mika had started up a whole new train of thought.

Interesting idea, right?

Twenty-Three

Clarus met us practically at the door. He was limping and he had various cuts and bruises and the beginnings of a beautiful shiner.

'We're fine,' he said. 'We're both fine, all right? Just don't go off the deep end, either of you, okay?'

I stared at him like someone had slugged me. Behind me I heard Perilla gasp. 'What happened?' I said.

Marilla had appeared at his elbow. As far as I could see, unlike Clarus's, all her bits were undamaged. I breathed a sigh of relief.

'We were attacked,' she said. 'In the Park of Pan. At least, *attacked*'s not quite the word. I think they were trying to kidnap me. Only Clarus got in the way.'

'Inside,' I said. 'Let's have this from the beginning.'

We were in our own bit of the house, the east wing. We went through to the big sitting area that looked out through the portico onto the garden courtyard, me in a numbed, guilty silence. Jupiter, this was what I'd been afraid would happen! The kids were evidently unhurt, or comparatively so in Clarus's case, but still -

When I next got in reach of the bastard responsible I'd kill him with my bare hands. Not if. When. I put it at two hours, max.

'Now,' I said, when we were settled on the couches. I was trying to be calm, and I knew I wasn't succeeding too well. Perilla, I noticed, was deathly pale and shaking. 'Tell us. The whole thing.'

'We'd -' Clarus began.

'We'd decided that it was such a nice morning we'd just take a walk,' Marilla said. 'Clarus didn't want to do any more sightseeing for the moment' - she glanced sideways at Perilla, and I found myself despite everything smothering a grin: the guy was human after all - 'so we went to the Park of Pan.' Yeah; like I said, that's the other high spot in Alex, mostly natural but part man-made. A half-wild area with plenty of walks and trees, where from the top there's a good view over

141

the city. 'It gets crowded later on, seemingly, but early in the day it's quite quiet. Anyway, we -'

'They must've followed us,' Clarus said. 'There were five of them, with clubs. Anyway, we were on one of the little paths that lead off the main spiral track to the top when they came at us from behind and grabbed Marilla. I managed to put one of them down, but two of the others grabbed me and the one who wasn't holding Marilla hit me.' He touched a bruise on his forehead.

'I managed to kick him in the -' Marilla hesitated. 'Well, I managed to kick him hard, anyway, and he didn't like it, but it meant one of the men holding Clarus let go of him. Then everything got a bit fraught.'

'We were shouting blue murder, of course,' Clarus said. 'There wasn't anyone else around that far off the main drag, but you must've been able to hear the racket half way to the town square. I was slugging it out with two of the guys, getting the worst of it, and the rest were dragging Marilla off, when a young local and a couple of his slaves came round the bend and piled in to help. That was it.' He shrugged. 'The men let Marilla go and ran off. End of story.'

Gods! 'You're not hurt, Clarus?' I said. 'Seriously, I mean?'

'Uh-uh. Just a sprained ankle and bruises, nothing that won't mend quickly. I'm a doctor, I know.' He shot Perilla a quick glance and smiled quietly. 'I, ah, won't be up to any more temples or monuments for the next few days, though. Unfortunately.'

'Certainly not,' Perilla said tightly. The lady had got her colour back, and she was looking grim. 'Marcus -'

'Yeah. Yeah, I know,' I said. 'You don't have to tell me.'

'Good. This has to stop.'

'It'll stop, lady.' I got up. 'I'll see to that.'

Her face changed. 'Marcus, where are you going?'

'To the fucking Palace. Where else?'

'Corvinus, no!' Clarus said. 'I told you: we're fine, and there's no harm done. We'll just be more careful next time we go out, take a few of Stratocles's slaves with us.'

I carried on walking. 'There won't be a next time, pal,' I said over my shoulder. 'I guarantee it. There shouldn't've been a first.'

...

I ought to have taken the carriage, but Frontis would've unharnessed the horses by now and I was too angry to wait. Besides, it was less than a mile in a straightish line, which was possible the way the city was laid out, and I'd got my bearings now well enough to use the side streets. What had been going on was pretty obvious. Marilla was right, it had been an attempted kidnapping, not an attack, and the guys had been armed with clubs, not knives, which showed they'd been told to injure at worst, not kill. Not that that made me feel any better. As I said, targeting me was one thing, I was fair game, but trying to put the pressure on through family was completely off the board.

The only problem was, who was I going for?

The obvious answer, on surface evaluation, would've been Flaccus: the theory held there, right enough. But after that talk with Mika I wasn't certain that Flaccus was the guy I wanted after all. There was what lawyers would call an area of reasonable doubt, and it centred on the business of the Jews' message of congratulations.

Oh, sure, I could see how it could be argued, and Mika had made the point herself: sending a separate, official message could be interpreted as an indication that Flaccus - and so Rome, since Flaccus was her representative - recognised the Alexandrian Jews as an independent, autonomous body, which politically they weren't. On the other hand, any governor with an eye to his immediate future career would think twice before actually suppressing it altogether, in any form. Especially if the intended recipient was a vain, touchy bugger like Gaius. Especially if he already knew he wasn't exactly flavour of the month already with said vain, touchy bugger. And especially, finally, because he'd already promised the Jews that he'd send their message on...

So maybe he had. Or thought he had.

We'd got another theory here, or rather we were back to the original one, which was equally valid: Flaccus was a complete innocent after all, and being set up for some reason with involvement in the fake Gemellus conspiracy. And after what Mika had said I could see how that worked.

Let's say someone in Rome - not Lepidus and Agrippina,

but high up all the same - wanted the Egyptian governor very, very vulnerable where the emperor was concerned; totally dependent on the someone's continued support and so ready to be manipulated by any agent they sent to Alexandria. If they could control the contents of the diplomatic bag that carried all the official correspondence between the Egyptian governor and Rome then because that would be what the governor was judged by back home they could engineer things how they liked. And to do that all they'd need was a key man at the Alex end. Someone who acted as the middle-man between Flaccus and the bag. Someone like the governor's aide, Acilius Glabrio.

Shit. It was beautiful. Flaccus hands the Jews' message of congratulation to Glabrio, telling him to put it in the diplomatic bag, and forgets about it, as he naturally would: job done, duty fulfilled. Only Glabrio, on instructions from X in Rome, burns it instead. Oh, official communications channels are much faster than the ones for the use of the ordinary punters, sure - the government has fast cutters, or triremes that can row against the wind, and once any message is on Italian soil there's the imperial courier service - but it had to be a clear month at least, probably a lot longer, before Flaccus smelled a rat and realised the Jewish letter hadn't got through. By which time it was too late to send a copy, not without providing a reasonable excuse with evidence to back it, which he didn't have. And even if he did it might just make matters worse: Gaius might well interpret the whole thing as a deliberate, studied insult on the part of a man he didn't like or trust in any case. Better, then - and I'd guess this was what Flaccus decided to do - to leave it alone and hope it would be quietly forgotten about. He wouldn't automatically think of blaming Glabrio either; why should he? Glabrio - as far as he knew - had no reason to monkey with the mail, and under the circumstances it'd be much more likely that the funny business had happened at the Rome end, where he knew he had real enemies; a passed-on message of congratulation isn't exactly hush-hush confidential stuff, so it wouldn't go direct to the emperor, for Gaius's eyes only...

I stopped. We kept coming back to the same area, like a tongue probing a bad tooth. I might not have a name for X, but I sure as hell had a job. Who, in Rome, besides the emperor, had unrestricted access to the contents of a provincial diplomatic bag? Who could control what went in and what came out; at least, if they were high enough up to get away with it? Who was likely to be Greek themselves, and so use a Greek as their prime agent? And who, finally, would be close enough to Claudius Etruscus for me to scare the willies out of him by turning up at civil service headquarters?

Right. X was one of his immediate colleagues, a top civil service freedman probably working at the same level or higher. No wonder he couldn't approach me through official channels, or *propria persona*. And no wonder the poor guy had been running shit-scared: if he'd found out somehow that one of his senior associates, maybe even his boss, was eyeball-deep in a plot against the emperor...

Only that didn't square, did it? Unless he'd been lying to me through his teeth and was the best actor since Roscius, Etruscus didn't know anything about the Lepidus/Agrippina plot. So what - to the best of his belief, anyway - was X up to?

Hell. I was so close I could smell it. Still, there was no point in speculating, not yet. And I was ninety-nine percent certain now that Glabrio was the man. Which in a way was a relief; even I could see that forcing my way into Flaccus's private office and punching an Egyptian governor's lights out was not such a hot idea.

I could see the roofs of the Palace up ahead now.

Here we went.

Twenty-Four

I had no problems getting past the front desk: appointments with the governor were controlled, sure, but evidently people were in and out of his aide's room all the time. Also, the clerk recognised me, so as far as he was concerned I was *persona grata*. He didn't even bother to send up an accompanying slave.

Which meant when I walked into Glabrio's office I took the bastard completely by surprise.

He was dictating to a secretary. He glanced up at me and blinked, but he recovered quickly enough.

'That's fine, Crito, we'll finish later,' he said. The secretary went out. 'Valerius Corvinus, isn't it? Delighted to see you again. What can I do for you?' He rose and held out a hand.

I didn't take it. 'You can explain why you didn't forward the Jews' letter of congratulations on the emperor's accession to Rome. What you, Isidorus and that poor sap Cineas that you use as your courier have cooking between you. How much you're being paid for helping to put the skids on the governor, who in the Roman civil service is doing the paying, and why. And finally, *pal*, what you meant by sending your thugs to kill me and - which is worse - trying to kidnap my adopted daughter and beating up her fiancé.'

He'd frozen, smile and hand together. Then he dropped both.

'Corvinus, are you out of your mind?' he said. 'Why should I -?'

I was over to the desk without being aware that I'd moved, one hand gripping his mantle and the other at his throat. He stiffened.

'Look, you bastard,' I said quietly. 'I'm not interested in lies, or protestations of innocence. All I want, barring at this precise moment to break your fucking neck, is some straightforward answers. But it wouldn't take much to make me put pleasure before business, so when I let you go you bear that very carefully in mind, okay?' I stepped back and he collapsed into his chair, gasping and rubbing his throat: I could see the red weals and where my nails had drawn blood, although I hadn't been aware of squeezing that hard.

'I can't...' he said at last. 'I didn't...' He swallowed. 'How dare you come in here and..?'

My fist came down on the desk, making the inkpot jump and spreading ink all over the surface. 'I warned you once,' I said. 'I won't do it again. You're up shit creek without a paddle, friend. I'm under personal instructions from the emperor to find out what's going on here' - his eyes widened - 'and if you don't tell me willingly then -'

The door opened; the secretary, back. Bugger!

'I'm sorry to disturb you, sir,' he said, 'but I had a question about -' He stopped when he saw our faces. 'Is there any problem?'

'No.' Glabrio straightened his mantle. 'No problem, Crito. But Valerius Corvinus was just leaving. Show him downstairs at once, will you?'

The guy gave me a suspicious look. 'Yes, sir, of course. Valerius Corvinus? If you'd like to come this way?' He waited.

I didn't move. I was still looking at Glabrio, whose face was the colour of old parchment. 'It doesn't end here, sunshine,' I said. 'Don't be a fool. You know where I am. I'll give you twenty-four hours to think it over and get in touch. After that I go to the governor, and believe me by the time I've finished with you that'll be the least of your worries. Have a nice day.'

I walked past the gaping secretary and down the stairs.

It took about three blocks for the fog of anger to lift and for me to start thinking clearly again. Not that, on sober reflection, I would've done things differently now: I'd known the minute I walked into the room and saw his face that he was our villain. Or one of them, at least. And every shot had gone home. When I'd let the bastard go he was practically gibbering.

That bit about having the emperor's commission had been a smacker, too, even if it wasn't quite true and I'd said it on the spur of the moment. Whoever Glabrio was working for ultimately in Rome - and I didn't have a clue who it might be - he wouldn't trump Gaius. It was an indication to Glabrio that if the game was up - which it was - then there was nowhere to run and no one who could protect him. He was well and truly screwed, and he knew it. I wasn't bluffing about going to the governor either: if I'd no actual hard proof the circumstantial stuff would be good enough, and if I was right it would all add up for Flaccus already. The only fly in the ointment was Isidorus; but then if Glabrio believed me about having Gaius's backing then I didn't see why Flaccus shouldn't as well, and if I didn't miss my guess the poor bugger would need every influential friend he'd got shortly.

So the chances were that Glabrio would be in touch as per instructions, especially if he had twenty-four hours to stew in his own juice and weigh the pros and cons of keeping his mouth shut. I reckoned I'd done a good - and certainly satisfying - day's work. If I could just ferret out the details of the Macro connection, now, we'd be off and rolling. It was a pity that Glabrio could only keep official documents out of the diplomatic bag, not put them in. That way he could -

The thought hit me like a hatchet. Oh, gods! Bloody Jupiter and the whole sodding pantheon!

Of course he could! Only not official documents, and not in the bag. Certainly not the first; in fact, you didn't get any more *un*official than these had to be, and that was what Cineas was for.

I was passing a horse trough fed by the overflow from a fountain: water's no problem in Alex, with the system of covered-over canals and ducts bringing it in from Lake Mareotis and the Nile, and there are more fountains than you can shake a stick at. Near the centre, at least. This needed thinking out in detail, and barring a convenient wineshop a seat on the edge of a horse trough would do me fine. I sat down and ignored the curious stares of the other pedestrians and the couple of nags who'd got there first.

A scenario. Let's say at the time of Gaius's illness Flaccus writes a perfectly innocent letter to Macro - who deals with provincial policy and who's himself written to the various governors apprising them of the situation - asking for instructions in the unfortunate event of Gaius's death; perfectly reasonable, because the odds on that happening at the time had been pretty good, and as the emperor's personal legate he'd be acting within his remit. X - we'll call him X, the civil service guy - handles the letter and sees his chance. He's already, for reasons I didn't yet know, targeted Flaccus and is looking for ways to burn him at some future date. The two men - Macro and Flaccus - are acquainted personally, as well as officially; and Flaccus, although he was a personal friend of old Tiberius, is already suspect with Gaius because he was heavily involved on the prosecution side in the trial of Gaius's mother Agrippina. Okay; so X decides to fabricate a conspiracy between them, one that neither will know anything about until it's too late, but will kill both birds with one stone: Macro literally, and Flaccus metaphorically, because by the time X has finished he'll be so stitched up in circumstantial evidence that he'll be a cinch to blackmail...

I stopped. Shit, no, that didn't quite work. If my theory was right, then X only wanted one bird, Flaccus: it was Lepidus and Agrippina who wanted rid of Macro, and if X had no connection with them, then...

Bugger. Leave it.

So anyway. X is sitting pretty. The evidence for the conspiracy will take the form of an exchange of letters, all forged, between Macro and Flaccus, having the first two genuine ones as their starting point. Only they won't be official, governor to imperial rep, but just Flaccus to Macro and vice versa, and they'll be carried *sub rosa* to and fro by a fall guy, Cineas, who if and when the shit hits the fan will be expendable. X will handle the Roman end, producing the 'Macro' letters; Glabrio, who's seen the governor's signature often enough to be able to forge it, writes the 'Flaccus' ones. Obviously, they never reach their ostensible recipients: Glabrio collects the former and X the latter. The whole package ends up eventually back in Rome, in X's hands. After Macro is chopped, X hands the package to Isidorus and sends him on his merry way to Flaccus with his blessing...

Shit, there was that glitch again, in a different form: if Gaius needed proof that Macro was conspiring against him, as he would, then it couldn't've come from the letters because the emperor, ipso facto, could never have seen them. We were still missing something here. Never mind, carry on.

Glabrio's safe enough. X - through Isidorus - would be careful to guard his part in things, and Cineas's: all Flaccus would know was that the letters were all forged; there'd be no reason for him to suspect his weren't done by the same guy who'd forged the Macro ones, his enemy in Rome, and Isidorus would be at pains to encourage the belief.

On the other hand, if push came to shove, Glabrio the faithful aide would be there to say he'd known for a long time that the governor was receiving clandestine letters via Cineas but that loyalty to his superior had forbidden him to etc etc. By which time Flaccus would be so far up the creek Gaius wouldn't believe him if he claimed the sun rose in the east.

It worked; it all worked. Sure it did. The only problem - and it wasn't an impediment, just a missing piece of the puzzle - was the connection between X and the imperials. If there was one. That part I just couldn't get my head around.

Well, enough for the day. We were getting there, certainly. I patted the noses of my fellow horse trough loungers and set off for home.

Twenty-Five

I needn't've worried. The message that Glabrio would see me the next morning arrived not long after I did: the guy was running scared right enough. Not at the Palace, mind, but at his home, which made sense. He gave an address in Bruchium, the other side of the Canopic Way, behind the Gymnasium.

I knew something was wrong as soon as I saw the house. There were cypress branches hung over the front door and draped around the pillars either side. That could only mean one thing: a death.

Shit.

The slave who opened the door looked frightened; not just frightened, terrified. He let me in, promising to go and fetch the major-domo, and left me in the main sitting-room with the body.

They'd laid him out on a formal death-couch, coins on the eyes and an embroidered coverlet pulled up to his chin. I couldn't see how he'd died but I twitched back the coverlet a little. Not a slit throat, anyway. There were the usual shears and basket for visiting mourners' hair-clippings, but I didn't use them. I wasn't that much of a hypocrite.

The major-domo came through: an oldish guy in his late fifties. He looked terrified too. He glanced at my unshorn fringe, then at the shears and basket, but made no comment.

'Valerius Corvinus, pal,' I said. 'I'd an important appointment with your late master this morning. Care to tell me what happened?'

'He choked on a fishbone, sir.' The guy's voice trembled. 'Last night, at dinner.'

Yeah. And I was Ptolemy fucking Sopater. 'Is that so, now?'

'There was nothing anyone could do. He was dead in minutes.'

'Were you there at the time, friend?'

He hesitated. 'Yes, sir.'

'Anyone else?'

'No, sir, barring some of the other slaves. The master was dining alone. We sent for a doctor - there's one a couple of streets off - but by the time he arrived it was much too late.'

It would've been. Whoever had stiffed the poor bugger - and I'd bet the process hadn't involved a badly-filleted Lake Mareotis pike, either - would've made sure of that. And made certain that none of the staff told tales into the bargain: the major-domo was twitching like he had the palsy.

'I don't exactly know how the local law stands on slaves covering up the circumstances of their master's death, sunshine,' I said carefully. I hated doing this, but it was the only way. 'But if it's the same as in Rome it means the strangler's noose. For the whole household. Now. You want to reconsider that fishbone?'

He swallowed like he'd got one lodged in his throat himself. 'No, sir. That was how it happened.'

Gods! If that threat didn't scare him then whatever one had was a beaut. And I'd a fair idea who'd made it. Not that, under the circumstances, I could do much about it.

Which didn't stop me trying, mind.

'Okay,' I said. 'Have it your own way, pal. I'll see myself out.'

I left.

I was as angry as I'd been the day before when I confronted Glabrio in his office. Angrier. The bastard hadn't even bothered to make the death plausible. A fishbone, a fucking fishbone! Oh, sure, I knew what had happened, it was clear enough: after Glabrio had sent to me to arrange the meeting the fool had had second thoughts or a crisis of conscience and run for advice to his co-agent Isidorus, who had naturally plumped for the obvious solution. Exit Glabrio.

I didn't know where to find Isidorus, but Flaccus would. And it was time to talk to the governor anyway. I'd start with the Palace.

What I couldn't get over was the casual way the murdering bastard had gone about things. Yeah, he wouldn't have had the time or the opportunity to arrange an accident that was half-way convincing, but even a fake suicide would've been more believable than this fucking fishbone nonsense. He was either mind-blowingly stupid with the imagination of a retarded gnat - and I knew he wasn't the first - or he thought it didn't matter one little bit whether I believed the story or not. And that was just plain insulting. Sure, it was worrying as well - it meant his hold over Flaccus was so strong he could laugh at the threat of an official investigation - but it made me furious all the same.

I got to the Palace, ignored the guy on the desk and went straight up the big staircase. Behind me it'd be an exaggeration to say that all hell broke loose, but we had the quiet equivalent all the same: two or three slaves no more than half a dozen yards behind me, plus the squaddies who'd been on guard outside the door half a dozen yards behind them. I kept on going, crossed the hallway at the top, and threw open the governor's door...

Flaccus had a visitor already, and he turned when I came in: a plump-faced smiling Greek with a narrow beard and moustache and the eyes of a rabid dog. Isidorus. It had to be. Which was fine by me, absolutely fine. Perfect.

'Valerius Corvinus!' Flaccus snapped. 'What's the meaning of this?'

The slaves behind me - and the squaddies - had stopped in a bunch on the threshold. One of the squaddies pushed through and grabbed my arm. I shook him off.

'That's all right,' Flaccus said to him. 'Leave him. And go back downstairs, all of you. I'll deal with this.'

He stood up. The squaddie saluted and backed out, closing the door behind him.

'I repeat, Corvinus. What's the meaning of this?' The guy was angry, sure, but there was something else in his eyes that looked very like fear. 'You have absolutely no right to -'

'Glabrio's dead,' I said.

'Yes, I know.' Flaccus broke eye contact and moved a pen from one side of the desk to the other. 'I was told first thing this morning. A tragic accident with a fishbone. What has that to do with -'

'Fuck the fishbone,' I said. 'He was murdered, and you know it. Or if you don't then your pal here certainly does.'

'I know nothing of the kind,' Isidorus said. We'd been speaking Latin, of course, but he'd obviously understood, even if he did speak now in Greek. 'And I find the implication totally insulting.'

I ignored him; my business at present was with the governor. Whatever his private situation was, officially he represented Rome, and I wasn't about to let him forget it. 'He was murdered because he'd arranged to talk to me this morning about the scam that this bastard here' - I stabbed a finger at Isidorus - 'has going to blackmail you about your involvement with Macro and the Gemellus plot.'

Flaccus's face had gone ashen. 'I had nothing to do with the Gemellus plot! Corvinus, you're raving!'

'Yeah, I know you didn't,' I said. 'Because the fucking thing never existed.'

Flaccus looked blank. 'Nonsense! Of course it did! I may not have been involved, but -'

'Believe me, pal. Not that it matters one hoot, because the emperor thinks it did, but it was a fabrication from beginning to end to get rid of Gemellus, Silanus and Macro.'

The governor sat down suddenly, like someone had cut his strings. 'What?' he said. 'Who by? And how do you know -?'

'I can't go into that,' I said. 'Take it from me, though, that it was a complete ringer from the outset.'

He stared at me, and his mouth opened and closed but nothing came out. Mika had told me Nikos thought Flaccus was losing his grip; I could see now that he might be right. Mind you, he had cause.

'This is nonsense!' Isidorus snapped: he was speaking Latin now. 'You said yourself, Governor: the man's raving!' He turned his mad-dog eyes on me and the hairs rose on my neck.

'I agree.' Flaccus was making a visible effort to pull himself together. 'I agree. Corvinus, go home, you're obviously unwell. I'll have someone -'

'I'm fine and you know it,' I said. 'And I'll go when I'm finished. Now. Anything I can say about this piece of dirt here you know already, so I won't bother: he's a blackmailer, a traitor, a killer and an all-round dangerous scumbag, but that's your concern, and if you want to keep taking his side and go to hell in a handcart then that's fine by me, it's your funeral.' He flinched but didn't answer. 'Still, I'm telling you formally that your aide, Acilius Glabrio, was in the pay of whoever your friend here works for in Rome, that he had been for the last sixteen months at least, and that it was his job to put the skids under you and supply him with the manufactured evidence. Think about it.' I paused; right, it had registered okay, Flaccus wasn't stupid. 'I'm also asking you formally, Governor, for what it's worth, to open an official investigation into his death. Now spit in my eye.'

Flaccus glanced at Isidorus. He was sweating, and a tic had started up on his jaw. 'I really don't think,' he said, 'that an investigation is either necessary or possible. Of course if -'

'Fine,' I said, turning for the door. 'Like I say, it's your funeral. Possibly literally. Just don't tell me later I didn't warn you.'

'Corvinus!' That was Isidorus. I turned back. 'Alexandria's a dangerous place these days. Perhaps it might be safer for you and your family if you put all this nonsense completely out of your mind.'

I counted to five before I let myself move or answer. If I hadn't the guy's teeth would've been all over the floor and I'd've legitimately been on the first boat out.

'Look, pal,' I said softly. 'You've tried twice and not succeeded, maybe through luck but never mind that. You want to try a third time? Because if you do, and it doesn't come off again, then you'd better run far and fast, because I swear by every god in the pantheon that I'll come after you and slit your fucking throat. Yours personally, no shilly-shallying, no questions asked, no quarter given. Understand?'

I got a look from those eyes that made my skin crawl, but the message had gone home. I meant it, and he knew I meant it. He didn't answer.

'Corvinus, I -' That was the governor, but it was all that he said. If ever I saw the face of a dead man walking then Flaccus's was it. Still, like I'd told him, he'd made the choice and if he wanted to stick with it then it was his funeral. He'd get no tears of sympathy from me.

I went downstairs and out, past the frozen tableau in the entrance hall.

So that was that: masks off, lines drawn. What I could do now I didn't know; maybe I might be as well going back to Rome in any case because there wasn't a lot left for me here except -

I stopped. Cineas.

He wouldn't know as much as Glabrio, sure, but he was better than nothing. And I needed a live witness. If our merchant pal was still alive: with Glabrio dead I wouldn't've put the odds on that being better than even. Still, it was worth a try, and his warehouse was only a short walk away.

I'd been wrong about Isidorus. Oh, no, nothing to do with his involvement, just the man himself: the guy was clever, sure, but he was a fanatic, and with that sort of bastard you don't expect logical thought. He'd wreck Alexandria without a second thought if it got him where he wanted to go, and he wouldn't think about little things like consequences or collateral damage. That was something else I'd got against Flaccus: the man was a Roman governor, he was far from stupid, and whatever his personal circumstances were letting a rabid animal like that have virtual control of local government policy was sheer -

Oh, shit!

Flaccus knew about the Lepidus/Agrippina plot!

He had to; it was the only explanation why he should be going so far out on a limb to back Isidorus, because it was the last throw he could make. Oh, he wasn't necessarily actively involved - or I couldn't see a role for him, anyway - but a change of emperor to one more sympathetic was his only chance of political survival. Probably, after the hash he'd made of things and the worse hash he looked like making over the next couple of months, of his physical survival too. Which meant that Isidorus knew, because he'd've had to be the one who told him. Which in turn meant that I'd got another clear link between X and the imperials.

I found the street with Cineas's warehouse on it. Okay so far: the place was open and everything seemed normal. Maybe I was going to be lucky after all. There weren't any slaves outside this time, so I made my way indoors and headed for the office.

No Cineas, but the clerks were there. After the circumstances of my last visit I wasn't surprised to see two or three gaping mouths and a lot of fingers suddenly busy with abacus beads.

The head clerk got up slowly and came over. 'Yes, sir,' he said. 'How can I help you?'

Stiff as hell.

'I was hoping to see Cineas,' I said.

'I'm afraid the master's gone to Athens. He left yesterday

156

morning.'

The day after we'd talked. Bugger. 'This would be a sudden decision, would it, sunshine?'

'Yes, sir. Very. But he may have had word from our agent there about something that needed his urgent personal attention.'

Yeah, I'd bet. 'He tell you when he'd be back?'

'No, sir. Only that he might be some time.'

Well, that was that. Hamster-face, very sensibly, had sniffed the air and headed for the tall timber. Maybe it was the best, because at least he was still alive and no doubt Etruscus or Gaius or whoever the hell I was doing this for could lay their hands on him at some future date if they wanted him. Even so, it was another avenue closed. Alexandria was just about played out as far as the case was concerned.

I left, and went home.

There'd been a message from Marcus Gallius in my absence. If it was okay with me and Stratocles he'd come round to dinner the next day.

Twenty-Six

He arrived promptly an hour before sundown. Stratocles had had a slight attack of chest palpitations that morning - he was prone to them, seemingly, now and again - and preferred to eat in his room, but he'd turned the main dining-room over to us and made sure before he left that everything would go smoothly. As I was sure it would, because although his chef wasn't quite in Meton's league he was well above the average hash-slinger. We were having poached snapper in a date sauce, quails with an almond-ginger stuffing and a purée of leeks and other assorted greens in a pastry mould, plus the usual sundries front and back. I'd reckoned we might make an appreciable hole in Stratocles's wine stocks over the evening, so I dropped in at the supplier's his head slave recommended and bought a jar of top-range Mareotis, plus a smaller jar that I'd give to Mika's Nicos when we left.

'Hey, pal!' I said when the slave led Gallius through to the dining-room. 'Nice to see you. Put on your slippers and park yourself on the vacant couch.' He did, and one of the dining-room skivvies offered him the hand-washing bowl. I made the introductions.

'Pleased to meet you, Tribune,' Perilla said.

'Thank you for the invitation, Lady.' Delivered dead-pan and super-polite, but with a smile: a well-brought-up youngster, Gallius. He dipped his hands in the basin, then dried them on the skivvy's towel while another slave poured him a cup of wine. I saw that he'd noticed Clarus's bruised face - the shiner had come up beautifully now - but he didn't comment. 'You're enjoying your visit to Alexandria?'

'Oh, very much. We all are. It's a lovely city.'

He turned to Marilla. 'So when is the wedding?'

'The end of October,' Marilla said. 'Not in Rome; we're having it in Castrimoenium, in the Alban hills.'

'Near Bovillae? I've an uncle with a villa outside Bovillae. Sallustius Calvinus. You know him?'

'Oh, yes.' Marilla smiled. 'At least, we've met. He was a friend of my Aunt Marcia's.'

'Fabius Maximus's widow? Well, well. He talks about her often. So you're *that* Marilla, the one who likes animals? It's a small world.'

I grinned. Yeah, it was, although the fact that they had an acquaintance in common wasn't surprising. The upper-class Roman network is pretty limited, and finding a connection somewhere in the course of the introductory small-talk isn't difficult. Which, of course, is how the empire's run, at base. Still, now we knew how we all fitted in, as it were, it made for a nice relaxed atmosphere. I signalled the slaves to wheel in the starters while Gallius, Marilla and Clarus chatted and compared notes about people and places they knew in common: Gallius was a few years older, sure, but they were the same generation and I was glad they'd struck it off together. When Clarus told him his father was the local doctor he didn't bat an eyelid. A nice guy, the tribune, like I said.

The starters came: raw vegetables, quails' eggs with a fish-pickle dip and an endive salad with a honey and wine-vinegar dressing.

'Did you find your bridesmaids' material, Lady Perilla?' Gallius said.

'Oh, yes. Actually, yes we did, at that merchant's warehouse you recommended. Absolutely marvellous. Thank you.'

'Cineas has some good stuff.' Gallius shelled an egg and dipped it in the pickle. 'We were lucky to spot him at the governor's. And if Corvinus here hadn't got himself involved in that fracas originally he'd never have -' He stopped and coloured. 'Uh, I mean -'

I was laughing. 'It's okay, pal. She knows. She had the whole thing out of me in practically five minutes flat.'

'Don't exaggerate, dear.' Perilla sniffed.

'Well, more or less.'

'I still don't understand it.' Gallius redipped the poised egg. 'For a Roman citizen to be attacked in the open street doesn't make any sense. It just can't happen.' I looked a warning at Clarus, but he didn't need it. He helped himself to endive salad and said nothing. 'Mind you, the city's in a strange mood these days, not itself. There've been a few muggings in broad daylight. People being beaten up for no reason at all.'

159

'Yeah?' I said, reaching for a stick of celery. 'People like who?'

'Jews, mostly. The occasional Greek, but mostly Jews.' He hesitated. 'One or two suspicious fires, too. Jewish property again, not in the Delta district where most of them live, up by the harbour.'

I set the celery down. 'You think there's going to be trouble?' I said quietly. 'Real trouble?'

He glanced at Perilla. 'Well...nothing major yet, but it isn't looking good. Hasn't done since that King Cabbage business. It'd help if the governor -' He stopped and looked uncomfortable.

'If Flaccus'd clamp down on it,' I said.

'Yeah. More or less.' A shrug. 'That's not just my opinion, far from it, and I'm not criticising. But we've been told to soft-pedal, ignore things. Agrippa still being here isn't helping matters, either.'

'He's shown no signs of leaving?'

'No. Not yet, nor of pulling his horns in supporting the Jews. And the Greeks don't like it. Particularly with Isidorus whipping them up.' He gave me a direct look. 'Corvinus, if I were you I'd leave yourself. As soon as you can. Maybe I shouldn't say that because the official line is that everything's under control and it'll all blow over, but there you are.'

I sat back. Shit. If Gallius felt strongly enough about it to give me the warning in front of Perilla and the kids then the situation was serious right enough. And I'd got my own inside information to confirm it. 'We talking riots here?' I said.

'We could be. Potentially.' It came out unwillingly, sure, but it came out all the same.

'Oh, Marcus!' Perilla set down her spoon.

'What do you reckon the time scale is?'

'A month. Maybe less, if things go on the way they are at present. We're getting more incidents every day, and the circumstances're worse every time. No actual deaths yet, but that's more by good luck than design.'

Gods! Maybe we'd better make enquiries about ships asap after all. Not that I'd be sorry to go, as far as the case was concerned: I suspected I'd got about as much out of Alexandria as I was going to, and the Roman end was showing signs of developing nicely again. Perilla'd be happy enough too, because she'd got her material and if things were going to spill over into outright violence she wouldn't want the kids anywhere near it, obvious Roman citizens or not. We'd have to have a serious talk later.

'So it seems you can forget the Rhine transfer,' I said. 'It looks as if you'll have your excitement after all.'

'I told you, Corvinus. I don't want excitement at that price. And action in Germany would be cleaner.'

'You're being transferred to a Rhine legion?' Clarus said.

'Uh-uh. Just a private joke. I wish it wasn't, mind.'

'Seemingly there's a big campaign coming up.' We'd just about finished the starters, and I signalled the slaves to clear away and serve the main course. 'Germany and beyond, over into Britain. The Rhine legions're providing the beef.'

'Yeah.' Gallius sipped his wine. 'Gaetulicus and Apronius have four each already, of course, but they're recruiting another two from scratch, plus the auxiliary support. It'll be the biggest Rhine force since Augustus's day, and if the emperor's thinking of taking three Eagles with him to Britain, minimum, they'll need every one of the rest to watch his back.'

Things went very quiet. 'Gaius is leading the expedition himself?' I said. 'In person?'

'Sure, Corvinus. I told you that.'

'No, you didn't, pal.' Shit! 'You only told me about the push. You never said the emperor was taking personal command.' I glanced at Perilla. The lady's eyes were wide: she'd got it, too.

'Yeah, well, he is.'

'When would all this be happening?'

'Next year, from what my Uncle Gaius said. Probably late summer early autumn, if preparations go according to plan.' Gallius was frowning: he'd noticed the change in atmosphere. 'Corvinus, what is this?'

'Nothing. Just interested.' I toyed with my spoon. 'So, ah, Gaius - the emperor, I mean - would be heading north to join the Rhine legions some time in the summer of next year, right? That's common knowledge?'

The frown disappeared and he grinned. 'I don't know about common knowledge. You obviously didn't know, for a start. Still, it's

161

no secret in army circles. My uncle's known about it for months, and so have I.'

Bloody hell! 'And Gaetulicus'll be in overall command, yes?'

'Until the emperor arrives, and unless he appoints someone else. But he's been governor of Upper Germany for the past eight years, and his brother was before him for years before that, so yes, naturally. And Apronius in the lower province isn't likely to contest the point. He's getting on a bit, Gaetulicus is his son-in-law, and they've been mates together since Gaetulicus took over.'

Oh, fuck! It felt like a trail of ants with frozen feet were marching up my spine. I didn't dare look at Perilla.

'That's...fascinating, pal,' I said. 'How's the wine, by the way?'

'Excellent.' He drained his cup and I motioned to the wine-slave to refill it. Mine, too: after that little revelation I needed the full jug.

Then the skivvies brought in the main course, and we talked about something else.

'Okay, lady,' I said, when the dinner was successfully over and we were alone and getting ready for bed. 'We've got a *terminus ad quem*. And a *modus operandi*. And the *criminis delictores*. The plan is to stiff Gaius next summer when he leaves Rome and joins the Rhine legions, right?'

'Marcus, he'll have the Praetorian Guard with him,' She wriggled out of her tunic. 'Or at least a fair slice of them.'

'I never said it would be easy.' I stripped my own tunic off. 'Still, Lepidus and Agrippina wouldn't have a better chance. And assuming they haven't already squared the Praetorian commander and his men and have to use force they've still got ten full legions on their team. That's a hell of a lot of muscle. You said yourself, the problem with killing an emperor was manoeuvring him into a position where he was vulnerable enough for you to do it and survive afterwards. I'd say this situation fitted the bill pretty well, wouldn't you?'

'Yes,' Perilla said softly. 'Yes, I'm afraid it would. The profiting-from-the-deed criterion is satisfied too, because even if the senate weren't happy with the situation Lepidus, as we said, would be far and away the likeliest choice for successor. In fact, the only choice that was

162

practical. Especially with ten legions behind him.'

'Yeah.' I threw the tunic down onto a clothes chest. 'Of course, we're assuming that Gaetulicus has a reason to play ball. If so, it's one we still have to find. I didn't want to press Gallius on the subject, because he was suspicious enough already and I couldn't go into the whys and wherefores, but he probably wouldn't've known anyway and we have other ways of finding out.'

'Such as?' The lady reached for her sleeping gown.

'Not here. Back in Rome.'

She paused. 'You think we should leave?'

'Don't you?'

'Yes.' She sighed. 'Yes, I'm afraid so, Marcus. We haven't been here any time at all, I know, but from what your tribune was saying the situation is going to get much worse, very quickly. It would be silly to stay and get caught up in things, so if you're happy to go then I am too. Besides, with the winds against us it'll take much longer, and we're on a very tight schedule where the wedding is concerned.'

'Mmm. Okay, so I'll take a walk to the harbour offices tomorrow, see what boats there are.' I went over and kissed her. 'You, ah, sure you want that sleeping gown on? Just yet, anyway. It's a warm evening.'

'Yes, it is, isn't it?' She kissed me back. 'Perhaps I might leave it off for a while longer.'

So she did.

Twenty-Seven

It took us almost exactly a month to get back, but we were lucky both ends: the *Latona*, the first passenger-carrying cargo ship out, had had a sudden last-minute cancellation (actually the punter concerned had come off second best in a scrap with a crocodile he'd poked with a stick in an attempt to impress his lady-friend), and also she'd be going to Puteoli, not Brindisi. It meant only the one cabin, mind, and with four of us squeezed in we'd've had to sleep standing up, but Clarus and I left it to the girls and bunked down with most of the other passengers in the scuppers.

Rome was still standing. After Alex it felt hot, cramped and crowded, and you noticed the smell, too. In Alexandria, in the summer especially, the prevailing wind from the sea keeps the air moving and fresh, and although it can get pretty niffy around the open canals the smell's nothing to good old Tiber effluent, especially south of the Sublician where it's had time to build up and where a lot of the big drains come out.

Even so, it was great to be back. Travel's all very well, but you wouldn't want to make a habit of it.

We spent the first couple of days recovering and getting into the swing of things again. We'd dropped Clarus and Marilla off at Castrimoenium on the way - I'd hired a travelling coach and driver in Puteoli - and Perilla had taken her precious material straight round to the dressmaker's off Julian Square to be made up. I sent Lysias on the mare down to Ostia with Mika's letter, plus various packages including a big one of stuffed dates for the kids and a promise to get over there as soon as I could and fill them in with the more general news in person.

I'd had plenty of time on the boat to think up a plan of action. For the immediate future, anyway. There was no point in getting in touch with Gaius or Etruscus: the first because I'd no solid proof of a conspiracy involving Gaetulicus yet, the second because if I was right

164

and our grey eminence X was one of his colleagues then showing up at Augustus House *propria persona* and asking for an interview would be just plain stupid. As, in retrospect, it had been last time, but there you go. Secrecy cuts both ways.

So the first item on my agenda was another talk with Caelius Crispus. If anyone could point me at a candidate for X, barring Etruscus himself, then it was that muck-raking genius. Whether he'd be so amenable second time round was a moot question.

No appointment here, of course. With Crispus, the element of surprise counted for everything, and if I'd warned him in advance I was coming he'd've gone to ground and not shoved his nose out from cover until spring. Accordingly, on the morning of our third day back I went over to the praetors' offices on the Capitol, gave the clerk on the desk a cheery nod and made my way to the shifty little bugger's room.

He was lifting a wax tablet out of his in-tray. When he saw me he froze.

'Oh, fuck,' he said quietly. 'Not again.'

'Hi, Crispus.' I shut the door behind me, walked over to his desk, pulled up a chair and sat down. 'Long time no see.'

'It's only been a month, you bastard.'

'Two months and four days. I counted.' I gave him my best smile. 'Doesn't time fly?'

'Too bloody fast, in your case. So what is it now, Corvinus? More about the imperials? Because if so I've already given you all you're going to get, even with the emperor's backing. And I'm still not certain that you've got that.'

'I swore, didn't I? I'll do it again, if you like.'

He waved an irritated hand. 'No, no. Forget it. I trust you. In a manner of speaking.' The piggy eyes narrowed. 'You're sunburned. You been away?'

'Alexandria. We've just got back.'

'A round trip in two *months?* Jupiter! You can't've had much -' He stopped. 'It had something to do with the case you're on, didn't it?'

'Yeah.' I crossed my legs and leaned back. 'To answer your question, though. About what I want. Jews.'

'How do you mean, "Jews"?'

'The name of a very senior civil servant, probably a Greek, who doesn't like them. Has something against them. Whatever.'

Crispus laughed and relaxed. 'Is that all? Easy, and no secret, either. Tiberius Claudius Helicon.'

I sat forward again. Gods! 'One name? Just the one? It's that obvious?'

'Sure it is. Plenty of Alexandrian Greeks in the civil service who don't like the Jews, but you said "very senior", and you don't get much more senior than Helicon.'

'He's Alexandrian himself?'

'Originally. He was one of the Wart's slaves, like most of the top-brass secretariat' - yeah; Etruscus must've been, too, from the shared part of their names - 'but he was freed five or six years back. Now he's one of Gaius's closest cronies. They play ball together. Literally, work out in the gym every day with half a dozen other kindred spirits.'

Shit. 'What does he have against the Jews? Specifically, I mean?'

Crispus shrugged. 'Nothing particular I know of. But he's an Alexandrian. If you've just been there you'll know what that means.'

Yeah, I did, and it was a fair point: being an Alexandrian Greek, he wouldn't need a specific reason. 'What's he like? In himself, I mean?'

'Clever bugger, too smart for his own good. Thinks a lot of himself and not very much of anyone else. A troublemaker for the fun of it. I'd sum him up' - Crispus smiled - 'as a malicious, objectionable shit.'

Very concise and pungent, and it fitted. I reckoned I'd got my X. 'Right. So how can I meet him? Unofficially and accidentally, of course.'

The smile disappeared. 'Come on, Corvinus! Information I don't mind, but I don't do introductions. Especially to bosom buddies of the emperor. Especially to one who's not going to thank me in the end for getting involved, which reading between the lines and knowing you he fucking isn't.'

'Crispus!' I spread my hands. 'It's no big deal. I'm not asking for a letter with your name on it here. Just point me in the right direction, no comeback, I swear. You can do it, I know you can.'

He fizzed for a minute or so. Then he said: 'You're sure you have the emperor's blessing?'

'Carte blanche. I told you. And it's important, maybe even vital. I'll swear that too, if you like.'

'Okay. It so happens he's having a birthday bash in five days' time. A big one, at his house on the Esquiline. You'd have to gatecrash, sure, but half of Rome'll be there. That's the best I can do; past that you're on your own. Now clear out, I'm busy.'

'I was going to ask you about Cornelius Lentulus Gaetulicus.'

He purpled. '*Out!*'

I grinned and stood up. Yeah, well, maybe I was pushing it. And I'd got a better source for info on Gaetulicus in any case, at least where the military side of things was concerned, and that was the place to start. I could always come back if something suggested itself, and I needed to keep Crispus sweet. If that wasn't an oxymoron.

'Okay, pal,' I said. 'Another time, maybe.'

'Not unless hell freezes first.'

Well, he didn't mean it. Not really. 'Thanks, friend,' I said, heading for the door. 'I'll see you around.'

'Bugger off.'

I wasn't doing too badly here: only three days back in Rome and I'd cracked the Alexandrian side of the case. Potentially at least. How I was going to handle the Helicon aspect of things I didn't know, but just having a name for X was a huge start, and it couldn't hurt at least to see the guy personally close up. When I gatecrashed his birthday party - as I would - I'd take Perilla with me. That lady is a born gatecrasher.

Fine. Now over to the Palatine, and Gaius Secundus.

Secundus was one of my oldest friends, well pre-Perilla and almost back into childhood. He'd been all set for a professional military career until an accident right at the start of it had shattered his leg and made that impossible, so he'd taken the civilian political route instead, ending up five years before at city judge level. Even so, the Eagles were in his blood, and when that appointment had expired he'd moved over to the imperial side and bagged a high-powered desk job in military admin. Which was where he now was. We split a jug between us, now and then, when our paths crossed, and although he wasn't the brightest button in the bag he was a very nice guy and about the best friend I had in Rome.

Fortunately, the military offices weren't in Augustus House, where I really didn't want to go. I gave my name to one of the clerks and kicked my heels for two or three minutes; after which Secundus himself came down the stairs to meet me.

'Hey, Marcus!' he said, clapping me on the shoulder. 'How's the boy? You're looking bronzed.'

'Yeah,' I said. 'Sea trip. We're just back from Alexandria.'

'That so, now?' He grinned. 'Have a nice time?'

'It was okay. How's Gemella?' Furia Gemella was Secundus's wife, a hot little number with a penchant for fancy earrings.

'We're divorced. As of last month.'

Oops. 'I'm sorry, pal.'

'Don't be. We never really fitted, us two, and when she took up with a finance officer we met in Baiae three months ago that was that. Mind you, the fact that I'd got very friendly with the finance officer's wife at the same time helped things along a bit.'

'Ah...right. Right,' I said. Well, he'd always been popular with the ladies, Gaius Secundus, and I'd found Gemella wearing myself. Maybe it was for the best.

'How's Perilla?'

'Blooming. And Marilla's getting married at the end of next month.'

'Yeah? To the doctor's kid? That's great.' He took my arm and led me towards the exit. 'I'll assume this isn't some sort of official visit and the idea's a wineshop, right?'

'Sure. If you've got the time.'

'The empire can run itself for a couple of hours. If the Parthians invade my secretary'll come and haul me out. Tasso's?'

It was the closest, at the foot of the Palatine on the Market Square side. Not my favourite place, but they served a decent Massic. 'Suits me.'

'My round.'

'Mine,' I said. 'I need some information.'

'Again? This in connection with one of your cases?'

'Could be,' I said cautiously. 'Only I'll tell you now, Gaius, it might be sensitive.' He was a friend: I needed to be up-front here from the start. 'You want to tell me to push off, now or at any point later, you just say so, all right? I mean it.'

He laughed. 'Forget that, boy. If you say you need the details of troop movements on the Syrian frontier over the next six months then you've got them, no questions asked.'

'Close, but you don't quite win the nuts.'

He stopped, and the laughter faded. 'You're serious?'

'Yeah, I am. Very.'

'Oh, shit.' He frowned. 'It's important?'

'A matter of life and death. Literally. Only I can't tell you any more than that.'

'Good enough for me.' He shrugged. 'In that case, it's definitely your round. And if you're after top-level military secrets you'll have to throw in some cheese and olives as well.'

'You've got it.'

We went to Tasso's.

Twenty-Eight

'Right, Marcus,' Secundus said when we'd got ourselves settled with the Massic and sundries in a quiet corner. 'Go ahead.'

'I want to know about the situation on the Rhine. Chapter and verse, the whole boiling.'

'Oh, fuck.'

'Yeah.' I took a sip of wine. 'Option's still open, pal. You can tell me to get lost now and I'll go like a lamb, with no harm done.'

'Sure I can. So where do you want to start?'

'There's a major campaign planned for next year, yes? Into Germany and over to Britain. The emperor's taking personal command.'

He nodded. 'He's bringing the eight Rhine legions up to full strength and recruiting another two, the Fifteenth and Twenty-second Primigeniae. Plus their full complement of supporting auxiliary infantry and cavalry.'

Yeah; I'd got that much from Gallius in Alexandria. Still, it was nice to have it confirmed. 'Who's commanding? I mean, before the emperor arrives?'

Secundus hesitated. 'That's a moot point at present, Marcus. Oh, sure, it should be Gaetulicus, or him and Apronius jointly. They're the two governors. But the word is that Gaius wants to appoint Sulpicius Galba. He'll replace Gaetulicus as the Upper Germany legate and Apronius'll take orders from him.'

Shit. The ice was forming on my spine. '*Gaetulicus is being recalled?*'

'I don't think it's been decided yet, not finally. But it makes sense. Galba's a good man, an experienced soldier. He's campaigned in Germany himself, he already knows the country and the tribes. If Gaius crosses over to Britain he needs to be sure of his back, and with Galba he can be.'

'But not with Gaetulicus.'

'Uh-uh. No way. Nor Apronius.'

'How so, pal?'

'Because he can't trust them, neither of them.' I shifted on my stool. 'Militarily, I mean.' Secundus's hand toyed with his cup; he hadn't drunk any of the wine yet, and barring that first sip neither had I. 'The truth is that the Rhine frontier's been going down the tubes ever since Gaetulicus took over. Before that, too, which was largely Apronius's fault.'

'Give me a for instance.'

'You know about the Frisian business, ten years back?'

'Not in any detail. Assume I don't.'

'The Frisians're one of the big tribes in Lower Germany. They revolted, crucified a detachment of troops sent to collect taxes, and made a push towards the Rhine. Apronius tried to stop them, found he couldn't and asked for help from Upper Germany. Gaetulicus's brother was legate then, and he sent troops in support. Apronius met the Frisians deep in their territory, lost the battle, and most of his men were slaughtered. He had to retreat to the Rhine leaving his dead behind him. It was practically Varus in the Teutoburg all over again.'

I was staring at him. 'This wasn't reported in Rome?'

'Not the full story, no. It would've caused an outcry, and Tiberius had troubles enough at the time as it was. That wasn't the worst of it, though. Seemingly - and this didn't come out until much later - when he'd retreated Apronius had left nine hundred men holding out, cut off from what was left of the main army. The lucky ones - just under half - managed to commit suicide when they were finally overrun. The Frisians took the rest prisoner and crucified them in one of their fucking groves. Every last one. Five hundred men.'

Gods! 'And Apronius wasn't replaced?'

'No. The Wart couldn't afford to tinker with the Rhine command, then or later, because between them the Gaetulici and Apronius considered holding it as their right. You know Apronius is Gaetulicus's father-in-law?'

'Yeah. Yeah, I did know that.'

'So it was practically a family perk. And they were - are - popular with the troops, largely because they let them do as they like.'

'Come on, pal!' This wasn't sounding good. 'The emperor's the emperor. Couldn't the Wart - or Gaius, now - just haul Gaetulicus and Apronius back to Rome and shred the buggers?'

'You're not listening to me, Marcus. Yes, I said, that's what he'd like to do, Gaius, I mean, in Gaetulicus's case at least, and it'd make good sense. But things aren't that simple. Tiberius considered it once, and when Gaetulicus got to know he sent a letter to the Wart saying he could depend totally on his loyalty as long as he kept his command. The emperor backed down, and Gaetulicus is still there. If Gaius wants to replace him with Galba - which he does - then fine, great, but he won't find it easy. The trouble is he's caught in a cleft stick. If he's to invade Britain then he has to build up the Rhine force, but if he doesn't winkle Gaetulicus out first he's handing the guy an extra stick to beat him with. An extra two sticks, plus auxiliaries.'

'You said Apronius is incompetent. How about Gaetulicus himself? I mean, if he's okay, then -'

'He's just as bad. Currently, the Upper Germany frontier is a joke. Or it would be if the situation was funny. The tribes're out of his control. A couple of years back raiding parties crossed the Rhine into Gaul because there was nothing to stop them, plundered a dozen towns and villages, stripped the countryside bare, killed a hell of a lot of people and escaped back over the river scot-free. That wasn't reported in Rome, either.' He looked down at his cup as if he was noticing it for the first time, lifted it and drained it. Then he was quiet for a good minute and a half. I didn't speak, I just waited: Secundus was a friend, and I wasn't going to push. Finally, he said: 'There's another aspect to things. One that's just come up. Not even the emperor knows yet, and if it's true it's worrying as hell.'

The back of my neck prickled. 'You want to tell me?' I said.

'No. But I will anyway.' He didn't smile. 'And look, Marcus, I'm levelling here in my turn, okay? If just a suspicion, the breath of a suspicion, that I told you this gets out then I can kiss my job and my career goodbye. I'd be lucky to get work scrubbing out the senate-house privy.'

I didn't answer. Waited. It was his decision to make, not mine.

'Calvisius Sabinus. Name mean anything?'

I shook my head.

172

'He's the Pannonian legate, next to the east along the Rhine-Danube line from Gaetulicus, only appointed last year. A good man, but hot on discipline and not too popular with his troops. You understand?' I nodded. Shit, I knew what was coming; I just knew it. 'He doesn't want to make trouble by reporting officially to the emperor, but he thinks Rome ought to know, so he sends directly to me and leaves it to my discretion.'

'Someone's monkeying with his troops,' I said.

'Right. Nothing obvious, tentative stuff. That's the problem, it could just be the usual squaddies' grousing that their mates under the commander next door are onto a cushier number than they are. But Sabinus is no fool, and he doesn't cry wolf without reason.' He hesitated. 'And that's not the full story, either.'

'Come on, pal! Spit it out!'

'It's not just the threat to his men's loyalty that's worrying him. He feels he's under pressure himself, personally. Sabinus is married, and his wife's in post with him. Her name's Cornelia, and she's Gaetulicus's daughter.'

'Shit!' I sat back. I understood what he was saying, all right: Pannonia had two legions, and with them on his side, if push came to shove, Gaetulicus would have the entire Rhine-and-Danube force under his control. Effectively, half the empire's Eagles.

'Marcus, I don't know what to do.' Secundus reached for the jug and filled his cup. 'I can't take this to the emperor as things are; and I can't *not* take it.'

'How long since Sabinus's letter arrived?'

'Ten days.'

'He got anything concrete to go on? Anything at all?'

He shook his head. 'No. I told you, that's the trouble. If he had he'd've reported it directly to Gaius. He's done what he could, tightened up, put his most trusted NCOs on their guard and told them to have a quiet word with the men. Also, he's warned Cornelia in no uncertain terms without actually accusing her that he's loyal to Gaius and staying that way. With luck, he's nipped any trouble in the bud.' He paused. Again, I waited. 'There's one thing, though. Not from Sabinus. It happened separately, and it predated Sabinus's letter by the best part of a month, but the paperwork came across my desk.'

'Yeah? What is it?'

'One of his tribunes, a guy called Titus Vinius, asked to resign his commission and come back to Rome. Family problems. His father's in poor health, seemingly, dying, in fact, and not up to making important decisions. Vinius is the only son.'

'You okayed it?'

'Sure, under the circumstances. It'll put paid to the guy's military career for good, naturally, because you don't just walk out of post when you feel like it, not for any reason, but that's his decision. So of course I did. Maybe I'm being over-suspicious, and certainly I've no reason to link the two things at all. Even so, it stuck in my mind.'

Uh-huh. That was interesting: he wasn't an imaginative guy, Secundus, quite the reverse, and if he'd made a connection then it was worth following up, even if it probably was a wild goose chase. 'You have an address for him?' I said.

'Not offhand. But I can get it and let you know.'

'Fine. You do that, pal.' I reached for the wine. 'Now let's just forget this conversation for the time being, shall we? I'll tell you about Alexandria, you tell me about your lady-friend in Baiae, we'll finish this jug and then have another. Meanwhile your secretary can run the empire for you. Okay?'

Secundus grinned. 'Suits me.'

So that's what we did, while I tried to ignore the cold feeling in my gut and wondered how the hell I was going to get proof enough to convince the emperor.

Twenty-Nine

'Gaetulicus is planning a rebellion, lady,' I said. 'That's definite.' We were sitting in the atrium, me with a cup of the Mareotis that I'd brought back and Perilla with some of the barley-water-and-mint concoction that Mika had given her the recipe for.

She set the cup down. 'You're sure?'

'He has to be. Oh, it needn't actually happen as such, in fact it probably won't, because if he's in with Lepidus and Agrippina it won't be necessary. Me, I think it's a ploy to put pressure on the emperor. At least, that's the surface scenario.'

'Explain, please.' She was staring at me.

'The guy's been in just this situation before, with the Wart. He made his position clear then, and he hasn't budged: so long as he's allowed to keep his command there'll be no trouble; mess with that proviso and the bargain's off.' I took a sip of the wine. 'Which is exactly what Gaius is threatening to do. He wants to replace Gaetulicus with Sulpicius Galba.'

'But Gaius is the emperor! If he tells Gaetulicus that he's being replaced then -'

'That's what I assumed, but like Secundus said it isn't that simple. Between them he and his brother've held down the job for fifteen years and he sees it as his right. Probably most of his men do, too, because all squaddies are conservatives at heart, especially where their own interests are concerned. The vast majority'll never have served under another commander, and they've had things easy ever since they signed up. The same goes for Apronius's legions in the lower province, and Apronius is in Gaetulicus's pocket.'

'Does the emperor have to replace Gaetulicus, then? I mean, if things are that sensitive -'

'Yeah, that's the problem. The guy's incompetent, and so is Apronius. If Gaius really, *really* wants his slice of military glory by

175

adding Britain to the empire - which he obviously does - then he has to use the Rhine legions to do it. And he's not going to risk things going to hell in a handcart at his back while he's on the other side of the Channel.'

'So effectively it's a power struggle. Gaetulicus is trying to force Gaius into keeping him on, hoping that, as Tiberius did before, he'll back down at the last minute.'

'Yeah. Only like I said that's just the surface scenario.'

'Lepidus and Agrippina.'

'Right. We keep coming back to Gaetulicus's main object in this, bar none: all he wants, all he's ever wanted, is to preserve the status quo. Gaius is a parvenu; he's young, he's inexperienced, he's only been in power for a year and a half, and compared to the Wart's twenty-three that's nothing. If Tiberius, who was a soldier himself and spent years on the northern frontier, was willing to leave him alone then he's not going to tamely walk out of post at Gaius's asking. It's a matter of pride. And if Gaius looks like forcing the issue that's too bad for the emperor.' I took another swallow of wine. 'Besides, he isn't going totally out on a limb. It's not like he's staging a full-scale military revolt and dragging us back seventy years to the civil wars. We said: if Gaius goes, whatever the circumstances - and you can be sure Lepidus and Agrippina'd make his death as unspectacular as possible - then Lepidus would be the only practical legitimate successor. *Legitimate* successor, and that's important. There'd be no need for strongarm stuff, none at all.'

'But isn't Gaetulicus taking a huge risk? I'd've expected that even a whiff of suspicion that he's disloyal would lead the emperor to get rid of him. Not through official channels; you know what I mean. Like Tiberius and Sejanus.'

'He's got no choice, lady. He's walking a very narrow tightrope. All he can do is stall, flex his muscles like he did with the Wart but without being too obvious and hope his friends at court will persuade Gaius to think again. Which of course Lepidus and Agrippina will be busting a gut to do, because their whole plan depends on Gaetulicus still being in post when the emperor goes north next year. They'll need all the help they can -' I stopped.

'Marcus? *Marcus!*'

'Jupiter, that's it!' I whispered. 'That's the connection!'

'What connection?'

'Between Helicon and the imperials. It's a trade-off. A quid pro quo.'

'*Who* is Helicon?'

Bugger, I hadn't told her about him yet. 'Our X. The guy in the civil service. He's one of the emperor's bosom buddies, and according to Crispus a five-star grey eminence.' Now I had the connection everything fell into place. Shit, I'd got the whole thing! Not in detail, maybe, but in essence, and the detail would come. 'There were two plots, running side by side, the one Helicon and his Alexandrian Greek civil service pals were hatching - that's the one Etruscus knew about - and the Lepidus/Agrippina conspiracy. How each side found out about the other I don't know, and it doesn't matter, but they discovered that for things to pan out they needed to work together.'

'Go on.' She was watching me closely and twisting a lock of hair around her finger.

'Okay. Take the Helicon plot first. The intention behind that's pretty straightforward, at least in Alexandrian Greek terms it is: they want to screw the Jews, not just in Alexandria but in the empire as a whole. Which means a change of policy at imperial level. *New* imperial level. And that means persuading Gaius that they're not just the joke he and most Romans think they are but a real threat who have to be stamped on and stamped on hard.'

'But Marcus, dear, if you're going to use the business in Alexandria to support this you have it the wrong way round. It isn't the Jews who're causing the problems, it's the Greeks.'

'There's such a thing as incitement, lady. Under the old policy - Augustus's, the Wart's, Gaius's up until now - the Alexandrian Jews've been perfectly happy. They're allowed to worship as they like with an indulgent eye turned to their little foibles, given their own courts and assemblies and so on outside the city's general admin structure. Protected. Privileged. The same goes for Jews everywhere else in the empire. So long as they don't meddle with the *pax romana* Rome's got no quarrel with them, and the Alexandrian Greeks have to sit on their hands and grind their teeth. Yes?'

'Yes.'

'Fine. Only recently over in Judea that's just what happens. The Jews there start getting political, throwing rocks at the troops and generally making themselves a pain in the backside. That gives Helicon and his pals their opportunity. Judea's useful up to a point, but who in Rome, including the emperor, gives a toss what a pack of backwoods goat-herders get up to? Especially if it's no real threat to the safety of the empire as a whole? Alexandria's different: it's the empire's second biggest city, and it's got a thirty-per-cent-plus Jewish population. If they can stir up the same sort of trouble there then they're really cooking.'

'So they set out deliberately to provoke the Alexandrian Jews into violence, hoping that it'll spread to other cities in the east and result in a pogrom and a change to a much more repressive policy.' She tugged at the strand of hair. 'Marcus, you're convincing me.'

'One gets you ten that it was Helicon who suggested that Herod Agrippa stop by in Alex on the way to his kingdom, too. There ain't nothing like a bit of positive incitement to riot on both sides to get things moving.'

'But it's dreadful! Completely irresponsible! And it could wreck the peace of the entire east!'

'Right. I'd bet that's exactly what Etruscus thinks. Only the poor bugger can't do anything to stop it happening, which is why he came to me. It's working, too. If all Helicon wants to do is cause the maximum mayhem then Isidorus is the perfect agent; the guy's a fanatic, a mad dog. You can't reason with people like that, and Flaccus knows it. He has only two choices, to co-operate all the way down the line - and Isidorus'll make sure it's a very long line - or Helicon slips Gaius the packet of whacky correspondence while they're scraping down after their matey game of handball and he finds himself chopped before you can say "Macro". Which brings us neatly to the link between the two plots.'

'Carry on.' I had her hooked good and proper. She'd started on another strand of hair.

'You said it to me yourself: you can't use Macro twice in different roles. Helicon and his pals couldn't do that either, and it was stymying them. On the one hand, they needed the fake treasonable correspondence with Macro to burn Flaccus, and ipso facto in that case Gaius couldn't know about it; on the other, unless the emperor was convinced that Macro was definitely implicated in the Gemellus plot and had him chopped as a result then they'd no stick to beat Flaccus with.'

'Oh, my!' Perilla tugged at the tuft. 'So they'd need another body of proof. To give to the emperor.'

'Right. Only - I'm guessing here - they jibbed at that. If they started, *propriae personae*, to mix themselves up in Palace politics it could quickly get them out of their depth. I mean, how far would they have to go before they could be sure the emperor was convinced? Besides, it was far too dangerous: Macro was the most powerful man in Rome after Gaius himself, he was no fool, and neither was Gaius. And both of them were on the spot, not half the empire away. It'd only take one of them to smell a rat and the whole thing would go down the tubes.'

'So they needed an ally. Someone to manage the Macro side of things for them.'

'Yeah. How they and the imperials found out about each other, like I say, I don't know and it doesn't matter. My guess is the impetus came from Lepidus, or maybe Agrippina, because she's the brains of the partnership like her mother was. Flaccus is on record as being a supporter of Gemellus, whatever the hell that is, he and Macro knew each other personally, it was common knowledge that he was out of favour with Gaius, and besides because he'd been instrumental in getting Agrippina Senior exiled she'd have her personal reasons for choosing him to put the knife into. He'd certainly make the top five on any list of candidates, however you slice it. And since he was currently in Alexandria sounding out the Alexandrian contingent in the civil service at Rome for a potential rotten apple would be a natural thing to do.' I took a sip of the Mareotis. 'In any case, that had to be what happened. Lepidus and Agrippina pulled the plug on Macro...'

'How?'

'Mmm?' I blinked.

'How exactly did they do that? I'm sorry, Marcus, but you can't just gloss over that part. If Macro wasn't killed because of his treasonable correspondence with Flaccus - and I'll admit that I agree that he couldn't have been - then why was he? What other proof could Lepidus and Agrippina offer?'

'Jupiter, lady,' I said irritably. 'I don't know. Or not exactly. The

179

civil service guys may've sharked up another letter to or from Gemellus or Silanus. Or a batch of letters, maybe. They could do that without breaking sweat, and so long as they didn't have to submit them to Gaius first hand, just give them to the imperials to use how they liked, they'd be well out of it. And remember Gaius was getting pretty jaundiced with Macro and Ennia as it was. Plus with two of his closest friends and his sister bad-mouthing the guy at every opportunity - as they no doubt did - it isn't difficult to see he'd be more than half-way likely to believe them to begin with.'

'Very well, dear.' Perilla sniffed. 'I suppose it's possible.'

'You have a better idea?'

'No.'

'Then clam up.'

She grinned. 'All right. So what now?'

'Now is the difficult part. Getting concrete proof that I can take to Gaius.'

'And how do you propose to do that?'

'Lady, I don't know.' I took a morose swig of wine. 'Oh, sure, he'd listen to me. With a great deal of attention and respect, what's more, because modesty aside and saving my blushes he knows from past acquaintance that I don't whistle through my ears. None the less, all I've got is circumstantial evidence and theory. *Good* circumstantial evidence and theory, sure, I grant you, but still. If I tell him that one of his best friends and both of his sisters are conspiring with another best friend and half the imperial civil service to put him in an urn, not to mention at least one of the top military legates in the empire, he's going to ask for hard proof before he blows his wig and starts chopping heads off. Quite rightly so. And if he doesn't, and goes ahead anyway, then the gods help Rome because we have a lunatic in charge.'

'What about Etruscus? Surely he would back you publicly now?'

'Jupiter, Perilla! You just don't listen! Etruscus has kept his head well down below the parapet so far and he isn't likely to stick it up now. With justification. He's no hero, he's just a conscientious pen-pusher with Rome's best interests at heart. Besides, I'd bet I know a hell of a lot more about this business now than he does. I wouldn't even ask him.'

'Then what?'

I sighed. 'I told you. I don't know. Oh, I've still got a couple more shots in the locker, for what they're worth: a tribune on the Pannonian staff to see, plus gate-crashing Helicon's birthday party in five days' time, but -'

'*What?*'

Bugger, I hadn't told her about that one either. 'Ah...'

'Marcus, if you think you can -'

'Dinner is served, sir.' Bathyllus, drifting in like a welcome ray of sunshine from the direction of the dining-room.

Saved by the apricot-stuffed duck with turnips.

Ah, well. We'd just have to see what transpired.

Thirty

A messenger came next morning from Secundus with Titus Vinius's address: the family house, hardly a ten-minute walk away on Head of Africa. Yeah, well; we might as well get this over with, and at least I didn't have to traipse over half of Rome to find him.

Good property: the family had money, which probably meant he'd had good reason to come back and oversee investments. There'd be a bailiff, sure, but even the best of these you have to keep an eye on, and if his father was at death's door and he was the only son then there wouldn't be anyone else to do it.

I went up the steps and knocked.

'Could I speak to Titus Vinius, please?' I said to the door-slave who answered. 'The name's Valerius Corvinus. He doesn't know me but -'

'Would that be senior or junior, sir?'

I frowned. 'Ah...junior, of course. I thought...Uh, forgive me, pal, but I thought Vinius senior was dying.'

He gave me an odd look. 'Of course not, sir. The old master's in perfect health. Come in, please. If you'd like to wait I'll tell the young master you're here.'

He left me in the lobby, sorely puzzled.

Shit, what was going on? Oh, yeah, people did make miraculous recoveries, especially if they'd kicked their doctors out at the first sniffle, but there's a big gap between *at death's door* and *in perfect health*. Something was screwy here.

The slave came back. 'The young master's in the garden, sir. Follow me, please.'

He led me through the atrium into the peristyle beyond. Nice garden. A bit over-regimented for my taste and cluttered with too many statues, but okay if you like that sort of thing. Vinius - I presumed it was Vinius - was sitting in a basketwork chair in one of the arbours.

'Valerius Corvinus?' he said. 'What can I do for you?'

Another slave had brought a second chair. I sat down.

He was a youngster, of course - being a tribune he'd have to be -, no more than early twenties, if that. I noticed two things at once. One, he was pretty - not good-looking, pretty, with what was almost a girl's face, long eyelashes and pouting lips. The second thing was he was frightened.

Not of me, or I didn't think so: his body was relaxed and there was nothing in his tone of voice. The look was in his whole face; withdrawn, slightly out of it, with something strange about the eyes. Like recently he'd been to hell and back, and hadn't got over it yet.

'Vibullius Secundus over at the military admin offices suggested I have a word with you,' I said; I'd thought about this, and it seemed the safest way to do things. 'See if I could get you to reconsider your decision to resign your commission.'

There it was; that frightened look again. 'No,' he said. 'No, I'm afraid not.'

'Even although your father's' - I paused, and chose the words carefully, without stressing them - 'no longer in danger of dying?'

Another flash; if he'd noticed the pause, or wondered how I'd known, he didn't comment. 'No. Not even for that reason.'

I leaned back. I'd have to watch how I played this, because there was something here. What it was I didn't know yet, but it was there in spades and I could feel the beginnings of a prickle at the nape of my neck. 'Care to tell me why?' I said. 'I mean, if the original reason was that you needed to look after the family affairs -'

'I think that's my business, Valerius Corvinus,' he said. 'I don't want to cause offence, but you've had a wasted journey.'

'Uh-uh.' I shook my head. 'I don't think that myself. Not at all.' That got me another scared glance, but this time it was meant for me personally. I gave things a moment, and then I said: 'So why did you resign? The real reason?'

I'd spoken quietly, but he was on his feet like he'd been jerked up on strings. 'Go now,' he said. 'Please. I've told you it's my business, no one else's, and -'

'Sit down, pal.' I still hadn't raised my voice or moved, and I knew if I did either he'd call for the slaves and have me pitched out

183

on my ear. All this was fright, pure and simple. The guy was like a frightened mare. He had to be gentled.

He sat, like the strings had been cut. He was breathing hard and fast, his eyes fixed beyond my ear.

'Now,' I said, still talking quietly, hardly above a whisper, 'I'm going to level with you. Secundus is a friend of mine, sure, but he's got nothing to do with this, nothing at all. I'm here off my own bat, on a commission from the emperor. No' - he'd shied away - 'nothing to worry about, so long as you tell me the truth and don't try to cover anything up. I'm not going to drag you off to the Mamertine or anything like that. But I need some information, and I need you to be frank or I can't help you. Okay?'

He swallowed. 'Okay,' he said. It was the ghost of a whisper.

'It had something to do with an incitement to the Pannonian legions to mutiny, didn't it?'

The look I got now was pure terror. He half-rose, and I pulled him down. Gently.

'I shouldn't've done it,' he whispered. 'I was a fool, a complete fool. But the chance...well, the chance was just too good to miss.'

Shit. The thought of this kid going round the barracks inciting two legions-ful of hard-bitten squaddies to mutiny against their commander just wouldn't stand up. They'd've laughed in his pretty face. Done it politely, mind, because kid or not he'd been an officer, but still -

'What chance?' I said.

He swallowed again. 'Corvinus, I told you: I've been a complete fool. I admit that. I've thought about nothing else for the past two months. I'm greedy, yes, and very, very silly, but I'm not a traitor. You have to tell the emperor that, convince him not to -'

'What chance?' No answer. 'Come on, pal! I'll do my best, I promise you, but I can't do anything until I know the whole story.'

He took a deep breath. 'Could you go inside and tell Sator - that's the slave who brought you through - to bring us out a cup of wine?'

I got up without a word and did what he'd asked. It was safe enough: he wasn't going to run out on me, I knew that. Besides, where could he go? Then I came back and we sat in silence until the guy had

184

brought the wine and padded off.

Vinius drained his cup in a oner. I waited, my own wine untasted.

'Now,' I said.

The kid wiped his mouth and took another deep breath. He was looking a better colour, but not by much. 'You know Sulpicius Galba?' he said.

I blinked but kept my voice neutral. 'Yeah. Yeah, of course.'

'He and I...well, we're friends. Good friends.' Oh, hell. I could see which way things were heading. Still, it didn't surprise me: I'd run across Galba five years back, when he'd been consul, the time of the business with the dead Vestal, and I knew where his predilections lay. Mostly from a conversation with his wife Aemilia, who was one of Perilla's poetry-klatsch pals. And from the looks of Vinius the next leap of the imagination wasn't Olympics standard. 'It was here in Rome, about four months ago, just before I went out to Pannonia.'

'You can't've been there long, pal,' I said. 'You've been back almost a month already.'

'No. Only a few days.' He ducked his head and smiled. 'But you're right. Me and the legions aren't cut out for each other. I discovered that very quickly, and it's another reason why I don't mind not -' He stopped. 'Anyway. I found out from Galba that the emperor was putting him in charge of the Rhine legions. Or rather, he didn't actually tell me, I put two and two together from what he let slip. Caesar had just told him, you see, and I think he was very pleased with himself. Also perhaps' - he blushed - 'at that stage of our friendship he was anxious to impress me. Could I have your wine, Corvinus? If you're not going to drink it?'

'What?' I'd forgotten that I was still holding the cup. 'Oh, sure. Help yourself.'

I handed it over. He didn't down it like the last one, but he took a good swallow and set the cup on the flagstones beside his chair.

'So I went out to Pannonia. You know the legate's wife - Sabinus's wife - is Lentulus Gaetulicus's daughter? Cornelia?'

Things were beginning to come together. 'Yeah,' I said. 'I knew that.'

'I thought that...perhaps...her father might be interested in

185

some information I had.' He lowered his eyes again. 'For a price. You understand? I told you: I was a fool, and greedy.'

I said nothing.

'She wrote to Gaetulicus, he wrote back agreeing on principle, and there you are. I told her what Galba had said. Or what I'd worked out, anyway. That he was to be her father's replacement for the coming campaign. Then she paid me. A hundred gold pieces.' He looked up. 'That's all that happened. I swear.'

'What about the incitement to mutiny?'

'That wasn't me. I wouldn't. And anyway, I wouldn't know how.' Well, that was true enough. 'Oh, Cornelia tried to persuade me to help, but she gave up after a while and said she'd arrange it herself. She's a very...*strong* woman, Cornelia.'

Yeah, I'd bet. Mind you, coming from that background and having spent most of her life in an army environment I supposed she'd have to be. A hell of a lot stronger, certainly, than this wilting violet. 'So why did you cut and run?' I said. 'Which is what you did, isn't it?'

'Yes.' His eyelashes fluttered. 'Corvinus, wouldn't you? Under the circumstances? It was only a matter of time before Sabinus noticed what was going on, and it was my fault. And Cornelia was trying to force me to get involved by threatening to tell her husband that I already was. The whole thing was a nightmare. I had to get out.'

'So you wrote resigning your commission,' I said.

'Yes. I didn't even wait for the reply. I went to Sabinus, told him my father was dying and that I was giving up the tribuneship, and he gave me leave of absence.'

'He didn't suspect anything?'

'No. Or I don't think he did. Why should he?'

Why should he? No; the kid was right. As an *agent provocateur* Titus Vinius was a non-starter. The thought wouldn't even have crossed Sabinus's mind.

'So...what happens now?' He was looking at me like I was the only drink of water in the desert.

I shrugged. 'I don't know. I honestly don't know. Oh, you have my promise: when I see the emperor I'll tell him just exactly what you've told me. Then it's up to him.'

'You think he'll understand?'

'Maybe.' Personally, I doubted it: Gaius wasn't exactly your understanding person, and he didn't forgive easily. The guy wasn't looking at the chop, mind - unless the emperor was feeling particularly vindictive - but exile was a distinct possibility. Still, he had it spot on: he'd been a greedy little fool and deserved all he got. 'I'll do what I can.' I stood up. 'Meanwhile, don't go anywhere. That's not advice, it's a warning.'

'Where would I go?'

Right. I turned to leave. Then a thought struck me, and I turned back.

'Did Cornelia happen to mention any names? Anyone at all?'

'Like who?'

'I don't know. Just anyone.'

'No, none.' He frowned. Then he blushed again. 'She said once when I'd refused to help that I was as much an innocent and a washout as Gaius Anteius sounded, but -'

'*Who?*'

'Gaius Anteius. I'd no idea who she meant. I still don't. Do you?'

But I was already heading for the portico and the front door.

Gaius Anteius.

Shit.

So: I'd got a witness. Not much of one, but at least Vinius was better than nothing. And his evidence would prove at least that Gaetulicus was trying to subvert the Pannonian legions.

The mention of Gaius Anteius had been a facer, though. The guy, if you remember, had been at literary hack Seneca's poetry reading the evening I'd been almost crushed by the runaway cart on the Staurian Steps: the squeaky-clean young North Italian quaestor with a penchant for poetry who'd mentioned Gaetulicus to us. And who had almost immediately thereafter been hauled off by Agrippina. Whom Crispus had later indicated he was possibly having some sort of an affair with.

Jupiter, it couldn't be coincidence. No way.

How exactly he fitted into things I didn't know, but it set up a very interesting train of thought. He was a friend of Seneca's, and Crispus had also told me that Seneca was currently screwing the emperor's second sister Livilla. Who was also - if the theory held - in on the plot. Obviously, if Cornelia knew his name, she'd have to have got it from her father, probably through one of his letters. And *innocent* fitted the guy to a T. He and Vinius - barring certain important differences - were birds of a feather.

Okay. I distinctly remembered him saying he'd been talking to Gaetulicus himself only a couple of months previous, and at the time the implications had slipped past me. Anteius was a North Italian, sure, but Mantua was still a long way from the Rhine. What opportunity would he have? Gaetulicus couldn't've come to him on his father's estate: a legate isn't allowed to leave his command except under very exceptional circumstances, and if he'd just been elected quaestor he couldn't've been lately out of uniform himself. Which left only one possibility.

He'd gone to the Rhine specially. Because Gaetulicus was using him as a courier to keep in touch with his imperial pals in Rome.

Maybe I'd got my second bit of living evidence.

Thirty-One

In the event I decided not to go for Anteius, or not directly: if Vinius had been right about Cornelia's summing up of him - and my impression when I'd met the lad confirmed it - then he was an innocent dupe in any case, and so not likely to be very informative. Besides, through him I had a much better prospect lined up: Annaeus Seneca.

I wasn't sure that Seneca was actively involved in the Lepidus/Agrippina plot, but if he didn't know what was going on and be providing at least his support and tacit approval then I was a blue-tailed Briton. The guy was the archetypal go-getting provincial on the make: politically and socially ambitious, a total snob, and with a conceited ego the size of the Capitol. One of those sad buggers who only see the height of the dung heap without caring about what it's made of or how much shit they have to swallow to get to the top. Which was fortunate: convince them that there's a danger that in a short space of time they're going to be back on the barnyard floor arse-up with their face in the mud and they revert from the roosters they thought they were to the chickens they really are.

The problem was, of course, that he'd know who I was, so knocking on his door and asking to talk to him just wasn't an option: at best he'd have his slaves give me the bum's rush, at worst he'd leg it for safer climes and stay there until the heat died down, leaving me to twiddle my thumbs. Probably warn his imperial pals that I was sniffing around again into the bargain. So I made my preparations. Finding where he lived was easy enough - a top-market rented property on the Esquiline - and I sent my smart-as-paint gardener Alexis over to hang around outside the house, follow him when he went out, and suss out my best chance for a private tête-à-tête. Then, when he reported back, I packed off another skivvy to Agron in Ostia asking if I could borrow him and a couple of his stevedore chums.

All this took four days. On the fifth - coincidentally, the day of Helicon's party - we were set to roll. The deal was simple. Every morning, fourth to sixth hours, Seneca used a bath house in the Carinae near the Porch of Livia. Me and Agron and his two chums would follow him in, paying our entrance coppers like ordinary punters; after which I'd hussle Seneca into a quiet corner somewhere for our chat while the other three made sure we weren't disturbed.

It went without a hitch. I collared the bastard in the changing-room and stiff-armed him while whispering in his ear that if he so much as squealed I'd dislocate his fucking shoulder. Then, with Agron and company in close attendance, I ignored the curious glances we were getting from our fellow would-be bathers and marched him down the corridor to one of the empty massage rooms.

Not that I need've worried about him squealing, in either sense of the word: when I let him go and he turned round his pudgy, jowly face was slack with terror.

'Okay, pal,' I said conversationally, pushing him back so that he sat on the massage couch. 'I'll start by telling you what I know, after which you can fill in the gaps, if any. That suit?'

'I don't know what you -'

'Been there. Heard it. Let's just skip that part, shall we, sunshine? You, Lepidus, Agrippina and Livilla are plotting with Lentulus Gaetulicus to have the emperor assassinated when he joins the Rhine legions for the British campaign next year.'

He gave a sort of mewling whimper. 'I'm not -'

'Involved? Sure you are. Right up to your greasy neck, which I am sure when I tell him Gaius will take the greatest pleasure in wringing.' He swallowed and clammed up. 'The only question is whether you're in over the eyeballs as well. For instance. Lepidus and Agrippina roped in bubblehead Livilla by threatening to tell the emperor that you were screwing her, right? Now I'd like to believe that the lady herself made the running and you only started the affair because getting an imperial into bed with you gave you an in, as it were, with the ruling family. Simple ambition, opportunism and social climbing, in other words. On the other hand, I have a very dirty and suspicious mind, and there's just the off-chance that the whole thing was deliberate from the beginning and that Agrippina suggested it to you. In which case, pal, you are really in schtook. You like to comment, maybe?'

He said nothing, but he went a shade greyer and his jowls wobbled. Bull's-eye!

'Fine. Now let's move on to Gaius Anteius.' That got me another scared look. 'As a courier between you and Gaetulicus he's perfect. He comes from Mantua, so if he takes the occasional trip north no one's going to be surprised, and if he overshoots by a few hundred miles, well, who in Rome would know about that? He's a fellow-poet, a friend of yours and an admirer of Gaetulicus, who also dabbles, so no one's going to question the relationship either end of the line, especially if one of you wants him to carry a message to the other. Least of all Anteius himself, who I doubt would recognise a treason plot if it jumped up and bit him. Particularly if the kid's all starry-eyed at being taken on by Agrippina and desperate to please.' I paused. 'How am I doing, by the way?'

He gave a strangled grunt.

'I'm delighted. So. The plan is that next summer Gaius will tootle off north to spearhead his triumphant campaign into Britain, probably taking - at his request - his good friend Lepidus with him. In the meantime his other good friend Claudius Helicon' - another terrified stare - 'plus *his* good mates in the imperial civil service have been working their little socks off to persuade him that sacking Gaetulicus, at least for the time being, is not a smart move. When he reaches Mainz the emperor will die in as unsuspicious circumstances as Lepidus and Gaetulicus can manage, the whole campaign and the changes to the command structure will be quietly shelved for the duration and Lepidus will return to Rome to be saluted by the senate and people as emperor, with Agrippina as his consort. Oh, and perhaps Annaeus Seneca as one of his chief advisors.' I smiled. 'There it is. What do you think? Have I missed anything? Any mistakes?'

The eyes that looked back at me were a terrified rabbit's. He swallowed.

'Lepidus was staying in Rome. Agrippina thought it'd be safer, he couldn't be implicated. Gaetulicus would arrange the whole thing.'

I didn't react, just nodded, but my heart had broken into song. Joy in the morning, I'd turned the bugger!

'I need you to talk to Caesar, Corvinus. Tell him I made a mistake, I never meant to involve myself in treason.' He was pawing at my tunic. 'Tell him it's all Agrippina's fault. She forced me.'

'You can tell him yourself, pal.' I backed away. 'Explain the whole thing personally. In fact, if you want to avoid the strangler's noose or an invitation to slit your wrists that's the course I'd recommend.' Not that I thought it'd do much good: the ladies, being Gaius's sisters, would probably get away with exile, but I reckoned the emperor would have Lepidus's and Gaetulicus's heads on a pole, and Seneca's too. Not that the stupid bastard had been using it for much recently barring keeping his ears apart, so I didn't have a lot of sympathy.

He made a little bleating noise. 'Corvinus, I can't! They'd...if she found out it was me who told the emperor Agrippina would -'

'Your problem, sunshine. I only make the recommendations. You think it over, I'll be in touch.' I paused, my hand on the curtain. 'Oh, and in your own interests I really, *really* wouldn't recommend passing on the content of this conversation to anyone, not even Livilla. The last guy I talked to who had second thoughts in that direction died suddenly of a fishbone in the throat.' He gave another little bleat. 'If it helps, just think of the loss you'd be to poetry.'

I went out. Agron and the other two were standing along the corridor with their backs against the wall, just out of earshot.

'Get what you wanted?' he said.

'Yeah. Skip the bath and split a jug of wine?' I looked at the two stevedores. Jupiter, they bred them big in Ostia! 'Better make that four jugs.'

'I thought you'd never ask,' Agron grinned.

I got back home in plenty of time to get ready for gatecrashing Helicon's party. Again, I'd done my homework carefully in advance: he had a big house on the Pincian, where a lot of the new money was, and the bash would start in the early evening, an hour before sunset.

We were doing things properly: best mantles, scent at a gold piece the tiny bottle, Perilla dolled up to the nines with the family jewellery out of hock and the litter slaves washed, polished and gleaming. I was even taking the bugger a birthday present, one of these little models of the Alexandrian lighthouse with an oil lamp in the top that the souvenir sellers in the agora insist you can't possibly go home without. Pure tat, sure, but I thought it was appropriate. And if we did get talking then it'd give me an excuse to introduce the subject of Alexandria.

'You sure you won't reconsider this, Marcus?' Perilla said as we got ready to board the litter. 'After all, you've got Seneca now, and that tribune, what was his name? Vinius.'

'Uh-uh. They're both on the other side of the case. Anyway, I want to see Helicon for myself, close up.'

'Well, I think it's silly. And possibly dangerous.'

'Lady, it's a party! There'll be a hundred people there, literally, probably more. And you never know what'll turn up.'

'All right.' She sniffed. 'On one condition. If there's any trouble, about admission, I mean, you leave it to me to solve. I am *not* having you indulging in a punch-up or slanging match with the slaves on the gate. It's not dignified and it would be counter-productive. And if we are turned away in the end then we go quietly.'

'Fair enough,' I said. 'Agreed.'

We set off.

The party was in full swing when we arrived just before sunset. Big house was right: it stood in its own grounds, with a wrought-iron gate and a carriage drive leading up to the main complex of buildings with various wings and annexes off to either side. There were marquees set up in the garden, a stage with fluteplayers and percussionists tootling, banging and tinkling away, and the busy hum of a large slice of Rome's great and good networking their socks off as they tucked into the drinks and nibbles.

Our litter lardballs set us down at the gate and we disgorged.

'Good evening, sir. Madam.' A slave in a natty red tunic with silver tassles came over. 'Your invitation, please.'

'Ah' - I patted my mantle-pouch - 'we seem to have come away without it, pal. Stupid, I know, but these things happen. Still -'

'Then I'm sorry, sir, but the master gave very strict instructions. Perhaps if you were to go back home and return with it, or send one of your slaves -'

'Now that is *enough!*' Perilla snapped. 'Young man, if you think that we are going to go all the way back to the Caelian for a silly bit of paper or sit out here while one of the boys fetches it then you are very sadly mistaken. Do you?'

'Ah...' The guy shifted nervously and glanced at me. I shrugged

and moved out of the line of fire: the poor bugger had asked for it, and
he was on his own.

'And look at your hands!' The gate slave put them quickly behind
his back. 'The nails are filthy! You will go straight inside, please, after
you've let us through, and give them a good scrub with a nail brush.
And comb your hair while you're at it, it's an absolute disgrace!'

'Yes, ma'am.'

'I really do not know what things are coming to these days. If
a high-profile slave like you thinks that absolutely strict attention to
detail where appearances are concerned doesn't matter and that it's
enough to -'

'Yes, ma'am.'

'- give your sandals a cursory scuff on the back of your ankles
before you greet the guests, then -'

'Yes, ma'am. Sorry, ma'am.'

'- I despair of the state of the empire. Now open that gate at
once, please.'

'Yes, ma'am.' He did, almost blurring in the process. 'I do
apologise, ma'am.'

'So I should hope. Remember, young man, I shall be checking
up on you when we leave, and if I do not see that there has been a
considerable improvement to your present slovenly turnout then I shall
be very seriously annoyed.'

'Understood, ma'am. Thank you, ma'am. And I can only
apologise again, ma'am.'

We went in.

Jupiter!

'Ah...well done, lady, nice job,' I said cautiously, glancing back
at the slave. He looked like someone had just hit him with the Capitol.
'What do you do for an encore? Chew iron and spit out nails?'

'Don't be silly, Marcus, you just have to be firm, that's all.' She
sniffed. 'Now what?'

'We mingle.'

So we mingled.

Thirty-Two

I hate these stand-up parties. You never know what to do with your plate, and if you set your wine down for a minute either some other bugger sinks it by mistake, an overefficient slave whips it off, or half the local insect population uses it to drown in. Plus spending the evening exchanging small talk over the canapés with Rome's great and good just isn't my bag. Perilla was okay; the lady's a natural stand-up party animal, she'd met one of her poetry pals early on, and they were in deep conversation about the Cyprian pastoralists. Me, I spent ten gruelling minutes with an ex-consul on the subject of his staffing problems (it was impossible, seemingly, to buy a chef who boiled your breakfast egg *just right*) and another ten with a horse-faced woman who kept trying to drag me into the shrubbery. That was enough. I disengaged myself politely, cadged a refill from a passing slave (Chian, but not bad. The wine, I mean) and drifted off to enjoy it in peace.

I'd been communing with Claudius Helicon's version of nature - bushes topiaried within an inch of their lives, separated by a gridwork of scrubbed flagstone paths, twee grottos and simpering statues - just long enough to be thinking about another belt of Chian when I spotted the birthday boy himself over by the huge ornamental fountain, chatting to a couple of broad-stripers: a fit, chunky guy in his early thirties wearing a freedman's cap and sharp Greek party mantle and looking more like a professional wrestler than a civil servant. I took my gift-wrapped Alexandrian lighthouse out of my mantle-fold and began to stroll over, rehearsing what I was going to say. I'd got to within a dozen yards when our pal the gate-slave moved in ahead of me, tugged at Helicon's sleeve and whispered something in his ear. Helicon looked up, back towards the gate, and I followed his eyes...

Which was when three things happened almost simultaneously.

The first was that I saw the man who the gate-slave had obviously

195

wanted to bring to Helicon's attention. He was hanging around on the fringes of the crowd - unseasonably thick travelling cloak, no party mantle, a visitor, not a guest - and I recognised him straight off. Our delinquent Alexandrian bridesmaids' dress material seller, Cineas.

The second thing was that Cineas saw me. His jaw sagged in horror and disbelief, and he turned to bolt.

The third thing was that Helicon saw him seeing me. He whipped round, our eyes met across a crowded patio, and I could just hear the clink of the dropping penny...

Oh, shit. I stopped dead. Out of the corner of my eye I glimpsed Cineas heading for the gate at speed, leaving a trail of indignant upper-class punters with freshly wine-stained mantles in his wake: too much of a lead, too fast to catch. Meanwhile, Helicon was pointing at me and talking urgently to the gate-slave and one of the waiters. Uh-oh; trouble was right. As they headed in my direction I took a step backwards. They wouldn't use violence, sure, or nothing obvious, not in this crowd, but -

I collided with someone behind me.

'Marcus, petal! What are you doing here?'

I turned. 'Ah...'

'Well, well, this is a surprise!' Gaius Caesar gave me a dazzling smile. 'A pleasant one, of course, apart from the wine you've made me spill down my mantle, but no doubt that'll come out in the wash, and if not I'll send you the bill.' Jupiter! 'I never knew that you were a friend of Helicon's. How's the investigation going?'

'Ah...' I looked back over my shoulder. The two slaves had paused, uncertain. 'It's, ah, -'

'You must tell me all about it.' Gaius linked his arm with mine. I glanced at the slaves again. They hadn't moved. 'Right now, please, because I could do with cheering up. Between you and me, dear, and much though I love Helicon, this party is absolutely bloody.'

'Actually, Caesar,' I swallowed, 'the investigation's finished.'

That got me a very sharp look. 'Is it, now?' he said.

'Yeah. Yeah, more or less.'

'Successfully?'

'I think so.'

'Then we'll certainly talk.' He hadn't let go of my arm, but now

196

there was a touch of steel in his voice. 'Somewhere private inside, I think. Helicon won't mind.'

I wouldn't bet on that; in fact, glancing over to where the guy was standing and seeing the look on his face I'd say that currently providing a venue for me and the emperor to have a quiet tête-à-tête was pretty low on the bastard's wish list. However, if the gods had decided to smile for a change then I wasn't going to complain.

'Fine by me, Caesar,' I said.

Gaius had the flustered major-domo show us to Helicon's study, ordered a jug of wine ('Not the rot-gut you're serving outside, cherub. Bring us something decent.') and when he'd done it told him to bugger off and make sure we weren't disturbed.

'Right, Marcus,' he said when the door closed. 'Let's have it.'

So I told him. The whole boiling, from beginning to end.

When I'd finished he said, very quietly: 'You can prove this, of course. I really hope you can, petal, because if you can't I shall be very seriously upset with you.'

Gods! The ice formed on my spine. 'Uh, yes, Caesar,' I said. 'At least I think -'

'Don't think, dear. Thinking isn't half-way good enough, not this time.' He stretched out on the couch, his eyes on the coffered ceiling. 'Gaetulicus I'm not surprised at; he's been a bore for years, incompetent into the bargain, and I'm glad of the excuse to have his head, especially now. Nor at Agrippina, because she's a scheming little bitch and always has been. I'll even grant you Livilla, because she's just an empty-headed fool who doesn't look beyond the next fuck. But Helicon and Lepidus are something else entirely.' He gave me a quick sideways glance. 'Do you know how many friends I have, Marcus? Friends, not hangers-on? No? Well, I can count them on the fingers of one hand. So you had better be able to prove it to the hilt, love, because if you can't then I'm afraid you're cat's meat.'

Oh, shit; he meant it, too. I swallowed. 'I've got Seneca,' I said. 'He can confirm the Gaetulicus side of things. Plus his pal Anteius, who acted as the link, and Titus Vinius who's willing to testify about the attempt to bring over the Pannonian legions. That should be enough for Agrippina and Lepidus.'

'And for Helicon?' He'd gone back to staring at the ceiling.

'Cineas. The guy I told you about, in Alexandria. I saw him outside not half an hour ago. You'd have to find him for yourself, Caesar, granted, but the bastard's in Rome and it shouldn't be too difficult. After all, where could he run to?'

'Alexandria excepted, anywhere in the empire you could name, petal. And Rome is a big place.'

Yeah; right. Still, I'd given it my best shot. Now it was up to him. I waited, held my breath and tried not to let the ice-cold gut fear that was building inside me show in my face.

He sat up suddenly. 'Very well, Marcus,' he said. 'I can't blame you for any of this, especially since I gave you permission to use that long nose of yours in the first place. In fact, I suppose I should thank you, and I probably will when I don't feel so bloody.' So it wouldn't be Lusitania or slit wrists after all. I let the breath out. 'That's conditional, of course, on your first three informants coming up with the goods on Lepidus and my sisters. As far as Helicon is concerned -'

He stopped. He simply stopped, his eyes fixed on the far wall. I gave the silence a good minute. Then I said:

'Caesar?'

'Hmm?' He blinked. 'Oh, yes. Helicon. Don't worry, dear, I'll have a little talk with Helicon. He's been very naughty, very naughty indeed.' I said nothing. 'Still, no real harm done, is there? And he does have a point about those Jews, they're nothing but trouble, always have been. Of course, Flaccus is another matter, he should've known better. I can't have my governors acting irresponsibly, whatever the excuse.'

'What about Macro?' I said.

'Oh, *Macro!*' Gaius sighed. 'Marcus, dear, I'm sorry, but you really are being a little tiresome there. Frankly I couldn't give a fuck about Macro. I'd've had him killed eventually in any case because he was becoming far too pushy. The same goes for Silanus. And Gemellus, for different reasons. Even if the plot was a complete fabrication - which I'm not entirely convinced of - then I can thank Lepidus and Agrippina for the excuse.'

'And Drusilla?'

I knew I'd made a mistake as soon as I said it. The look I got was from eyes that were pure cold steel.

'If you're right that Lepidus was behind her death,' he said, '*if* you're right, then I'll have the bastard in an urn. Agrippina too, if she was involved.' I swallowed. 'But you said yourself: Helicon had nothing to do with that side of things.'

'No, he didn't, but -'

His hand came crashing down on the small table beside the couch, toppling the wine cup and spattering the mosaic floor with wine. '*I will not lose two of my friends!*' he snapped. 'Not at once. Not for you, not for anyone, not even for fucking Rome herself. Whatever the truth of things. Is that perfectly clear?'

'Yes, Caesar,' I said.

'Good.' He lay back again and closed his eyes. 'Now bugger off, there's a love, and leave me alone. On your way out you can tell the major-domo I want to see his master.'

I turned to go.

'Marcus?'

I looked back. 'Yes, Caesar?'

'Thank you. Awfully well done. Congratulations. Now go to hell, please.'

I left.

'So what did he say?' Perilla said when we were ensconced in the litter and on our way back to the Caelian. 'The emperor?'

'He congratulated me and told me to go to hell.'

'Oh.' She pulled back the curtain and watched the scenery.

'Why is it always so fucking unfair? Helicon's responsible for framing a chief advisor, blackmailing a governor, thanks to him probably by this time in Alexandria there's rioting in the streets and they're lynching Jews and burning them out with Flaccus's fucking blessing, and Gaius bloody Caesar plans to let the bastard off with a good talking-to and a fucking smacked wrist. That's not justice, lady, it's -'

'Gently, Marcus, gently.' She hadn't turned round. 'You haven't done too badly. The emperor owes you his life, for one thing. And you did solve the case.'

'Yeah. I'll bet wherever Macro is now that's a great consolation to him. Maybe I shouldn't've bothered.'

She turned to face me. 'Listen,' she said. 'Macro never asked for your help in the first place; you knew that letter was a forgery right from the beginning. And Claudius Etruscus has got what he wanted. Oh, perhaps not yet, but he will: Helicon has been stopped, Flaccus will be recalled, and it's all thanks to you. So let's have no more recriminations and self-pity. It's over and done with, just forget about it.' She kissed me. 'Besides, we still have a wedding to arrange.'

I half-smiled. Oh, the joys. Still, she was right: I'd done my best, the case was solved, and how Gaius intended to take things from here was his business, nothing to do with me. It might even turn out, in the end, to be all for the good of Rome. If you believed in flying pigs.

Ah, well; onward and upward. At least I'd seen Alexandria, and I had a couple of jars of good Mareotis in the wine cellar that I wouldn't've had otherwise. Life wasn't too bad, at that.

I kissed her back, and we went home.

The End